CW01646253

Cold Secrets

V. J. Randle

Copyright 2024 V. J. Randle

The right of V. J. Randle to be identified as the Author of the Work has been asserted by her in accordance with the Copyright, Designs and Patents Act 1988.

First published in 2024
Print ISBN 978-1-0685714-1-1
E-book ISBN 978-1-0685714-0-4

Apart from any use permitted under UK copyright law, this publication may only be reproduced, stored, or transmitted, in any form, or by any means, with prior permission, in accordance with the terms of licences issued by the Copyright Licensing Agency.

All characters in this publication are fictitious and any resemblance to real persons, living or dead, is purely coincidental.

To my lovely Dad, Ethan Greenhalgh; my hero, forever, and always in my heart.

Who can stop grief's avalanche once it starts to roll?
Euripides, *Medea*

Map of Findrussie

Prologue

Clara Rowley knew she should be afraid. But as the end of her life drew near, she struggled to believe that any of this was really happening. Perhaps it was the cold. Maybe it numbed feelings as well as flesh. Or perhaps it was the shock. As she lay on the filthy floor of the bothy, staring up while her attacker steadily approached, she couldn't understand how someone could be so familiar yet also so strange and dangerous.

The tears kept her face warm, at least. She had tried shouting already; it was no use. She thought about all the things she could say, but words seemed useless at a time like this. It was best, she thought, to let her mind wander to happier places. She closed her eyes, willing herself to stop whimpering. For the first time in her life, she understood what was meant by time standing still.

The footsteps stopped.

Opening her eyes, she saw two boots planted inches before her face. From this angle, she could see the fresh, sculpted shards of snowflakes on the leather, quite like the Christmas decorations that hung on the tree back at the house.

How long would she have to lie here? She squinted at the

boots, her neck too stiff to twist upwards, and asked the only question that came to mind: 'Why?'

She never received an answer.

As the blade swung downwards, the last sound she heard was the soft swoosh of metal through the freezing air. The last sensation she felt was a very brief, but overwhelming, eruption of pain, before the vast expanse of nothingness.

Chapter One

Robert Begg hated Hogmanay. In his office of mismatched plywood furniture, he listened to the joyous buzz from the adjoining bar and wondered how he could possibly be the same species as these partygoers. It wasn't that he didn't enjoy the odd drink – his mug was filled with tepid mulled wine – but crowds were a problem for him. Specifically, small crowds ... or, to be honest, any type of social gathering. He felt comfortable enough with some people – namely his staff and a couple of regulars – but he had never got his head around the idea of socialising with strangers. This, he knew, was how most people struck up new friendships, but there seemed to be a set of hidden rules surrounding such interactions that continued to elude him, despite his best efforts. For example, when was the appropriate point to start a conversation? In a group of, say, four, who was he supposed to address when speaking? Was he expected to shift his gaze periodically, so he didn't leave anyone out? The questions were endless, but everyone, apart from Robert, appeared to have the answers.

He sighed and took a sip of wine. This wasn't looking good, not good at all. He jabbed an index finger at the calculator again, as if pushing the buttons harder would make any difference to the numbers on the screen. He lowered his forehead to the desk and tried to ignore the relentless beat of the music from the other side of the wall. There was no hope of concentrating over that racket. He breathed deeply, trying to get a hold of himself. It wasn't his customers' fault that his business was falling into financial disarray. It wasn't entirely his fault either, for that matter.

He tilted the chair back and stared at the photograph above the computer screen: a father teaching his son how to fly-fish. The boy was about ten years old, barely a year before his mother had left. His serious, pointed face almost scowled at the camera. Robert remembered the bright, cool day clearly. He had struggled to catch anything and concluded there must be some secret technique he had yet to master. He had tried counting the ripples on the loch, mentally noting the number of concentric circles and attempting to calculate when and where the fish were most likely to bite. His mother's call for a photograph had interrupted his concentration. In contrast to his serious son, his father had beamed at the camera and placed a large arm around Robert's shoulders. The excitement apparent in his crinkled eyes suggested he already knew another fish was about to take the bait.

'Give it to Robbie!' His mother had laughed, winding on the disposable camera. 'Let him pose with it!'

His father had shaken his head firmly and, squeezing Robert's shoulder, said, 'He needs to do it for himself. He'll learn it soon enough.'

But Robert never did learn how to fish. Just as he never learned how to drink, joke or hunt properly – all shortcomings that had served as niggling disappointments to his father.

Bennie Begg: beloved of all in Findrussie, locals and tourists alike. The internet was teeming with positive reviews of the family business, the Pine Needle Bar, and guests travelled miles to sample Bennie's famed pickle-backs and pine-infused gin collection. He was the life and soul of Hogmanay, treating his friends to unlimited drinks until the morning, when the surviving revellers would strip, run the short distance from the bar to the loch, and submerge themselves in the icy water.

Unfortunately, though, running a successful bar demands more than being liked. As the on-the-house drinks stacked up, the Pine Needle became about as profitable as its namesake. Now, looking at the sums, Robert gave it less than six months. It seemed inevitable he would continue to disappoint his father, even after death.

'Oh no! Looks like you need a top-up.'

Robert twitched as Eilidh barged her way through the office door. She brought the smell of the party with her: smoke, sweat and drink. A large cheer erupted from the bar and Eilidh raised her glass to the ceiling, enacting what Robert could best describe as a jiggle.

He looked at his feet, wishing he could think of something fun to say. 'I'm working on the accounts.'

'On Hogmanay?' Eilidh stared past him to the screen.

Robert quickly exited the spreadsheet; he had no desire to ruin the staff's big night. 'Just catching up,' he replied, managing a weak smile.

Eilidh's face softened, her large, heavily made-up eyes resting on the fly-fishing photograph. 'I know it's hard,' she said. 'He used to love tonight.'

Robert felt his shoulders freeze as an uncomfortable jolt rippled through his stomach. He did not enjoy this sort of conversation – the sort where emotions were discussed. It should be obvious how he was feeling. No need to dwell on it.

'Yes, well...'

'He'd be pleased you carried on the tradition,' Eilidh continued, smiling gently. 'Like father, like son.'

'He wished,' Robert said, a little more aggressively than he had intended.

There was a short silence before Eilidh raised her eyebrows. 'Now that's the ... err' – Eilidh grabbed the mug from the desk and took a swig – 'mulled wine talking. No wonder you're feeling down. I'm sure we can find something a bit stronger to cheer you up.' She pretended to search the office, picking up old books and folders. 'If only we could find—'

'Eilidh, I'm fine, really.'

'Ah!' She stamped her foot and cocked her head as if she had just come up with a brilliant idea. 'I've got it! Is that not...' She sniffed the air, enjoying every second of her performance. Robert couldn't help but smile. 'Is that not a *bar*, merely metres away? A fully stocked, *free* bar? And is it not Hogmanay? Tonight!' She tugged on his arm and pulled him from the chair. 'And are you not throwing the party of the year?'

Robert allowed himself to be dragged from the office. Eilidh's enthusiasm was infectious, as always. She had a way of brightening up even the darkest moments.

The bar was rammed with familiar faces, as well as some strangers. The Christmas break was *the* peak tourist season, and the Pine Needle's Hogmanay was always a sell-out. A few of his father's old friends noticed Robert's entrance and gave him a stoic nod as he followed Eilidh towards the bar. He suddenly realised this evening would be hard on them, too – the first big event without their best mate.

'What are you having?' Eilidh effortlessly jumped up and swung her legs over the counter.

Robert shook his head, resisting the urge to protect his ears from the deafening music. 'Is there any mulled wine left?'

Eilidh threw her head back and laughed. 'No!'

'Are you sure?' Despite his reservations, Robert could feel himself smiling broadly now.

'I'm sure!' She grinned and reached for a bottle of the best local malt. 'Double?'

'All right.' Robert shrugged as she poured two enormous measures. How did she manage it?

They clinked glasses and Eilidh took a long, gleeful sip.

'How was your set?' Robert asked.

Eilidh placed a hand on her chest. 'You mean to say you missed it?'

'I ... I was in the office,' Robert stuttered.

Eilidh prodded him. 'Don't be stupid – I'm joking. You've seen me do it about thirty times.'

More like sixty, Robert thought, but he chose not to correct her.

'It was great. Easy crowd.' She gestured around her. 'Like always.'

Robert looked down at his glass, unsure of what to say. She had been dropping hints about growing restless for a while. There were only so many opportunities for ambitious singers in Findrussie and the surrounding area. But there was no real reason for him to miss her if she left – they only ever talked at work.

'Ten minutes!' Justine, whose cheeks were a deep shade of red, bustled into the centre of the bar.

For as long as Robert had known her, she had always given the impression of being permanently rushed off her feet. Predominantly the bar's cleaner, she had babysat him after his mother had moved away. He glanced at the table by the window where he had once done his homework. Somehow, in between her cleaning duties, Justine had always found the time to bring him a sandwich and deliver a pat on the back. After his mother had left, she had quietly taken care of him as his father had scrambled to make ends meet. Now, as she urged everyone to their feet, it was obvious she was trying to make the evening as bearable as possible for him.

The crowd cheered as the band gathered on the small stage at the rear of the bar, but Robert suddenly felt very hot. He tugged at his collar and hoped he was not sweating through his shirt.

'Justine's enjoying herself,' Eilidh said, grinning.

'Deserves it,' Robert replied. 'She's been working in the kitchen *and* the bar as well as cleaning non-stop.'

'We should hire more staff,' said Eilidh. Robert merely nodded, unable to meet her eye. She seemed to sense his discomfort and changed the subject immediately. 'Well, I need a dance partner,' she said, holding out her hand.

'Absolutely not,' said Robert. There was little he liked less than dancing, as Eilidh well knew.

'Come on!' Eilidh spun around on the spot, slapping her thighs as she landed the turn. Her proficiency did not boost his confidence.

'I'd best be getting back...' He made to return to the office, but Eilidh grabbed his arm and pulled him towards her. He squirmed as he felt the heat of her body, unsure of what to do. His arms went limp; his feet seemed ten sizes too big.

'It's easy,' Eilidh insisted. 'And no one's looking anyway.'

The band began to play an energetic melody, pints sloshed out of glasses, hands clapped and a large circle formed. The noise seemed far too large for so small a space. Robert knew his hands must feel sweaty in Eilidh's. He yearned to shut himself away with one of his favourite books and let the night pass him by.

'*Five* minutes!' Justine was carrying a large tray in each hand, distributing Bennie's speciality shot – the Pine Needle Pickle-Back. She hurried over to them and handed a glass to

Robert. 'Cheers, Robbie. Here's to your dad,' she said, her eyes welling up. Robert swayed slightly but accepted the drink, blinking at Justine's friendly, rosy face. She shook her head and he understood immediately that he was not expected to respond. 'You're all right, Robbie,' she said in her gravelly voice, which comforted him somewhat. 'You're all right.'

'Cheers,' he said, pouring the briny liquid down his throat.

'*Two* minutes!' Justine nudged him in the ribs and winked at Eilidh. 'You never know. New year, new opportunities...'

Robert spluttered, spitting his drink down his shirt. Justine chuckled. Eilidh, thank God, was either enraptured by the band or had decided to ignore the comment. Robert shot Justine an exasperated look.

'*One* minute!'

Eilidh downed her shot and placed the glass back on Justine's tray. 'Right, I'm off for a dance!' With that, she disappeared into the mass of bodies.

'She won't hang about forever, you know,' Justine said, raising her eyebrows.

'No idea what you mean,' replied Robert, uncharacteristically considering a second drink.

'Oh!' Justine cried. 'The photo! I forgot to do it at dinner. Hang on!' She slammed the trays onto the nearest table and extracted her phone from her jeans. 'Lift me up, will you, Robbie?' she said after failing to climb onto the table under her own steam. 'Quick!'

Robert dutifully pushed her from behind and she shimmied onto the tabletop. He chuckled, pleased she had remembered this particular tradition. The midnight photo was a Pine Needle Hogmanay staple. 'All right, you lot, look this way!' Justine hollered over the bouncing heads as she blinded everyone with a series of rapid flashes. "Let's do another, that's right...and another one! Smile!"

The final countdown was already under way and the building's wooden beams were shaking with the excitement of the New Year.

'Five, four, three, two...'

'Happy Hogmanay!' The band burst into 'Auld Lang Syne', which some enthusiastic English tourists took as their cue to stand on their tables and start bellowing.

'Happy New Year!' Justine called to Robert just before she fell from the table and into his arms. He caught her with a considerable struggle, and she repaid him with a huge hug. He breathed in the familiar scent of hair-dye and cigarettes. Even with all his biological family now gone, this place was still very much home. 'Now, are you going to ask this old lady to dance or what?' Justine laughed and pulled him towards the ceilidh. She kept her phone in one hand as she moved, whooping with delight as she continued to take photos of the party in full swing.

He followed her and his inhibitions began to dissipate. He allowed his body to respond to the music, if not enthusiastically, then at least respectfully. Justine, a middle-aged woman of curvaceous proportions, fully embraced the opportunity to boogie. She sprang into action, leaping from foot to foot, with no worry about whether she was in time, or even performing the correct routine. 'You see?' she wheezed. 'It's not difficult!'

Robert's knees began to relax. Justine and Eilidh were going to such efforts to lighten his mood, and anyway, most of the tourists had no idea what they were doing. The person next to him linked their arm into his and swung him round, almost knocking him off his feet.

'There you go, Robbie!' Eilidh shouted as she passed him by, caught in a similar spin and posing for Justine's photo. He was about to respond to her, thinking he might say something witty about having one whisky too many, when a scream cut through the celebrations.

A current of whispers started rippling from those nearest the entrance and spread rapidly across the dance floor. A cold blast of air followed. Someone had clearly opened the doors, allowing the snow to billow inside. Before Robert could ask what was happening, he heard a chilling wail. The band stopped playing as a figure staggered through the doorway. Her face was stained red, her hair tousled, her eyes wild. The suddenly subdued guests craned their necks, some taking a step back, murmuring beneath their breath.

Robert wished he was imagining the whole scene, but there was no escaping the woman's ragged, yet thunderous, words.

'He's dead!' she screamed. 'Dead!'

Chapter Two

Robert walked towards the porch, keeping his eyes on the woman. He didn't rush, partly because he didn't want to cause a scene, partly because he was frantically considering what to do next. As he moved closer, he saw she must have been in her sixties, with grey-blond, bobbed hair. She was dressed inappropriately for the freezing weather, with only a pashmina covering what looked like frail shoulders. Glancing behind him, Robert realised all eyes were on him.

The woman rocked slowly back and forth, her teeth chattering manically. She watched Robert carefully, with a wound-up tension that gave him the impression she might pounce at any second.

He cleared his throat and stepped through the doors, folding his arms tightly. 'Excuse me ... are you ... all right?' He hunched his shoulders, knowing how inept he must sound.

The woman flinched and raised her eyes to his. Her cheeks were tainted with mascara, but thankfully the red smear across her mouth seemed to be no more than lipstick.

'Can I help you?' Robert persevered.

On the opposite side of the forest road, the bushes rustled

and a towering figure clad in a dark, full-length waxed coat emerged from the shadows. Robert recoiled for a moment until he realised it was just Hammy, his seventy-year-old neighbour, out for a late-night walk with his huskies. With his usual wide grin, Hammy raised his free arm to wave but stopped as soon as he spotted the woman.

'He's dead!' The woman repeated, pointing to the bottom of the steps.

It was too dark to see anything, but Robert's mouth still felt dry. He fought every instinct telling him to run far away from whatever horror this woman had seen. The thought of another pair of blue lips, another set of stone-cold limbs, filled him with dread. The guests behind him were silent now. Eilidh and Justine were telling them to remain inside in a futile attempt to distract them from the scene in the porch. Robert took a deep breath, felt his hands begin to shake, and started the short walk down the steps.

'What was that you said?' Hammy asked as he crossed the road and whistled for his dogs to sit. Oddly, he did not seem in the least perturbed by the dead body that was supposedly lying just feet away from him.

Robert glanced back at the trembling woman, followed her gaze and braced himself for the worst.

He almost laughed when he arrived at the foot of the steps and realised the woman was pointing at his father's memorial plaque, which had been installed the previous month. He let relief wash over him, thanking the universe for the misunderstanding.

'You knew my dad?' He asked as he looked at her curiously, wondering what on earth his father would have had to do with this person. Judging from her accent, she was both English and very well-to-do.

'And you are?' Her voice was no less urgent.

'Now then...' Hammy said, glancing at Robert. 'Can we take you anywhere? Where do you stay? Kinlogie's only a short—'

The woman whipped her head around towards Hammy and hissed, 'I know all about Kinlogie House!'

Hammy pouted, shrugging. 'I don't doubt that.'

Robert wrapped his arms more tightly around himself. By now, he was wishing that he had remained in his office. He couldn't in good conscience leave this woman stranded outside in the middle of the forest; she'd have next to no chance of finding a taxi at this hour. Hammy's guess was a good one: she was just the type to be staying at Kinlogie.

'I'm Robert,' he stammered, 'Robert Begg.' He pointed to the plaque. 'Bennie was my dad. I'm very sorry if this is a shock, but he died a couple of months back.'

'It's no shock, really,' she said. Her demeanour seemed to have flipped in an instant from mania to irritation. 'I just needed it confirmed. I ... I apologise for being a tad over-dramatic. But I got your attention, didn't I? Forgive me ... the champagne...'

Robert suppressed a smile as Hammy rolled his eyes. They could both smell the alcohol on her breath.

She continued in a slightly slurred voice: 'Tell me, how did he die?'

Robert was caught off-guard by her tone. She seemed almost angry, accusing.

'Now, that's enough...' Hammy said, moving a step closer. The tightness in Robert's gut relaxed a little. Describing his father's unexpected demise to a stranger was not high on his list of enjoyable New Year pastimes. The sky thundered with the explosions of fireworks and cheers echoed from the bar, the forest, the loch's beach and beyond. The huskies whimpered, and Hammy knelt down from his great height to comfort them. 'Noise kept them up. Thought a walk would do them good.

Obviously not, though. I'd best be off,' he said, giving Robert a long stare. 'You all right? Justine about?'

'She's inside,' Robert assured him. Hammy clearly felt that he wasn't up to the task of handling the woman on his own, which may well have been true.

'So, so strange. Couldn't be a coincidence...' The woman was mumbling to herself now.

'Give me a call if you need,' Hammy said, brushing the snow from his beard. 'I'll be in tomorrow regardless.'

Robert watched as Hammy, dogs in tow, disappeared into the path carved between the snow-clad pines. He turned around and started to offer the woman his office telephone but then realised he was standing alone, talking into the darkness. She seemed to have evaporated into thin air, leaving only two dainty footprints behind.

Chapter Three

The last of the Pine Needle's customers finally stumbled from the bar at 5.00 a.m., some still wrapped in towels from their moonlit swim. Justine was napping on the bench by the wood-burner as Eilidh helped Robert clean up. They would be opening for lunch in a few hours' time, which meant none of them would be getting much sleep.

'She'll be fine,' Eilidh said. 'Probably just wandered away from the hotel. She looked like she'd had a few...'

'I should have walked her home,' Robert said, struggling to scrub some dried candle wax from the bar. 'It can be dangerous if you don't know where you're going.'

'She said she knew Bennie?' Eilidh asked.

'Sort of. Probably came here on holiday. People tended to remember him.'

Eilidh laughed. 'Aye, that's for sure.'

They both smirked when Justine gave a huge snort as she rolled over.

'It was all right, wasn't it? The party?'

Robert nodded, his face close to the counter as he continued to scrub. 'Everyone seemed to enjoy themselves.'

'Did you?' This was Eilidh's special talent: she had the ability to switch from light-hearted chit-chat to heartfelt conversation with no warning whatsoever.

'I suppose so.' He felt Eilidh's eyes scrutinising him from behind, but he had no clue what she wanted him to say. 'You can go,' he said. 'I'll finish up here.'

Eilidh looked quite disappointed at the prospect of going home for some rest. Her reactions never ceased to confuse Robert.

'Really,' he insisted. 'There's not much left to do.'

She began collecting her belongings, which seemed to be strewn haphazardly around the bar. Zipping up her coat, she hesitated for a second before flinging herself around him in a tight, unanticipated hug. Robert thought it was a distinct possibility that she was still completely drunk. 'I love working here, Robbie,' she said with the sort of enthusiasm that could only be attributed to the vodka shots she had poured for the swimmers on their return from the loch.

A guilty lump rose in Robert's throat. 'Great job tonight, Eilidh' was all he could manage.

Eilidh reacted with what sounded like an exasperated sigh, but it could just as well have been a tipsy hiccup.

After Eilidh had roused a bleary-eyed Justine and led her out of the bar, Robert took a seat at the nearest table and rested his head in his hands. If this were a book, he thought, this would be one of those pivotal moments when the protagonist reaches for a bottle of whisky, pours himself a large dram, and experiences an intense revelation. Unfortunately, he didn't feel like another whisky. More to the point, the narrators of his favourite, much-thumbed walking memoirs always seemed to have access to endless pots of money, or at least no looming bills to pay. Perhaps that was why he liked them so much: they were safe and familiar adventure stories.

His penchant for the genre had begun with a title one of the customers had donated to the bar's windowsill library: *The Living Mountain*. He remembered reading the first sentence as a child: 'Living on the high plateau can be delectable as honey; it can also be a roaring scourge.' Robert must have read it over a dozen times, enjoying the rhythm of the colourful, poetic depictions of a dangerous world, before suddenly realising that the author was describing the place where he himself lived. Thereafter, he had become an avid collector of similar tales of treks along windswept coastal paths and mountain trails.

He gave the bar a final, cursory wipe, accepting the whiff of stale alcohol and smoke would linger for a few days yet. Back in the office, just as he was reaching under the desk for his satchel, he heard footsteps.

'Eilidh?' he shouted with more than a hint of annoyance that she had ignored his instruction to get some rest. Nobody replied. He stood up, slipped the satchel over his shoulder and walked out of the office, closing the door behind him. He scanned the bar for Eilidh, but it was empty. Shaking his head, he turned to lock the door, then heard more footsteps in the kitchen.

'Who is it?' he called. 'We're closed until midday.'

Most likely, a tourist had found himself locked out of his accommodation and was looking for a warm place to grab a few hours' sleep. Robert shook his head again and made for the kitchen. 'Hello? We're closed but...'

The back door was swinging gently on its hinges. Whoever had snuck in had now snuck out. Striding towards the door, Robert slammed it shut and locked it. Enough funny business had happened last night. Why couldn't people just behave properly? He rubbed his eyes, wishing he was already tucked up in bed with a nice cup of tea, before reluctantly inspecting the kitchen. Everything seemed in order: clearly his visitor had not intended to steal anything ... or had been disturbed before he could.

The bar seemed exceptionally quiet. At this early hour on a winter's morning, not even the trees rustled in the wind. It was as if the mountains slept for a while until the hares darted at the first shimmering, pale light of dawn. Robert usually loved the sensation of perfect solitude, but this morning he felt uncomfortable, as if he were being watched. It was silly, he knew, as most people had passed out by now, or were so drunk that their senses had left them. But even the smiling faces of his father's treasured photographs on the walls seemed to be spying on him, recording every move.

'Time for bed,' he said, gratified that at least his voice sounded strong against the silence. He glanced about the bar one last time and began the short walk home.

It was still dark but the sky had taken on a blue-grey hue, which made the snow appear almost fluorescent. The lane ran alongside the woods and past the campsite, which was closed until spring. Robert used to enjoy taking the loch's beach path, which boasted a fine view of the mountains carving their great forms into the sky, but these days he kept strictly to the forest track. His boots trudged methodically through the snow with a pleasing crunch while the freezing morning air stung his tired eyes. Without thinking too much about it, he started to hum one of Eilidh's songs, but by the time he reached the chorus he realised he was in too high a key and his voice started to crack. He cleared his throat and was about to try again when he heard the unmistakable sound of snapping twigs in the trees beside him. He stood stock still, expecting a deer to dart from the foliage. The uneasy sensation of being watched returned. He crossed his arms around his chest and pushed onwards, just about resisting the urge to run. Yet, there it was again – another loud rustle – only this time it sounded far too clumsy to be an animal.

'Who is it?' Robert called into the shadows, spinning around on his heel. His breathing quickened as he waited for an answer, but none came. It was best to walk with purpose, he decided. That way, any troublemakers would be deterred. He was sure a teacher had told him that once. He could just about make out the roof of his timber-clad cabin, one of a handful scattered throughout the forest. Ploughing on through the snow, his breath was clouding before him in an opaque fog. The trees seemed to lean inwards on either side. 'One foot in front of the other,' he told himself. 'One foot in front of another.' He tried to convince himself that he was just exhausted, that no one was following him ... but he couldn't quell the anxiety.

After almost skidding a couple of times on the icy path, he finally lurched towards his front door. His hand was already grasping the keys as he checked over his shoulder before shakily unlocking it, glad that nobody was there to witness his jitters. Once inside, he rested his forehead against the door and began to recite today's words under his breath: 'Stoat, squirrel, starfish, snake, skunk...' Tomorrow would be a 'T' day; then it would be 'U'. He had developed this method for remaining calm at school, shortly after his mother had left. It enabled him to focus, to re-centre his world. He had thought about stopping around the age of sixteen; then again at eighteen; then again at twenty-two. Yet even now, at twenty-nine, he still kept track of the letter days and recited the animals whenever the need arose. As far as quirks went, he felt it was a perfectly reasonable one.

The radiators were starting to gurgle and spit, which meant it must be past six already. He shuffled towards the couch and lay on his back, staring at the ceiling beams. His father's voice echoed in the deepest recesses of his brain: 'Robert, get your boots on! It's time for a walk. Just a wee one.' He closed his eyes. He had always dragged his feet during the New Year's Day walk, moaning that he was tired. Now the house groaned with the absence of his father's enthusiasm; all that was left was his own lonely body. Blowing air through his lips, he pushed himself from the couch and made for the stairs, trying to forget he'd have to be up again in a few hours.

He had just about reached the landing when he realised what was happening. For a second, he thought a distressed bird must have fallen down the chimney, and the sound he could hear was its frenetic, flapping wings. But birds don't tend to open front doors. Nor do they make clunky footsteps on the stairs. Nor do they smell of alcohol and smoke. Nor do they grab your shoulder with an iron-cold hand.

'What the—' Robert fell forwards, onto the landing, scrambled to regain his balance, then turned towards the intruder.

'Don't worry. I won't hurt you.' The voice was surprisingly calm ... and familiar.

As his eyes started to make sense of the situation, Robert recognised the woman standing at the top of the stairs as the same one who had interrupted the Pine Needle's Hogmanay celebrations. Her hair was still ruffled, lipstick was still smeared around her mouth, but her eyes seemed softer, her face pale and frail.

Robert swore loudly as the adrenaline coursed through his body. 'Sorry!' he said, holding up a hand to reinforce the apology. He suspected she was not the type to appreciate profanities. 'You, err, you startled me.' He peered behind her, hoping that she had not invited any more unwelcome guests into his home.

'Don't worry,' she repeated. 'It's just me. Please, there's no need to be frightened.' At that moment she took a step forwards, which, although he was almost certain she didn't mean him any harm, caused Robert to scramble towards the bathroom, half-thinking he could slide down the drainpipe if need be.

'Now, really!' she said, rather petulantly. Robert's lack of trust was clearly starting to irritate her. 'There's no need—'

'What are you doing?' he interrupted, surprising himself with the ferocity of the question. 'Look, I'm sorry, I didn't mean to shout. But you are in my house, so—'

'Yes, I *know* that.' Her annoyance was palpable now.

Robert sighed. He had dealt with people like her many times before; though, to be fair, they were usually complaining about the service in the pub, rather than breaking into his home. Nevertheless, he knew he should let her say her piece. The quicker she got whatever it was off her chest, the better.

'Tea?' As soon as the word left his lips, Robert realised it was both the most natural and the most ludicrous suggestion in the world, given the circumstances.

'That would be lovely,' the woman replied, albeit in a tone that implied he should have thought of it much sooner.

He followed her down the stairs and into the kitchen. She was still quite wobbly on her legs.

'It's freezing,' she said, wrapping the shawl tightly around her shoulders.

'The heating will be on soon enough,' he replied, boiling the kettle. 'Always takes a while to warm up.'

She didn't respond. Instead, she stared at him for far longer than was comfortable.

'So,' Robert continued as the silence became unbearable. 'What can I do for you? You said you knew my dad.' There was still a slight tremor in his voice.

'He lived here?'

'Aye, we both did. Now it's just me.' He poured the tea. 'How did you know him?'

The woman took her tea and sipped it with a small, sharp pout. She smacked her lips, then stared deep into Robert's eyes. 'Your father – Bennie – you said? No, I didn't know him, apart from visiting the bar a few times.' She drew herself even straighter, if that were possible, and cleared her throat. 'I believe his death may provide me with some information.'

'*Information?*' Robert was struggling to fight the cloud of tiredness that was descending over him.

'Yes, information. I am Mirabella Rowley. You might...' Her voice trailed off and she nodded grimly. Clearly, she had recognised the dark shadow of comprehension that had swept across his face.

There wasn't a soul in Findrussie who had not heard of the Rowleys. Robert vividly remembered the day himself. He'd been – what? – six or seven years old, sitting in the corner of the bar, staring through the window. Then, he had seen the flashing lights and his mother had called out, 'Odd day for sirens.' Even now, he didn't know precisely what she had meant: odd because it was New Year's Eve or because it was such unseasonably beautiful weather? Either way, they'd heard the news soon enough.

'No!' his father had screamed. '*No!*'

'Daddy?'

His father had picked him up then, protectively, his eyes darting about the bar. 'It's all right, son. Nothing for you to worry about.'

But it had been something to worry about; something very much to worry about. The sirens had signalled the discovery of a teenage girl's body in the Ryvune bothy, not five minutes from the Pine Needle. Thereafter, events unfolded in a nightmarish manner: the childlike magic of the winter holidays was chiselled away as ever more police turned up, yellow-and-black ribbons cordoned off the forest and everyone was instructed to remain indoors. The next day, it was confirmed the victim was seventeen-year-old Clara Rowley, whose family were staying with friends for the week.

'He didn't do it.' Mirabella's cut-glass voice sliced through Robert's memories. She studied him with penetrating eyes. The words sounded rehearsed, as if she had said them a million times before. She was referring to Toby Rowley, Clara's elder brother, who had been convicted of her murder. The incident had shocked the community, not to mention the nation. It had been how Robert had learned the meaning of the word 'sororicide'.

Unsure of what to say, he took a long gulp of tea, then muttered, 'I'm so sorry.'

'Of course. Everyone is.'

There was another long pause during which Robert contemplated how this woman's life had turned out. Losing one child to a brutal murder, and another to a life sentence, was unimaginable. How had she managed to carry on? Yet, here she was, in his living room.

He cleared his throat. 'My dad—'

'Yes,' she interjected. 'I read he had passed not long ago. I have always known that Toby didn't do it. He was falsely accused, you see. Framed. I am quite sure of it. Your father's death was ... sudden, yes?'

'That's right,' Robert replied, wishing she wouldn't probe like this. For the last two months he had tried – and failed – not to think about it.

'Unusual,' Mirabella said, 'in a village this small, no? I've been wondering if his death might have something to do with my family's tragedy. That's why I'm here. I want to get to the bottom of it. There's a possibility the two events are linked, you see.'

She spoke with such clarity and assurance that it seemed almost reasonable to think she was not talking complete and utter rubbish.

'Please, Mrs Rowley. I sympathise, I really do. But my dad's death had nothing to do with any—'

'And you know that, do you?' Mirabella's eyes narrowed.

'Well, yes, I do. There was nothing suspicious about it. I think you might be...' He searched in vain for an alternative to 'clutching at straws'. As far as he knew, the investigation into Clara Rowley's murder had been closed for decades. The evidence against Toby Rowley had been irrefutable. He had even been found alongside his sister's body. Robert winced at the thought.

'I don't mean to make you feel uncomfortable,' Mirabella said, although, from her tone, Robert suspected she didn't mind too much.

He knew grief could have strange effects on people, but now was certainly not the time to entertain this poor woman's delusions; nor was he qualified to counsel her. 'You should speak to the police,' he suggested gently. 'I'm sure that they will listen to any ... ideas you have.' He was even more sure they would be able to direct her towards some professional help.

'McCrae!' She almost spat the name, causing Robert to flinch. 'He did next to nothing twenty-two years ago. It grinds my bones that he's still in a job. Useless, is what I say. He's the reason why both of my children are dead and my daughter's killer is still out there, running free.' As she spoke, she massaged the tops of her arms, obsessively kneading her scant flesh.

Robert felt his eyelids drooping as he struggled to keep up. 'I'm sorry,' he said. 'Did you say that *both* of your children are—'

'Dead. Yes.'

'But...'

'Toby hanged himself. It wasn't long before he reached the

end of the road in prison. He started to ask me whether he might have done it after all. He was truly helpless. Driven mad.' Her eyes flashed with an emotion Robert couldn't quite identify – somewhere between sorrow and icy rage.

Although Brian McCrae was not his favourite person, Robert had never heard him accused of incompetence ... professionally, at least. As far as he knew, he was now a high-ranking detective in Inverness. And he was sure he would have done a thorough job during the Rowley investigation, even as a relatively junior police officer. Either way, though, he couldn't understand what any of this had to do with him. He stared at Mirabella. 'I'm so sorry, Mrs Rowley, but I don't know how I can help you.'

'You might have some crucial information without realising it.' Her voice was raised in something approaching desperation. 'But even if you don't, I've needed a local's insight for years. There are lots of secrets in places like Findrussie, crevices that outsiders never see, never hear about. If you would just listen to me, you might understand that your father may well be the key.'

'I highly doubt that, Mrs Rowley. And, well, he's not here any more, is he?' Robert heard his voice crack and he looked away before Mirabella could see the tears in his eyes. He was not about to break down in front of her. 'I can't possibly know how awful this has been for you, but right now, I'm exhausted, and my next shift starts at midday.'

'Goodness, you should get some rest then.' There was an edge to her tone that left Robert feeling rebuked.

He blinked at her. 'Yes, I should,' he said firmly.

She pulled the pashmina tightly around her shoulders in readiness for the blizzard that was swirling outside.

'Do you know where you're going?' Robert asked. However, as she had been sufficiently crafty and sober to stalk him here, he reckoned she could probably find her way home.

'I'm fine,' she said, snorting.

With that, she walked to the door, flung it open and stomped into the snowflakes nose first, giving the appearance, Robert thought, of a keen hunting dog. The door slammed shut behind her. Robert locked it, checked it three times, then finally dragged his tired limbs up to bed.

Chapter Four

'What do you mean, "just outside"?' Justine asked. She was surprisingly chipper, given the amount of alcohol she had consumed the night before.

The same could not be said of Eilidh. 'For crying out loud, Justine,' she grumbled. 'He's explained it a hundred times.'

'On the steps.' Robert pointed to the front of the bar. 'She must have come straight here from my place and left it there.'

'She's gone in the head,' suggested Hammy, flicking the top of his pint glass with a fingernail. Robert knew what the signal meant, although he was reluctant to give Hammy a third pint before 1.00 p.m.

The four of them were huddled around the bar, looking at a tightly packed A4 envelope that was stuffed with photographs, dates, computer printouts, newspaper cuttings and general musings relating to Clara Rowley's murder. It had also contained a smaller envelope, addressed to Robert, which he had yet to open. He had told them almost everything about his two encounters with Mirabella, aside from her suspicions about his father's death. He didn't like the way she had brought him into all this, and there was no need to upset the others.

'I remember it on the news,' Hammy said. 'It was everywhere back then.'

'Imagine what it was like here in Findrussie,' said Eilidh. 'My brother told me I'd be murdered in my sleep.'

'That's horrible,' said Justine distractedly as she scribbled notes on a play script. '"I would rather stand beside my shield three times in battle than give birth once,"' she recited quietly, peering deep into the page.

'What's she saying?' Hammy asked, nodding at Justine.

'Lines,' said Robert. 'First read-through is tomorrow, apparently.'

'*Apparently?*' Justine's eyes flicked up from under her glasses. 'You'd best be there, Robbie. It's a good one this year. I'm taking us in a whole new direction.'

'Stole Mr Tiggs. Told me he'd been taken by the murderer.' Eilidh shook her head, lost in memory.

'Mr Tiggs?' Hammy asked.

'My teddy,' explained Eilidh. Her eyes were glassy and bloodshot.

Robert slid her another pint of water over the countertop. 'Of course she wants to believe her son didn't do it,' he said. 'Who could live with that? If I were her, I'd be searching for any reason that might prove his innocence, too.'

'Sorry, I wasn't listening...what was that?' Eilidh asked.

Robert groaned. This conversation was proving impossible.

'Any mother would do the same,' Justine agreed, turning a page and running her index finger down the lines. She looked up with a start, as if she had just remembered something important. 'My God, I remember it like it was yesterday. The noise that woman made.'

'Who?' asked Hammy.

Robert needed no explanation. Mrs Rowley's terrifying, banshee-like screams could be heard from this very bar.

'The mother,' Justine said patiently. 'Mirabella Rowley. It must have been terrible for her. Closest I've come to that sort of grief is losing Pickles.'

'He was a good little cat, Justine,' said Hammy, patting her arm.

Justine's eyes welled up as they normally did whenever she thought of her bygone pets.

'What's the play, Justine?' Eilidh asked.

Justine grinned through her wet eyes and sniffed, pushing her glasses to the bridge of her nose. 'It's a good one this year, sweetheart. Ancient, but very good. If you don't mind, I'd like to leave it as a surprise ... announce it tomorrow. Don't worry, though, there's definitely a juicy role for you.'

'He was definitely guilty?' interrupted Hammy. 'This Toby?'

'I'm certain,' said Eilidh. 'They found him in the bothy, standing over the body, weapon in hand, blood all over him. I'm sure you'll find it all in there.' She gestured to the large envelope.

There was an awkward pause as Eilidh, Hammy and Justine eyed the smaller envelope in Robert's hands. He raised his eyebrows. 'She's a very sad and misguided individual,' he said. 'There'll be nothing of any substance in here. Probably just more delusional rubbish, like last night.'

'You're right, pet,' said Justine. 'Don't let it bother you.' She returned to scribbling her notes.

'Always worth a look, though, no?' Hammy huffed. 'I'd be happy to—'

'Hammy!' Justine exclaimed, jabbing her pencil towards his chest, although her interest had clearly been piqued.

'Eilidh!' Robert shouted and nudged her in the ribs.

She gingerly raised her forehead off the bar. 'What do you want?' she asked, looking more than a little green.

'You know what you need, lassie?' Hammy said, draining his glass. Justine giggled; Robert sighed. 'Hair of the dog.'

'Oh, no,' Eilidh replied, as if even the thought made her nauseous.

'Suit yourself. But I'll take another. It's New Year after all.' This was met with muted cheers from a few of the other customers.

Robert slid off his stool to grab a clean glass. He was in two minds: he had no interest in reading any more of Mirabella's desperate fantasies, but he still felt compelled to open it. Perhaps it was simply a case of morbid curiosity. Then again, he liked the thought of opening a handwritten envelope. When had he last done that? The walkers in his books always enjoyed receiving letters, too. He handed Hammy the beer and picked up the envelope again, rubbing it between his fingers. 'She doesn't like Brian, that's for sure.'

'Ha! Who does?' laughed Justine. 'Less we say about him, the better.'

'Something you and Mirabella have in common, then,' said Eilidh, still struggling to keep her head upright.

'I say open it,' Hammy persisted, after a deep swig. 'Worst that happens is we burn it, forget it ever existed. Go on...'

Robert shrugged and, blowing through his teeth, tore open the envelope. Inside was a single sheet of fine writing paper, headed with an elaborately printed 'Mirabella Rowley' above an address and a mobile number.

'That paper probably cost more than the shoes on my feet,' Justine said.

Robert read the words slowly but seemed unable to process them. He read them again and instructed his eyes to convey some sort of coherent message to his brain, yet still he failed.

'Come on!' urged Hamish, leaning forwards.

'Robbie, are you okay?' asked Eilidh.

Robert noticed his hands were shaking as he lowered the letter onto the counter. The message it contained had finally sunk in.

'Robbie, my God, what is it?' Justine reached for the letter.

He lowered his voice and steadied himself against the countertop. 'She's offering us money in exchange for information about who murdered her daughter.'

'*What?*' Eilidh peered over Justine's shoulder.

'He's right,' Justine said. 'Says here: "Thank you for meeting with me last night ... trust you appreciate the gravity ... I know you will now understand the loss of a family member ... blah, blah ... ample remuneration."'

'*Remuneration?*' Eilidh repeated.

'Cash, Eilidh,' Hammy said, rubbing his hands together excitedly. 'Now *that* makes this interesting.'

'What's this about your dad, Robbie?' Justine asked, tapping halfway down the sheet of paper.

'She said she knew him, remember?' Eilidh muttered, massaging her forehead. 'When she came to the bar last night.'

'But she's quite specific here,' replied Justine, flicking her eyes over the letter again. 'It says, "I've kept an eye on news from Findrussie over the years and, like I said, your father's death struck me as peculiar." What does she mean by that, Robbie?'

Robert realised he had to tell them. But he supposed there was no harm in it, as none of them would think for a second that it was true. 'She has some stupid idea that Dad's death is linked to Clara's murder.' He was pleased that it sounded even more unlikely in his own words. 'I didn't want to tell you because ... well, it's hardly worth entertaining, is it? The police said there were no suspicious circumstances. I was annoyed she brought it up, to be honest.'

Eilidh rolled her eyes and blew through her lips. 'Right...'

'Don't listen to a word of it,' Hammy said, stretching out an arm to pat Robert's shoulder. 'She's a crackpot.'

'Half-gone, if you ask me,' agreed Justine. 'Although that's understandable.'

Robert nodded and looked at each of their faces in turn before finally resting on Justine's. 'Anyway, she's offering a hundred grand. That's what she says, see?' He pointed to the foot of the letter. 'Fifty thousand now, fifty thousand later. I have until tomorrow to decide.'

'I'm telling you, she's crazy,' Hammy declared, rocking backwards on his chair, laughing.

'Do you think she's got that sort of money?' Eilidh asked, staring at the letter.

'Aye, I'd say so, judging from that accent,' Hammy replied.

'And that paper,' Justine agreed, eyeing it suspiciously.

'A hundred grand, though,' said Eilidh. 'Seems a bit excessive.'

'Would do a man for life,' said Hammy, swirling the beer in his glass.

Robert cast a quick glance at the bar's most frequent patron and wondered how much he knew about its finances. 'All right,' he said, calling a halt to the chatter. 'This is ridiculous. I say we forget all about it, put it down to New Year madness. Clearly, Mrs Rowley needs some kind of help.'

'Sounds sensible,' said Justine, nodding. 'No need to start a wild goose chase.'

Justine and Robert nodded, but Hammy drummed his fingers on the countertop until he finally exclaimed: 'On the other hand, she is offering fifty grand *for nothing*.'

A few of the punters turned their heads towards them. Robert felt flustered as he tried to stuff the letter back into the bulging A4 envelope.

'Keep your voice down, Hammy,' said Justine in a faux-whisper that was just as loud, if not louder. More heads turned and they both started to chuckle.

'Well, I'm glad you two are enjoying this,' said Robert.

'I'm just saying it might be worth exploring.' Hammy held Robert's gaze, which meant he was about to impart something he, at least, considered to be deep wisdom. Robert braced himself. 'Your dad loved this place, Robbie. I reckon that kind of money could spruce it up, give it a once-over, you know? It might not be the worst idea.'

Once again, Robert wondered how well he had concealed the bar's dire financial straits. It was true it had been his father's pride and joy. It had been just a shack when he'd bought it, before Robert was born, so he had literally built the business with his own hands. The thought of losing it was not only sad but terrifying. Selling the bar would almost feel like losing his father all over again. The final let-down.

'But I don't know what this woman expects me to do,' Robert replied. 'I'm no private investigator. I can't believe we're even discussing it. This was a murder' – he lowered his voice – 'that happened decades ago ... *and* it was solved. Mrs Rowley can't possibly know anything that the police haven't already discovered and dismissed. It would be cruel, not to mention insane, to entertain her ... theories. She'll believe anything to convince herself that her son didn't do it.'

'Fine.' Hammy shrugged, draining the rest of his pint. 'Would have been something to do, that's all.'

Eilidh laughed. 'Fancy yourself as a detective, Hammy?'

'Aye, me and the dogs. It would have been good to have a wee distraction. Something to turn the cogs, you know? Anyway' – he patted Robert on the back – 'I trust you'll work out what to do for the best. I'll be seeing you tomorrow.'

Robert felt a twinge of guilt. Hammy had lived alone ever since arriving at Findrussie from the West Coast some fifteen years earlier. He had bought a plot of land near the green loch with a plan to set up a seasonal sledging business. He still did the occasional excursion during the winter season, but otherwise his life seemed to revolve around walking the dogs, sitting at home, and drinking at the bar. Despite his twinkly disposition, Robert suspected he must be very lonely.

Justine slid from her stool and wedged the script under her arm. 'Duties beckon.' She waggled a finger at Robert and the semi-conscious Eilidh. 'Half-past six ... sharp!'

'I'll be there,' Robert assured her with a grimace after his mind had tried and failed to come up with a plausible excuse.

'Oh, I know you will,' Justine chuckled as she disappeared into the kitchen.

'I need a nap,' moaned Eilidh, pushing herself from the counter. 'I *really* need a nap.'

'Use the office if you like,' said Robert, trying his best to sound disapproving. He handed her the envelope. 'And take this with you, will you? We don't want the customers seeing it. It's hardly appropriate New Year's Day reading.'

Eilidh shook her head slowly. 'It's a lot of money, Robbie.'

'She's probably not even serious. If she wants the case reopened, there are plenty of people she could ask.'

Eilidh yawned, nodding, 'True,' she agreed. 'But she's asking you, Robbie.'

Chapter Five

The Findrussie Amateur Dramatic Society was a phenomenon no mortal could fathom. Never exceeding twenty players – of varying degrees of acting ability – the performances had acquired a somewhat legendary status, with people travelling from as far as Glasgow to see the annual productions. Justine had been at the helm for the past five years, and she had proven herself a surprisingly competent director. Robert wasn't sure where or how she had gained such an in-depth knowledge of the dramatic arts between her various cleaning jobs, but every year she bedazzled the players with new and exciting ventures.

The entire company was sitting in a circle on the village hall's blue plastic chairs, clutching flasks of tea, listening intently. 'Now, you may think me a mad old whatsit,' began their leader, 'but I've chosen a play which I think will really stretch us – emotionally, technically and as a team.'

Robert smiled as he watched her in full flow, wondering how many times she had rehearsed this speech.

'It's a story about love, really – just as all stories are in the end.' Justine winked at Ruth McLuckie, Robert's old Primary Six teacher, who jumped obediently from her seat and started handing out the scripts. 'But it's also about anger,' Justine continued, 'the terrible anger only a woman scorned can feel ... and what she decides to do with that anger.'

'Media?' asked one of the players.

'*Medea*,' Justine replied, with passionate relish.

Robert flicked through his script, feeling a rising panic as he saw that one male role involved a lot of long, heartfelt soliloquies.

'Bit serious, isn't it, Justine?' piped up Colin, shuffling in his seat.

Justine, clearly prepared for such questions, simply shrugged and shot him a proud pout. 'The Findrussie Am Dram is a serious business.'

'Right...' replied Colin, glancing about the room.

'When are the auditions?' asked Eilidh, who was practically standing, seemingly ready to burst into a monologue.

'I suggest we familiarise ourselves with the script tonight, then you can submit your preferences to me. We'll run the auditions later this week.'

Eilidh nudged Robert in the ribs. 'Who'll you go for?'

'No idea.'

'Jason?' Eilidh jabbed an index finger at the script. 'He's got some cracking lines. Here, look at this...'

Robert frowned at the lengthy speech. 'Absolutely not.'

Eilidh rolled her eyes. 'You've got to go for someone.'

'Is there a character who spends most of his time off-stage? Perhaps all of his time?'

Before Eilidh could respond, there was a shout from the back of the hall. 'Robert Begg! I said Robert Begg!'

Justine stood up and retrieved the glasses that hung about her neck so she could see who it was. 'Excuse me! This is a private rehears—'

'Oh, don't mind me. Please, remain seated.' Mirabella Rowley made her way towards the circle.

Her appearance was in stark contrast to the last time Robert had seen her. She was wearing a pale pink cashmere jumper tucked into a pair of tight, blue chinos, and her hair was styled into an immaculate bob. The rest of the Findrussie Am Dram Society watched her with an odd sort of reverence as she glided towards them. Robert merely sighed deeply. How on earth had this woman not got the message? Although, now he thought about it, something about the way she held her head, with the chin tilted slightly upwards, suggested that she had heard him loud and clear. She had simply chosen to ignore him.

'Robert Begg!' she repeated, as if she had never met him.

'This is Robert!' Ruth almost squealed, pointing at him deferentially.

Mirabella made a great show of resting her eyes upon him. 'There,' she purred.

Robert looked desperately at Eilidh, who shrugged and stood to make room for the new arrival.

'Can we help you?' Justine was watching Mirabella intently through the thick lenses of her glasses.

Mirabella spun gracefully on her heels to respond. 'Why, yes, you can. You see, I have been in discussions with this young gentleman,' she gestured towards Robert, who felt his cheeks glow, 'about a business proposition that has the potential to affect the whole community. The thing is, he had until today to inform me of his decision.' She cocked an eyebrow at Robert. 'Tick-tock, tick-tock,' she said, wagging a finger back and forth, then clasped her hands tightly in front of her narrow waist. Most of the group leaned forwards with interest; a few sat back, arms tightly folded.

'This is hardly the pla—' Justine began, shooting Robert a nervous look.

'I am very fond of this village,' Mirabella interrupted, holding up a polite, yet stern, hand. 'I find it has an original, unique beauty. My family used to visit often.' She spoke with such poise that you never would have guessed that one of those visits had ended in such appalling tragedy.

Robert squirmed in his seat. Mirabella's new-found composure was unnerving.

'Like most visitors, we enjoyed the Pine Needle Bar very much.' She paused to ensure that everyone's attention was still firmly focused on her by studying each of them in turn from beneath coy eyelids. 'That is why I was so disheartened to hear of its demise.'

'*Demise?*' Colin asked, followed by a chorus of similar questions and exclamations.

Robert stared at his knees, sure that he must be scarlet by now. These people had all been close with his father; the Pine Needle was their social hub. The idea that Robert would let it crumble was nothing short of shameful.

'Oh!' Mirabella placed a manicured hand in front of her mouth. 'It seems I have put my foot in it. Silly me.'

'Well, if you're quite finished,' Justine said, pushing herself up from her chair, 'I'd like to get back to our read-through.'

'You mentioned a business proposition?' Colin prompted.

'Oh, yes.' Mirabella took a dainty step forward. 'I think that's for Robert to share with the rest of you.'

Eilidh leaned sideways and whispered in Robert's ear, 'For God's sake, say something!' Her eyes were wide and expectant.

Robert knew what she was thinking: everyone wanted an explanation. He thought back to the early hours of New Year's Day, when he had heard someone in the bar. Mirabella must have rifled through the office, seen the accounts, found his weak spot. She was more ruthless than he had realised.

'Is it true, Robert?' asked Ruth. 'Your dad's bar?' The question sent another round of mumbles through the group.

Robert shook his head, unsure whether his legs were twitching through anger or embarrassment. He clutched the sides of his chair, sat upright, and admitted, 'There have been some .... cash flow issues.'

'But it's always full!' exclaimed Colin.

'That's true. Unfortunately...' Robert closed his eyes, wishing he could be anywhere else but here.

'What's *she* got to do with it, though?' Colin pointed at Mirabella, who looked like she might take issue with the gesture, but then let it slide.

'I've offered Mr Begg some money,' she explained smoothly. 'Enough to tide him over for a few months, at least.'

This was met with a chorus of mixed emotions: a few appreciative murmurs, some suspicious grunts.

'Consider it a donation to an area I have grown to love. Trouble is, I am having real trouble convincing him to accept it.'

'Take it, Robert!' insisted Ruth without hesitation, beaming at Mirabella. Most of the group started to nod in agreement.

'No room for pride, Robert,' added Colin. 'Don't look a gift horse...and all that.'

'You see' – Mirabella was still addressing the room – 'when Robert's father di—'

'We can speak in private!' Robert cut her off abruptly and rose to his feet. These people had been some of his father's closest friends. He didn't want them to hear Mirabella's ridiculous fantasies just as they were starting to recover from their grief.

'Of course,' said Mirabella, nodding to the group and shooting Robert a smug smile. 'Wonderful to meet you all.'

'You too!' called Ruth.

Robert led Mirabella out of the hall and into the car park.

They walked in silence past the flower boxes the village committee had planted the previous spring to brighten up the space. Now they were just dry, hard mounds of earth.

'I'll call the police,' he said suddenly, rounding on her, his fists clenched inside his coat pockets. 'I don't know what you want from me. I've told you I can't help you. This is way over the line. Too much!'

'*Too much?*' Mirabella raised a bored smile. 'How do you mean?'

'You are practically stalking me,' Robert exclaimed, forcing himself to meet her eyes. 'I haven't done anything to you.'

'I haven't accused you of anything.'

'Then why are you doing this?' He knew he sounded desperately childlike. He checked the door over Mirabella's shoulder and was grateful that no one had followed them outside. 'Why bring my dad into it? He was a good man, respected. We're all only just getting over his death. You can't just show up here and begin talking nonsense about how he died, no matter how upset you are. And he certainly had nothing to do with your daughter's death. The police knew what they were doing. You don't have any right to overrule them.'

She remained silent for a moment, standing like a sculpture in the stony air. 'No right? You think you know about rights? You know nothing. I have had everything – *everything* – stolen from me, without just cause, without justice.' She stepped closer, until he could feel her hot breath against his face. 'You loved your father?'

'Of course I did,' he said, trying to suppress the tremble in his bottom lip.

'Good,' she snarled. 'Then listen to me. After twenty-two years of watching this place – where, I think you'll agree, nothing, and I mean *nothing*, normally happens – I read that Bennie Begg has died suddenly. In the loch, wasn't it?'

Robert tried to nod through the dizziness he suffered whenever he thought of that day. He closed his eyes, wishing he could dispel the flickering images from his mind. He could still hear his own screams, the crunch of the pebbles beneath his feet.

Mirabella continued, 'The loch he swam in every day, more or less. He was fit and healthy, wasn't he? No reason to suppose his body might fail him.'

'Stop...' Robert pleaded.

'But no questions were asked, am I right? Everyone just accepted that your father suddenly – magically – drowned, out of the blue. Do you know what I think, Mr Begg?'

Robert knew by now that there was no point in protesting. He held his hands tightly against his sides.

'I think he discovered something. I have always thought that the secret behind my daughter's murder lay buried here. Someone must have known something. I believe that your dad stumbled across—'

'You can't be serious,' Robert interrupted, stepping away from her. 'It's all in your head, Mrs Rowley.'

'Perhaps,' she acknowledged. 'But if that's the case, how do you explain *this*?' She reached into her purse, extracted her mobile and held the screen in front of Robert's face.

He frowned as he stared blankly at the call log. 'What's this?' he asked.

She said nothing. Sighing irritably, Robert started to look at the list of calls more closely, then caught his breath as he recognised one of the numbers.

'That's the Pine Needle's landline,' he said, snatching the phone from her hand. 'This says you were called on...'

Mirabella nodded slowly as Robert's voice trailed away. He expected her to be smug, but instead her eyes were inflected with pity. 'The day your father drowned,' she said softly. 'I had a strange message from him. It was a short one, I thought it was a mistake at the time. All he did was introduce himself before the line went dead. I forgot all about it for a while. Then I saw the announcement of his death in the local news; I follow the news of Findrussie meticulously to this day. Something clicked. So, I Googled his number and it showed up at the Pine Needle and ... well, here I am.'

Robert blinked at the screen and bit his lip. It was certainly peculiar, but didn't necessarily indicate anything untoward. 'I ... I don't know why he would have—'

'I'm sure it was your father,' Mirabella insisted.

He shook his head. 'I'm not sure that this means anything, Mrs Rowley. We can pass the information on to the police, but otherwise I'd rather just move on with my life.' Then he paused as a question occurred to him. 'How would my dad have got your number, anyway?'

'That's simple,' said Mirabella, in the now-familiar tone that suggested he really ought to keep up. 'My number has been in your visitors' book for years and it's never changed. I've drunk at your bar for decades, on and off.'

Bennie Begg had insisted that they must maintain the visitors' book, no matter how much Robert had insisted it was an antiquated system. To this day, it was still in the top drawer of the office desk, precisely where it had always been.

'Mr Begg, let me get this right,' she said. 'I have evidence that casts suspicion over your father's death, and you are telling me that you'd prefer to do nothing about it?'

'I ... I don't know...' Robert winced at his own indecision as well as the fact that he was clearly losing this argument.

Then she delivered the *coup de grâce*. 'And I'm sure your

friends would be very disappointed to learn that you had turned down my kind offer to save the village bar.'

Robert was left in awe of her verbal dexterity. Her voice was low and ominous. She cocked her head towards the hall, which was, sure enough, full of people who would be more than a little annoyed if Robert allowed the bar to fold.

'You've already made sure of that,' said Robert, narrowing his eyes.

Mirabella shrugged casually. 'So, do you accept my offer?'

Robert stared up into the night sky and considered his options. Mrs Rowley would surely keep pestering him until he agreed to her proposal. She had also proven herself well capable of calculated manipulation, which was not something he wanted to experience again. And although he felt it was neither here nor there, he would like to know why his father had called her on the day he'd died. He assumed that there would be a reasonable explanation for that, at least.

'I'm still not entirely sure why you think I can help you but ... fine. It seems I don't have much choice, anyway,' he said, thinking of Colin's reaction were he to reject Mirabella's lifeline.

'Oh, you have a choice,' she said. 'Just not the sort of choice you want to make. I'm accustomed to those myself.'

'I'm just a barman, Mrs Rowley. I can't promise I'll find anything.'

'Call it a hunch,' she said. 'I feel you might have more to you than meets the eye.'

Robert shifted uncomfortably on the spot. Did he detect the tiniest compliment buried somewhere in there?

Mirabella continued, 'There's a kindness in your eyes. That's something else I have learned over the years: how to distinguish between the honest and the duplicitous. It's now a finely tuned skill.'

'I'll look through the notes you left at the bar,' Robert assured her.

'In your own time,' she replied, although the implication was clearly 'As soon as is humanly possible,' especially as she added: 'We'll meet tomorrow at the Pine Needle. I'll come after closing. Ten o'clock on Tuesdays. That's right, isn't it?'

Robert nodded, speechless. This was not how he had expected his New Year to begin.

'Splendid,' she said, and with that brushed past him, stalked through the car park and headed onto the main village street.

'Wait!' he shouted.

'Yes?' She stopped and turned, silhouetted beneath the orange glow of a streetlamp. It made her hair seem translucent.

'Can I bring some friends along?'

❄

Later that night, Robert stared at his bedroom ceiling and watched a spider make its way from one corner to the other. The book he had planned to read lay unopened; his tea was cold on the bedside table. He had exhausted his list of 't' animals, which would normally have sent him straight to sleep, but not tonight. The faces of the Am Dram Society revolved around his bedroom, looking down on him through the pale moonlight. Each person was wearing a different expression, some smiling, some frowning, disappointed in him.

He sighed and kicked the duvet off his legs. He had planned to save Mirabella's notes for the morning on the assumption that they would make poor bedtime reading. But the knowledge that they were sitting in his wardrobe drawer made sleep impossible. He fetched them, carried them downstairs, and boiled the kettle.

As expected, the details were shocking. The report of Clara

Rowley's face being unrecognisable due to the ragged wound that sliced right through the middle of her skull was terrible. Robert gulped and took a sip of tea. The envelope also contained copious notes on all of those who had been involved in the case. Inevitably, Brian McCrae – and especially what Mirabella viewed as the shortcomings of his investigation – featured heavily. Several meticulously constructed sections – some more convincing than others – attempted to explain why Toby could not possibly have killed his sister. The final item in the envelope was a scrap of paper with the Pine Needle's telephone number and a short note – 'Called on October 28th' – written alongside it. Robert's eyes began to sting as he pored over reports of blood spatters, descriptions of Kinlogie House, maps of Findrussie, photographs of almost all of the locals. But after two hours of intense study, he couldn't understand how Mirabella had reached the conclusion that Toby had not murdered his sister. Her whole case seemed to be based on nothing more than a mother's intuition.

He massaged his temples and, with a heavy sigh, dragged his feet back up the stairs. Just before he fell into a broken sleep, he pictured his father. His beard was longer than Robert remembered, but his eyes were the same: bright and full of promised fun. 'Dad,' he whispered. 'What's going on? What on earth have you got me into?'

Chapter Six

Robert had never liked the dark mornings that haunted Findrussie's winters. His father had religiously dedicated every one to a run along the low mountain path that swept through the forest near Hammy's lodge, back around the loch, up to the higher ground, then the descent with expansive views of the highest mountains on the other side. Robert had joined him, always a few paces behind, even as his father grew older, throughout the spring and summer, but never in the winter.

'The way is gritted,' his father would argue.

'It's still dangerous in the dark.'

'Then wear a head torch; I have a spare.'

'I'm all right. You go,' Robert would chuckle, but only to distract himself from the frown of exasperation on his father's face. Bennie Begg had always been what people might call 'hardy', but when his wife left him, he took to outdoor pursuits with a sense of single-minded determination. It was almost as if he were trying to prove himself as more of a man, or at least a better man than his wife's new lover.

Despite his misgivings, a month after his father's death, Robert had decided to see what he was missing. He left the house at 6.00 a.m. and jogged his father's route alone. At first, he felt pathetic: his legs almost gave way up the very first hill and thereafter he took tiny, timid steps, scared of slipping on the icy path. However, as he pushed on, he found that the darkness, far from being an enemy, started to embrace him like an old friend. The loch loomed below in a mass of silvery shadows. He had avoided it for weeks, keeping his distance from his father's watery grave, but seeing it from above, with his father's torch strapped to his head, he began to feel that he just might be able to live with it again.

That first winter run had been precisely a month ago. Now, as he performed his stretches in the kitchen, his phone buzzed with a message. He reached for it warily, praying the text was not from Mirabella. To his surprise, it was from Eilidh: 'Do you mind if I join you on this morning's jog?' followed by runner and sunrise emojis, as if the question itself did not contain all the necessary information. He was typing his response – including a gentle dig that the sun would not be rising for at least another couple of hours – when there was a knock at the door.

'Let me in, Robbie. It's freezing out here!' Eilidh was standing on the front step, dressed in a pair of brightly coloured leggings and a pair of plimsolls. She grinned. 'Thought you'd say no, but I reckon you could do with some company.'

'How do you know I run in the morning?' Robert asked, stepping to one side.

'Hammy sees you,' Eilidh replied. 'He's always up with the dogs.'

Robert nodded, frantically trying to remember when and where on the route he broke into fits of unabashed song. 'Do you ... *can* you run?'

'Won't know until I try, will I?' She craned her neck inside the doorway and looked around the house. 'Like what you're going for here...'

Robert followed her gaze to the piles of laundry on the sofa, the discarded mugs on the coffee table, the empty pizza boxes stacked beside the wastepaper basket. He felt himself reddening as he edged past her. 'Well, are you coming or not?'

'Let's go!' she said and sprinted ahead.

Unsurprisingly, shortly after her initial burst of speed, Eilidh requested a 'power walk' for the rest of the route, which amounted to a moderately brisk stroll. Still, Robert enjoyed the company, especially after the last couple of days. It also gave him an opportunity to broach the topic of the upcoming meeting, which he was hoping Eilidh would attend.

'I don't understand,' she said. 'Are you saying Mirabella wants you to solve her daughter's murder?'

'Pretty much,' Robert said, glancing down at her footing in the snow. 'That's what she says, anyway. I've only agreed to meet her again to get her off my back ... although I must admit that fifty grand would come in handy, too.'

'It's all so crazy.'

'I know,' Robert said. 'But that phone call from the Pine Needle is ... weird. I'm not saying I agree with all her theories about the murder, but *that* is a mystery.'

'Sounds like you might be starting to believe her...'

'God, no. But someone rang Mirabella from our office phone and I'd like to know why, just ... in case.'

'In case of what?'

'I don't know!' He checked himself. None of this was Eilidh's fault. 'Sorry, I didn't mean to shout.'

'No bother.'

They were approaching the best view of the loch. The inky blues swelled in the centre of the water, calling to the mountains to emerge from the darkness.

'It's so beautiful,' said Eilidh.

Robert nodded, interlocking his hands behind his head.

'So, you're going to accept the offer, then?'

'I suppose I am.'

Eilidh turned towards him and nodded, puffing slightly.

'She's coming to the bar later. I was wondering if you'd like to ... No, it's a stupid idea. You've probably got plenty of other things going on.' He stumbled over his words as Eilidh frowned. How could he have missed the mark so badly? Why on earth would she want to spend an evening going over a brutal murder case with a mad old lady and him? She had a life outside the bar, filled with parties and friends and ... boyfriends, probably. Which, he reminded himself, shouldn't bother him at all.

'Robbie...'

'No, no, you're right. Stupid suggestion.'

'Oh my God! We're going to be detectives!' She jumped into the air, laughing from her belly. 'You're serious, aren't you?'

Robert began to smile, his lips twitching at the idea. 'It's utterly ridiculous, isn't it? But it could be interesting. And we could all do with the money.'

'Hammy is going to love this.'

'I thought we could share the cash between us. Fifty thousand divided by four is still loads.'

'Who said anything about *fifty* thousand?' Eilidh asked, looking him squarely in the eye.

'That's what she's offering, remember? It was in the letter.'

'No ... it's fifty up front, *plus* another fifty when we identify the murderer.'

Robert stared at her. 'Eilidh,' he said firmly, 'Toby Rowley was convicted and sent to prison. *He* was the murderer. We'll just have to ... go through the motions, and hopefully find out why Dad called Mirabella. That'll be the end of it.'

'Unless ... she's right!' Her eyes were wide now. He was

about to protest again when she held a finger to his mouth. 'Hear me out. You've seen the phone records. You know that she received a call from the Pine Needle. Affirmative?' She paused, waiting for a response.

'Yes,' Robert agreed. Eilidh raised her eyebrows. He sighed, rolling his eyes. 'Affirmative.'

'Excellent, thank you. We both agree that Bennie was a sane man?'

'Ye ... affirmative.'

'Good. And that he wasn't in the business of randomly calling strangers for no reason? Especially the mothers of teenagers who had been murdered in his village?'

'Affirmative.'

'So...' Eilidh tried to click her fingers, but it ended up as more of a finger waggle in her thick gloves. 'This all suggests to me, as a rookie detective, that there is at least some mystery to be solved here, Mr Begg.'

Robert frowned towards the shadowy mountains. Above them the sky was clear, pierced with sharp, shimmering stars. 'So, you think Dad might have discovered something, too?'

'It's not impossible, is it?'

'No, but ... You know what this means, Eilidh? You know what you're saying?'

She pursed her lips and grabbed hold of his arms. 'I do. I'm sorry, Robbie. That was insensitive of me.'

'No, it's fine...' he whispered. His face felt numb, and not just because of the cold. He had been so busy telling himself that Mirabella was talking nonsense he had ignored the logic of her argument. If even just some of her theories were correct, then his dad's death may not have been an accident. He let out a small groan.

'Robbie,' Eilidh rubbed his upper arms, 'if there's any

chance what she's saying is true, don't you think we owe it to Bennie to investigate?'

'You mean actually try to do this *properly*?' He closed his eyes and willed his racing heart to slow.

'No other way to do anything, Robbie.' With that, she turned on her heel and started to retrace her steps, back towards an archway of snow-laden trees.

'Eilidh, it's this way,' Robert called as she disappeared beneath the branches.

'Justine's at Hammy's,' she shouted over her shoulder. 'They've got breakfast waiting. They'll want to know where to begin.'

Robert followed her, shaking his head in disbelief at what had just happened.

Chapter Seven

The day sped by in a blur of food orders, hiking recommendations, pint-pulling and mopping up spillages.

Justine worked her usual magic, hurried off her feet, yet somehow gliding through the bar and cracking jokes with the customers. She especially delighted the tourists, exaggerating her accent and teaching them the proper pronunciations of the nearby landmarks. Should one of them dare to ask if they could throw an extra log on the fire, she would reply, with just as much enthusiasm as the first time she had delivered the line, 'Trying to bleed us dry, are you? It's not as if they grow on trees, you know.'

Hammy sat at the bar from lunchtime onwards, with his dogs – all eight of them – lying patiently at his feet in a shaggy mountain of white fur. Eilidh pulled pints with her usual vigour, then happily sloshed them across the bar to the eager punters. Robert divided his time between taking orders and working in the office. All four of them had fallen into a peculiar pattern of sharing surreptitious, sideways glances whenever they walked past one another. Robert was amazed that none of the customers had noticed and asked what the big secret was.

When the last bill was settled, Eilidh cleared away the plates while Justine fetched the couple's coats and jostled them towards the door, 'Lovely night,' she trilled, looking at the full-blown blizzard through the window. 'Bracing!' The man seemed about to ask if they could stay awhile until the weather had eased off, but Justine opened the door for them before he had the chance. 'Hopefully see you soon. Glad to hear you're enjoying it up here. Do try the Coire trail, as I said.' She let out a tremendous sigh as she closed the door behind them.

'She'll be here any moment,' Eilidh said, rushing to load the dishwasher.

'Aye,' said Hammy, helping himself to another pint from behind the bar. 'You ready, Robbie?'

Robert could hardly speak. His stomach knotted more tightly every time he thought of Mirabella. He had never foreseen himself in this sort of scenario and, unfortunately for his nerves, today was a 'U' day, which always proved problematic. He dragged the old noticeboard from the office, but instead of the usual staffing rotas and scribbled orders, it was covered with the contents of Mirabella's 'Murder Pack', as Hammy had christened it.

'Wow!' said Eilidh.

'We've certainly got plenty to get through,' said Hammy, ruffling a dog's head.

'Well, it's taken me twenty-two years to reach this point, so it should be substantial,' announced Mirabella from the doorway. 'Shall we get started? I will need a whisky, Mr Begg.'

❄

The other four sat before the noticeboard while Robert talked them through what he had gathered so far. He got off to a slow start, mumbling over the initial details, until Mirabella first ordered him to speak up, then declared, 'And good heavens, stand up straight!'

Robert cleared his throat and did his best to comply. 'So, to run through the night in question again. It's 31 December 2000. The Rowley family – Mirabella,' he nodded at her nervously, 'her husband Anthony—'

'Now deceased!' Hammy interjected.

Robert cringed and cast a worried glance at Mirabella.

'Oh, please,' said Mirabella, wafting a dismissive hand in the air. 'I assure you that comes as no surprise to me.' Her notes on the case had included full details of her husband's descent into depression in the wake of their children's deaths and his subsequent overdose at the family home.

Robert continued, '...their eldest child Toby, twenty-one at the time, and their daughter, Clara, who was seventeen – are visiting their old friends Felicity and Peter Montgomery—'

'Also deceased!' Hammy exclaimed.

'Yes,' Robert agreed. 'Peter is also now deceased. Thank you, Hammy. They are staying at Kinlogie House, which the Montgomerys own. On Hogmanay, the Rowley family visit the Pine Needle Bar for pre-dinner drinks.' Again, he looked directly at Mirabella, who retained her steely expression, though her eyes had drifted to the series of Hogmanay photographs on the wall behind the bar. They dated back decades; the one Justine had taken earlier that week would be added soon enough. Robert suddenly realised that Mirabella's family would probably be in the 2000/2001 photo. His father always took it early in the evening so as not to interfere with the midnight celebrations.

'At eight o'clock, they leave the bar and return to Kinlogie, where Felicity Montgomery has prepared a Hogmanay dinner. The meal lasts about two hours and, when they have finished dessert, Clara asks her mother if she can meet someone in town.'

Mirabella was nodding methodically now, her eyes glazed. Robert took this as confirmation that his account was correct, so he continued: 'Mirabella is just about to ask who Clara is intending to meet when Toby, who has drunk too much, starts to cause a scene.'

Mirabella's left eye twitched and she turned her head sharply to face Robert. 'I should have paid more attention,' she said robotically. 'She was trying to tell me something. She was always sneaking out to meet some boy or other. She never asked permission, always just left the house without a word. There must have been a reason why she tried to tell me that night.'

Robert nodded and scribbled a note on the board. 'It's impossible to know precisely when Clara leaves Kinlogie, as Anthony and Mirabella have their hands full with Toby, who needs to be put to bed. And Felicity Montgomery is doing the same with Peter, who is suffering from early-onset Alzheimer's.'

'There must have been staff though?' Eilidh asked. 'That place is huge.'

'No.' Mirabella shook her head. 'Your classic landowners' problem. Felicity and Peter were asset rich but had next to nothing in the bank, as far as I know.'

'Aye.' Justine nodded solemnly. 'I cleaned the place a few times when Felicity needed help. Poor woman. Some of the rooms were an inch thick in dust. She offered to pay me in whisky. What with looking after Peter and running that big old house, she had her hands full, I can tell you that.'

Robert made another note on the board. 'It gets to eleven-thirty. Toby has been put to bed by his parents. Anthony is in the study drinking whisky. Mirabella is in the drawing room, err...'

'Crying,' Mirabella added. 'As usual, the evening had not been the happy occasion that I had imagined.'

'...and Felicity and Peter are both in bed.' He took a deep

breath. The next section was the part he was dreading. He caught Mirabella's eye and she nodded curtly. Her lips were pursed together so tightly that the skin around them was turning white. 'Mirabella decides to go on a walk, to let off some steam.'

Eilidh shuffled in her seat, her face ashen. Robert tried to reassure her with a grim nod. 'She sees a light coming from the Ryvune bothy…' He walked across to the map above the bar and pointed to a spot between Kinlogie House and the Pine Needle. 'She notices footprints in the snow leading to the bothy entrance.'

'I thought…' Mirabella stared into the mid-distance, unblinking. 'I thought it was Clara, just messing about with a boy.' She emitted a noise that was halfway between a yelp and a sob.

Justine moved her chair closer and placed a comforting arm around Mirabella's shoulders. 'We can take a break if you like,' she said, shooting Robert a worried look.

'No.' Mirabella spoke so sternly that Eilidh jumped and the dogs whined. 'No,' she repeated. 'Carry on.'

Robert glanced towards Hammy, who rotated his hand as a signal to continue. 'Okay,' he said, feeling queasy. 'Mirabella follows the footprints and opens the door to the bothy. There, she finds her daughter, Clara.' He swallowed audibly, looked back to the noticeboard and decided to spare Mirabella the gruesome details of the murder scene. After all, she had witnessed it first hand; and the others already knew how she had found her daughter, with the axe still lodged in Clara's skull. Toby, covered in his sister's blood, and out of his mind on whatever party drugs he had taken after going to bed, was kneeling over the body, cackling. 'Sardonically' was the word Mirabella had used in her initial interviews with the police, something that no doubt had contributed to his conviction.

'Mirabella tries to drag Toby back to Kinlogie, but he

refuses to move, so she runs back alone, calling for her husband. Seeing his wife inconsolable and covered in blood, Anthony rings the police before he is fully aware what has happened. The police arrive after Mirabella has led Anthony to the bothy. Toby is still there, with Clara's body. He is taken into custody that night.'

'It wasn't him,' Mirabella said, her voice shaking.

'Which is why you are – *we* are – here,' agreed Robert swiftly, noting the disbelief in the others' eyes. He knew exactly what they were thinking: when the events were laid out in black and white, it was inconceivable anyone else could be the culprit. He pressed on regardless: 'There are some noteworthy points of interest. Mirabella, you say Clara mentioned running into an old friend?'

'Yes.' Mirabella nodded. 'She didn't say who, though.'

'Did you ask?'

Mirabella folded her arms. 'No. You must understand that I was preoccupied with my son. He was ... struggling. University hadn't done him any good at all. He left for Oxford as a bright, energetic young man. He came back after his first year a different person. Thereafter, things went from bad to worse. We tried everything: rehab, counselling, therapy. Nothing helped. When we were invited to Kinlogie, I thought a family trip away from his London crowd might do him good. Besides, Clara had some friends here. As you know, we'd visited a few times throughout her life.'

'So, you've no idea who the friend was? The one she said she was meeting?'

'I told the police it might have been an old boyfriend she'd seen on and off during previous visits.'

'No name?' asked Eilidh.

'I'm afraid not. Everything I know is in my notes. Clara was very secretive about her private life, like a lot of teenage girls.

But I think one particular boy bought her alcohol as she often came back tipsy.'

'It would be good if we had a name,' said Eilidh, scratching her forehead.

Mirabella nodded. 'Yes, I am well aware of that, young lady.' She glowered at Eilidh. 'I'm not paying you to judge me. I've had long enough to ponder my shortcomings as a mother, believe me.'

Robert wrote 'Boyfriend' on the board before Eilidh could respond. 'You identified him as a possible suspect.'

'Of course,' said Mirabella. 'But the police didn't even bother to find out who he was.'

'Ah,' said Robert. 'Which leads us to—'

'McCrae,' said Mirabella.

'Brian McCrae,' repeated Robert, writing the name on the board. 'He led the investigation into Clara's murder and you felt he was ... lacking?'

'He was next to useless,' corrected Mirabella. 'To him, it was an easy deal. He had a conviction handed to him on a plate and didn't bother listening to anything my husband or I had to say. He was happy to throw Toby to the wolves. I tell you, that sort of incompetence would never be tolerated in England.'

Robert shuffled awkwardly as Hammy made a small motion with his hand that instructed one of the dogs to lift its tail and break wind in Mirabella's direction. 'I'm so sorry,' he said, patting the dog on the head. 'That's enough, old boy. The dogs are Scottish, I'm afraid.'

Mirabella scowled. 'I always thought he could have done more. I complained many times over the years, of course, but no one listens to a hysterical woman.' She sniffed and added, pointedly, 'Especially when she's criticising a respected man.'

Robert summarised, 'So, we are dealing with a mysterious boyfriend and an "incompetent" police officer. Anyone else?'

She shook her head. 'But I'm open to suggestions.'

Robert took a step away from the board. He didn't like the idea of scrutinising the rest of the local community. Hammy, however, seemed to have no problem with it. 'We should add Felicity Montgomery to the list,' he said.

'That wild woman in the woods?' Eilidh asked, rolling her eyes. After Peter Montgomery's death, Felicity had sold Kinlogie and moved into what she called an 'eco-hut' but everyone else categorised as a semi-derelict shack.

'Worth speaking to her,' Hammy insisted, taking the marker pen from Robert and adding Felicity's name to the board. 'She might have noticed something important.'

'Right,' Justine said gently, her arm still around Mirabella's shoulders. 'So that's the boyfriend, McCrae and Felicity ... for now.'

Mirabella nodded and blew her nose loudly. 'Thank you,' she said, primly. 'I'll transfer the money first thing tomorrow.'

Robert sighed and looked around the bar until his eyes rested on the photograph of his dad serving the Pine Needle's first ever pint. His smile was as wide as ever, full of honesty and kindness. Robert knew what he would say if he were here, and he took the momentous decision to echo him: 'I won't take a penny, Mrs Rowley. My dad never would have accepted your money, not even to save the bar. So you don't need to pay me, either. It's what he would have wanted.'

Hammy seemed about to protest but checked himself and settled back in his chair. 'I agree,' he said finally, sounding only slightly put out. 'Bennie would be proud of you, Robbie.'

Robert felt a lump rise in his throat as he studied the noticeboard again. 'I don't know about that, Hammy,' he replied. 'Maybe if we can manage to solve ... whatever this is. But I'll understand if you lot don't want to help any more.'

'Don't be daft!' Eilidh rose to her feet. 'I'm still in, payment or not.'

'Aye, me too,' Hammy said. 'Nothing else going on, like I say.'

'You're like a son to me, Robbie,' Justine said. 'Of course I'll help.'

Robert gulped, overcome with an urge to scoop them all up into a giant hug. 'That's settled, then,' he said.

Mirabella had made her way behind the bar and was studying the photographs. 'One for every Hogmanay,' she said.

'Sort of a tradition. Dad started it when he opened the bar.'

Mirabella leaned in closely to study the 2000/2001 picture. She searched the image for a few seconds, then raised a shaky finger to it. 'She looks happy, doesn't she? Don't you think? She looks happy there, at least.' Her stoic exterior evaporated to reveal a sorrow that still seemed painfully raw. She began to sob. It was a terrible sound of pure heartbreak.

The group stood awkwardly for a moment before Eilidh broke free and approached Mirabella. 'Come on,' she said. 'Where are you staying? We'll take you.'

Mirabella looked at her as if she had completely forgotten where she was. Then, gathering herself, she declared, 'Kinlogie,' and held her hands out in defence. 'I know, I *know*. It's strange. But I felt I couldn't stay anywhere else. It doesn't feel the same at all, of course. Everything has changed. I never would have recognised it.'

'My flat's that way. Eilidh, you away too?' Justine rummaged in her bag for her car keys.

'Yeah.' Eilidh looked at Robert. 'If we're all done here?'

Robert nodded as he began to feel the slightest glimmer of confidence in his belly. 'For now,' he said. 'But then we've got to track down this mystery boyfriend.'

Chapter Eight

The auditions for the Findrussie Am Dram Society production of *Medea* were in full swing, with Eilidh, as usual, the only real contender for the leading role. Robert had agreed to assist Justine with the administration in exchange for exemption from playing the male lead.

'Just ask their names and write them down once they've finished, before they're away,' she instructed. 'Make sure you copy the main gist of my notes next to each one. We want all my comments in one easy-to-read document.'

'But I already know everyone's name,' he argued.

She fixed him with a firm stare. 'Just ask. It gives a sense of formality, trust me.'

Justine scribbled away excitedly as she assessed each performance before tearing the pages from her jotter and scrunching them into Robert's chest, but he found the notes almost impossible to decipher.

'What does that say?' he whispered as Mrs McKay shuffled from the stage.

'She might need to sit!' Justine hissed under her breath. 'She'll need to be in the Chorus so she can have a rest at the back. She does amazingly for her age, but she can't be on her feet all night.'

'Sorry,' Robert said as he received yet another page of scrawled notes. 'Can we slow down a bit, please?'

'No. I have a hair appointment soon. Sandra's opening the salon late specially. And Colin's next. He emailed to ask if he could read the whole scene as a monologue.'

Two hours later, Robert thought he could probably recite most of the main speeches himself. It was certainly a different direction for the company. Justine had explained it was written by an Athenian playwright over two thousand years ago, but modern adaptations were apparently all the rage. The denouement was particularly grisly. While fetching Justine a cup of tea, Robert had heard Ruth McLuckie whispering feverishly, 'Do you know how it ends? I like Justine, she's a good friend, but I think she should change that bit. Nobody wants to see that sort of thing on stage. People like our Noël Cowards and our Alan Ayckbourns.'

Treacherously, Robert had found himself agreeing. The main character ended up killing her own children in revenge for her husband's disloyalty. It didn't sound like something the local schools – which usually made up most of their audience on opening night – would be keen to attend. But he had to admit that Justine hadn't let them down yet, and she seemed convinced this play was a stepping-stone that would enable the company to reach 'the next level'.

He read out the preliminary cast list to Justine as she sat in the hairdresser's chair, waiting for her brassy-red tint to take effect.

'Eilidh is our Medea, obviously,' Justine confirmed. 'But what about Jason?'

'You didn't really like any of the male applicants,' said Robert, rifling through her notes.

'What about Daniel Bell?' she suggested. 'He didn't exactly light up the stage, but I reckon I can work with him.'

'All right.' Robert scribbled down the name.

'Enough about that, though,' said Justine in a dramatic, hushed voice, pushing the audition notes to one side. 'We should be talking about our investigation.'

Robert checked the mirror and saw Sandra was on the phone behind the front desk.

'Have you made any progress at all?' Justine continued.

Robert scratched his head. 'We only had our first meeting last night,' he said defensively. 'I was at work all day, then the auditions...'

'Murderers don't hang around for you to get yourself organised, Robbie.'

'Shhhhh!' he hissed, then checked to see if Sandra had heard. 'Anyway, this one's been hanging around for more than two decades.'

Justine jabbed his chest with a fingernail. 'Don't give me that sort of lip. Obviously, there's a reason why I asked you to come here.'

He nodded, looking at the audition notes. 'Yes, to go through the cast list.'

'Don't be silly. I've known who I want ever since I chose the play,' she said breezily, seizing the notes from him.

Robert narrowed his eyes. Much as he loved the woman, she could be infuriating.

'Tell me, Robbie, who knows the most about everyone in Findrussie?'

'Err...'

'Correct – the hairdresser.'

The heater beeped, which prompted Sandra to hang up the phone and make her way over. 'Now, let's see what we've got here. How are you, Robert?' she cooed. 'You haven't been in since you were wee.'

'Hello, Sandra,' said Robert as he held Justine's gaze in the mirror, wondering what she was about to say.

'Sandra,' Justine began. 'Can you tell Robbie how long I've been coming here for my colours?'

Sandra beamed. 'Longer than I can remember, Justine.'

'That's right. I make it just over thirty years, give or take. I was about your age when I moved here, Robbie.'

'Always had the same colour,' said Sandra as she started to remove the foils from Justine's hair. 'This is a woman who knows what she likes.'

'Aye,' agreed Justine, admiring Sandra's handiwork in the mirror. Then, with a flick of her eyes to Robert, 'Who else do you do, Sandra? Anyone as long-standing as me? Or am I special?' She laughed but Robert saw that she was watching Sandra's expression carefully.

'Oh well, let me think,' replied Sandra. 'There's Lesley McKay. She's been coming here for her rinse every month for thirty years.'

'Amazing,' said Justine, shaking her head as if in disbelief. 'Anyone else?'

Sandra laughed, clearly bemused by the strange turn the conversation had taken. 'I'm not sure...'

'The stories you must hear...' Justine pressed, still eyeballing Robert in the mirror. 'You know, I reckon Sandra could help you with your wee project, Robbie.'

'*Project?*' Robert's mouth suddenly felt very dry.

'Aye, the one you were blethering about earlier. That love-letter you found.'

'Err...' Robert saw his eyes widening in the mirror and hoped Justine planned to elaborate.

'Love-letter?' said Sandra, placing both palms on her cheeks in mock-excitement. 'Sounds intriguing.'

'He found it under a floorboard in the bar,' said Justine smoothly.

Robert watched in admiration as she continued to spin the story.

'It was addressed to "C", wasn't it, Robbie? Whoever wrote it said that they had never experienced a love quite like it before. Very romantic, if you ask me. That's what makes it such a great shame.'

'A shame?' Sandra began wrapping Justine's hair in a towel.

'Well, you said it was still folded tight, didn't you, Robbie? So it probably never reached the intended recipient.'

'Oh, you're right. That *is* a shame,' said Sandra. 'I'd be buzzing if someone wrote me something like that.'

'Me too,' agreed Justine, shooting an encouraging look at Robert.

'I just thought I should try to deliver it, finally,' said Robert, holding Justine's gaze as she nodded along to his words. 'Would be a nice thing to do. Might give someone a bit of a pick-me-up, especially at this time of year.' He was trying his best to sound as casual as possible, but his tongue felt huge and clumsy inside his mouth.

'Imagine! A love-letter that was never delivered,' mused Justine.

Robert raised his eyebrows: she was clearly relishing this opportunity to exercise her dramatic skills.

'Do you have any clues?' asked Sandra. 'Is there a date, for example?'

'Well, that's the main issue,' said Justine. 'Isn't it, Robbie?'

'Yes, that's the main issue,' he repeated as he tried to work out where she was going with this.

'It was written years ago,' said Justine, shaking her head

forlornly while Sandra attempted to check her roots. 'I've told him there's almost no hope.'

'How many years ago?' Sandra asked.

'Over twenty,' Robbie cut in, worried Justine was getting a bit carried away with her performance. He didn't want them to be too precise.

'I see,' Sandra said absently, lost in thought.

Robert looked at Justine, who shrugged.

'The letter "C", you said?' Sandra asked, finally.

'Never mind. Could be anyone. Might even be a pet name no one else knew. It was just a nice wee idea of Robbie's.'

Sandra cocked her head to one side, as if she were considering something deeply. Justine leaned forwards, barely able to contain herself. Sandra wheeled over a chair and sat down, joining them in a discreet huddle. 'Well,' she whispered, even though there was no one else in the salon, 'something does spring to mind. But I really shouldn't say...'

'We wouldn't want to get you into any trouble,' said Justine, although her voice was more eager than ever.

'It's no bother, Justine,' said Sandra, the colour rising in her cheeks. 'Just keep it to yourselves, okay? I'm no gossip.'

'Of course,' agreed Justine.

'Absolutely,' said Robert.

Sandra placed an arm around their shoulders and pulled the two of them towards her. Robert almost choked on the strong smell of ammonia from Justine's tint but swallowed hard, afraid he would divert Sandra's train of thought. 'You know Karen McCleod, from the coffee van, over by Glenmurchie?'

'I do.' Justine nodded.

'Well, she's been coming here for almost as long as you, Justine. Always the same, too: a half-head of highlights. Now, her brother—'

'Kevin?' Robert asked. 'He used to do our plumbing.'

'Exactly. Well, Calan Stuart was his apprentice a long while back, would you believe?'

Justine's eyebrows looked like they might disappear into her hairline at the mention of Calan. Robert was equally intrigued. Calan Stuart was notorious locally, often found drunk out of his skull, looking for a fight outside the Ionic in Currenbridge.

Sandra continued, 'Well, Karen said ... and this is going some time back too ... You're sure I can trust the both of you?'

'Yes!' insisted Justine and Robert in unison.

Sandra was momentarily taken aback by their vehemence, but she settled back into her story soon enough. 'I'm just thinking, you said the letter was addressed to "C"?'

Robert frowned in confusion, then quickly remembered the invented love-letter. 'Yes, that's right.'

Sandra lowered her voice even further, her eyes darting excitedly between the pair of them. 'Well, Karen mentioned that Kevin had told her that Calan was seeing some English girl who visited Kinlogie from time to time. Karen was worried, see, as the girl was a bit young for him. She didn't think it was quite right. He would have been about ten years older than her.'

'Do you know the name of the girl?' Robert asked, his heart beginning to quicken.

'It was that poor Clara, the one whose brother murdered her. You remember?'

'Aye,' said Justine, shaking her head.

'Clara ... Rowley?' asked Robert, as if dredging the name from the depths of his memory.

'Could be what that "C" stands for, don't you think, Robbie? But obviously that's not much help to you.'

Robert was momentarily perplexed, given how exceptionally helpful she'd been, and found himself asking, 'Why?'

Sandra sighed and clipped him playfully about the ear.

'Because the poor thing's dead, isn't she, God rest her soul. So you won't be able to deliver that letter any time soon. Anyway, Karen never mentioned it again after ... well, you know. And I don't suppose Calan wanted it to become common knowledge.'

'No,' said Robert, grabbing his coat, 'I don't suppose he did.'

'Right,' said Sandra, clapping her hands. 'Let's get you out of the rest of those foils, Justine.'

Chapter Nine

Sandra's Salon was on Findrussie's main street, opposite the Deli Shop and a short distance from the village hall. Robert crossed the road with some difficulty, shuffling over the icy surface in a cumbersome skating motion. Once on the other side, he waved goodbye to Sandra and slipped down the alley between the deli and a cottage that led to a back route, along the side of the woods, to the bar.

Eilidh would be locking up around now. He was desperate to tell her about Calan Stuart. It wasn't often he found himself in possession of exciting news, and he imagined how it would feel to begin the conversation with: 'You'll never guess what I've just heard...' He quickened his pace, keeping one hand against the wall to stop himself from slipping. As he moved, the light from the main street shone through the gaps between the houses, illuminating the snow on the ground in golden, glowing stripes. He heard Hammy's dogs barking through the trees. His house was near, only about 100 metres away, but concealed by the snow-laden branches.

The alley opened onto the forest road and Robert stopped and checked carefully in both directions before crossing; cars often skidded round the bend here. As he leaned around to get a clearer view beyond the overgrown trees, a figure loomed from the darkness only inches from his face. Robert jumped, nearly falling backwards, and thankfully managed to suppress an embarrassingly high squeal. 'Brian!' he spluttered, attempting to compose himself. 'You startled me.'

'Robert,' said Brian McCrae curtly, as if Robert had committed some offence simply by being there.

Robert averted his eyes. He still found it extremely awkward to be in Brian's presence, especially when it was unexpected. He noticed that the policeman's shoes were scuffed and the hem of his left trouser-leg was torn.

'What were you doing back there?' asked Brian, squinting into the alley.

'Err...' said Robert, his mind suddenly blank. Then he remembered: 'I was at the hairdresser's.' He paused as Brian's eyes raked over his unkempt hair. 'Not for me. For Justine, she wanted some company ... and the cast list ... new play...' He realised he was gabbling and took a deep, shaky breath. It had been a long few days and Brian McCrae, although he was a person of interest in the case, was the last person Robert wanted to meet right now.

'Where are you off to?' Brian asked, calmly. His eyes shifted from Robert to the trees behind him.

Robert wasn't sure whether it was because Brian was a detective, or because of their personal history, but he took issue with the question. Why was it any of Brian's business what he was doing? He certainly wasn't up to anything suspicious ... aside from secretly investigating one of Brian's old cases, of course.

'Back to the bar,' said Robert, trying to keep his voice steady. 'To close up with Eilidh.'

'I see.' Brian looked along the road, his bushy, grey eyebrows frozen at the edges. Robert noticed a fresh scratch that stretched from his temple to his cheekbone.

'Are you waiting for a lift?' Robert asked. 'Looks like the weather's closing in.'

'Yes,' Brian replied, folding his arms.

'Right, well...' Relieved that Brian didn't seem to want to talk, Robert moved to cross the road, but the policeman caught his arm.

The pressure just below his elbow transported Robert back to a day he never wished to remember. His parents' closed bedroom door. A strange, deep voice that didn't belong to his father. A nauseating, high-pitched giggle from his mother. He had known, even as a child, that he shouldn't open the door. But he had been worried, and perhaps a little curious. The shouts of surprise had been terrible.

'Robbie, away with you!' his mother had shrieked.

Sure that he'd seen something he shouldn't, Robert had run downstairs into the living room and crawled under the kitchen table.

'He's not a baby,' the unfamiliar voice had shouted from the top of the stairs, followed by chillingly loud footsteps.

Robert had held on to the table leg, hoping that they wouldn't realise he was there.

'Robbie!' his mother had called softly before lifting the tablecloth and resting her eyes on him. 'What are you doing down here, then?'

Robert had shaken his head, not wanting to talk just yet, just wanting to stay hidden, under the table. He hadn't meant to cry, but big, drooping tears had started to roll down his cheeks.

'Are you going to come out?' his mother had asked.

'For God's sake, I'll get him...' Then those big, rough hands had reached under the table and pulled him out.

As an adult, there was no need for Robert to put up with

Brian's bullish ways. He glared at him, batted off his hand and pulled away from his grip. 'Get your hands off me,' he managed, acutely conscious that his throat was clenched and tight.

Brian held up his hands in a sham apology. 'You're not up to something, are you, Robbie?' he asked, his eyes piercing and bright, almost as if he were mocking him. 'Wouldn't want you to get caught up in anything, would we? I know it's hard, what with your dad—'

'Don't talk about him,' Robert said, his voice low and firm.

Brian laughed, revealing a set of yellowing, chipped teeth. 'Let bygones be bygones, boy. No use in worrying about ancient history.'

Robert stood perfectly still. He would not allow this man to talk down to him ... not again. He watched as Brian eased himself onto the roadside bench and noticed he was moving gingerly, as if his flesh were tender.

'Be on your way then,' Brian barked, his eyes glowing darkly. 'I hear the bar needs as much help as it can get.'

Robert clenched his fists, furious that he could not think of a cutting retort, and crossed the road.

'Let me know if there's anything I can do,' Brian called after him. 'It would've killed your dad to know the bar was closing.'

❄

'What's he doing back in town?' Eilidh poured them both a dram as they sat before the wood burner.

'No idea.' The whisky burned through Robert's chest, distracting him for a moment from his meeting with Brian McCrae.

'He's getting on a bit now, isn't he?' Eilidh said. 'I'm surprised he's still working.' Robert grunted and took another long sip. 'Hey...' Eilidh took the glass from him and placed it on the table. 'Might want to slow down there.'

Robert sank into the armchair. 'I just hate the way he looks at me. He makes me feel like a wee boy all over again. I wish he'd just leave me be.'

Eilidh grinned. 'Think how mad he'd be if he knew what we're doing.'

'He'd be raging.' Robert laughed as Eilidh let out a blood-curdling growl in her best impression of Brian's gruff voice. 'It's a coincidence, though, isn't it?' Robert added.

'What?' Eilidh wiped her eyes, still giggling.

'Brian turning up right after Mirabella.'

'Well, you heard what she said. She thinks he covered something up.' Eilidh waved her arms in the air and said in a theatrical, spooky voice, 'There is no such thing as coincidence.'

Robert laughed. 'You're not wrong. You know, he looked like he'd been in a scuffle or something. I wish I'd seen where he came from, but he appeared out of nowhere. Looked like he was snooping about.'

'He is a detective,' Eilidh reminded him. 'It's his job to snoop, remember.'

'Something just seemed a bit off.'

'All in good time, Robbie,' Eilidh said, drawing her knees to her chest and frowning. 'I reckon we should focus on Calan for now. Justine performed some magic for us there.'

Robert nodded, reaching for his whisky again. 'Dad didn't like Calan in the bar. Said he was bad news.'

'My friend Dom got caught up with him at school, do you remember?'

It was well known that Calan was the main supplier of various drugs to the area's teenage population.

'Dom was beaten up, wasn't he? In Senior Six?' asked Robert.

'And some,' Eilidh said. 'Ended up in hospital. He'd been growing weed in his parents' basement and selling it. Stepped on Calan's toes.'

A log wheezed merrily as Robert wondered how on earth someone like him was supposed to negotiate a world of drug dealers and a man who beat up school kids. 'Maybe we should keep our distance,' he said.

Eilidh stretched her legs over the coffee table, saying lazily, 'Sure, if we want to get absolutely nowhere.'

Robert sank even lower into his chair. 'What can we do? He'll get suspicious if we ask him outright. Imagine that? "Hey, Calan, did you by any chance have a relationship with an underage girl? Oh, and while we're asking, did you murder her, too?" That sounds like an excellent way to end up in hospital ... or worse.'

Eilidh smiled, then drained her whisky. 'Don't worry. I have a plan.'

'Oh?' Robert looked at her. In the flickering light her face, which usually danced with a sense of unrestrained mischief, seemed heavier, more serious. 'There's no point doing anything dangerous, Eilidh.'

She opened her mouth to reply when a flash of blue light flooded the room. Sirens wailed. Robert and Eilidh ran to the front windows and pressed their noses against the cold glass.

'Police,' said Robert.

'That explains McCrae,' Eilidh murmured.

'They're parking by the woods,' Robert said. 'It looks like...' His mouth grew dry and bitter with the tang of whisky.

'They're heading for Hammy's house,' Eilidh said, throwing Robert his coat. 'Let's go.'

Chapter Ten

The body swung gently in the wind against a backdrop of sinewy branches. One end of the rope was fastened tightly around the neck while the other was tied to a thick branch. As the body continued to sway, the tree seemed to moan in sympathy. Robert wept, his arms folded tightly, his feet heavy upon the ground. Eilidh tried to comfort him, though her own face was pale and pinched. Neither of them could stop staring at the feet dangling loosely in the night air.

The woodland outside Hammy's house was swarming with fluorescent, white and brown coats. Robert wondered, as he had wondered once before, how the police officers could treat this as just a job. The most emotion he detected upon any of their faces was a slight frown. That didn't seem right at all.

Detective Chief Inspector Brian McCrae stood at the centre of the operation, issuing orders in quiet, short barks. He avoided Robert's eye but sent over a colleague to ask him and Eilidh to stand behind the police tape, which they did; and then to go home, which they did not. Short of cordoning off the entire national park, there was not much McCrae could do.

Hammy's dogs howled into the night as the disruption

outside their home showed no sign of abating. 'Here you are.' Hammy handed Eilidh and Robert a steaming flask of coffee each. 'They said they'd be finished in a minute,' he said, nodding towards his house, which was surrounded by uniformed officers, searching the grounds. 'I've told them they won't find anything. The dogs would have picked up on anything unusual long ago. Thanks for sticking around, though. It's nice to have some company.'

'Hammy,' Eilidh said, her hand trembling as she raised the flask to her lips. 'I swear I thought—'

Robert nodded grimly. He had thought the same thing. They had been running down the narrow lane that led to Hammy's house when they had seen the shadowy figure hanging from the branches, like an enormous, misshapen bat. At first, he'd felt sure it must be Hammy.

'What did they ask you?' Eilidh said, taking a step backwards as another throng of white overalls entered the area.

Hammy shook his head. 'What you'd expect, I suppose. Did I see anyone? Did I notice anything unusual? I said yes, obviously.' He nodded at the body. 'But they meant beforehand.'

'And did you?' Eilidh asked.

'No,' Hammy said as he scratched his head. 'Fell right asleep after taking out the dogs. Stone cold, I was. It was their barking that woke me. I looked out the window and...' He let out a deep sigh. 'Terrible,' he said.

'Did they say what they thought had happened?' Eilidh asked.

'Not to me,' Hammy replied. 'Looks like she hanged herself though, doesn't it? Chose a secluded spot, not too far to walk. And that tree wouldn't be difficult to climb.'

Robert, who hadn't spoken a word since entering the woods, blinked repeatedly at the hideous sight in front of him in the hope he might be able to make it disappear. Death was so inconsiderate. He had thought the same when they'd dragged his father from the loch. His once jovial eyes were white and alien. His face was engorged, as if death were mocking him, punishing him for that final beer, that final party. The same was true of Mirabella, although, in her case, death had stripped her of all her confidence and self-assurance. Now, she was a waif of a woman; weak. Her limbs seemed brittle, as if they would shatter at the merest touch. His eyes lingered on her gnarled and bent hands. Just one finger, left middle, was pointing eerily into the distance. A rising heat crawled up Robert's spine and he swayed backwards. Hammy intervened to stop him from falling to the ground, propping him up with his powerful arms.

Eilidh nudged Robert in the ribs as two police officers walked past them, deep in conversation.

'Straightforward suicide, he said,' murmured the woman.

'Looks like it,' agreed the man, who then noticed Robert, Eilidh and Hammy and shot them an exasperated look. 'We have asked you to clear the area.'

'Aye,' said Hammy. 'The dogs are upset, is all.' The mound of white fur at his feet rolled onto its back and gave an indulgent yawn, evidently bored rather than upset.

The officers shook their heads, the man audibly muttering, 'Sick thrill seekers,' beneath his breath.

'I think we should take the hint,' said Eilidh, looking at Robert. 'Let's go home.'

'Did she seem suicidal to you?' Robert asked, finally turning away from Mirabella's body. His mind began to spin with fatigue, whisky and confusion. 'She was sad but...'

Hammy shrugged, his eyes thoughtful. 'She'd been through a lot, Robbie. You never know. Being back here where her daughter was ... it may have been too much for her.'

'What does it mean?' Robbie asked, his voice breaking. 'Do we wind up the investigation?'

Hammy scanned the crime scene with concern. Robert swallowed hard, suddenly realising that he should have kept his voice down. The last thing they wanted was McCrae overhearing and asking questions.

'We can talk about that in the morning,' Eilidh whispered. 'But Mirabella wasn't the only reason why we're doing this, remember?'

Robert nodded, rubbing his eyes with the back of his sleeve.

Eilidh cast a worried look at Hammy. 'Time to go,' she said. 'It's late. Hammy, you'll be all right?'

'I'll be fine. Poor woman,' he added, looking at Mirabella again, then bowing his head towards the trees.

❄

Robert couldn't sleep. He read the same paragraph over and over again, barely digesting it, until his mind became a muddle of random words: 'scree', 'clouds', 'grass'. He normally revelled in the sense of isolation the narrators created as they trudged along their solitary paths, but tonight it was making him uncomfortable. No matter how much he tried to enjoy the author's account of the farmland on the Dava Way, he kept imagining Mirabella approaching the forest, alone and desperate, wringing her hands around a long, coarse rope. The landscape, about which his favourite books waxed lyrical, had not been kind to the Rowleys; nor, ultimately, to his father. Far from protectors, the mountains had been shadowy witnesses, dower testaments to three people's deaths.

He rolled over, letting the chilly air creep under his duvet. He was unable to shake the image of Brian McCrae from his mind, too. Robert wasn't prone to jumping to conclusions, but McCrae had behaved undeniably suspiciously. Not to mention his torn trousers and the scratch on his face. What were the chances of him being only metres away from the scene of Mirabella's death at precisely the time it must have happened?

A gust of wind shook the window frame and Robert pulled the duvet tightly to his chin. He tried not to let his imagination run away from him. Although McCrae was not well liked, he was respected among the local community. There could be a thousand reasons why he was on the roadside earlier. Likewise, he probably caught his trousers on a sharp branch, which caused him to stumble and scratch his face. Mirabella had killed herself. 'Straightforward suicide,' as the police had said. And why would McCrae want her dead, anyway? There was no rhyme nor reason to it. He was a senior police officer, for goodness' sake! The thoughts cascaded into a tangle of fears and suspicions, culminating in a vision of his dad whispering into a telephone. If only he'd worn a life jacket. If only he'd not waded so far out. Robert blinked into the darkness. Such exhortations were useless, he knew. Yet they resurfaced often, murky and fluid.

'There's not much choice, is there?' Robert said to no one.

Only the window frame replied, with another rattle. He shut his eyes and tried to clear his mind. A pair of deaths. One classified as accidental, the other as suicide. And a single missed call connecting the two.

Chapter Eleven

Over the next few days, word of Mirabella Rowley's death spread through Findrussie. People spoke about her in the bar in hushed tones, each version of events told with varying degrees of accuracy. 'Completely tragic,' Robert heard one woman say. 'She never recovered from her daughter's murder. Who could? Came back to where her daughter was killed to die herself. So sad.'

'She was found in the trees...'

'I heard she was naked...'

'She did it with an axe, like how her daughter was killed. But to do that to yourself...'

'People can do crazy things...'

Robert ignored the rumours as best he could. Justine, on the other hand, had no problem scolding the gossips: 'Don't mind me. I didn't realise we were hosting the weekly policing debrief. Please, continue.'

Eilidh provided Hammy with a steady stream of pints. He hadn't said as much, but discovering Mirabella's body had clearly affected him deeply. He would come to the bar straight after walking the dogs in the morning, then read the paper until closing time. Robert suspected he was struggling to sleep too, given the dark circles that had formed beneath his eyes.

The rehearsals had begun as planned, although Justine was conducting them with a sort of dogged resilience rather than her usual ebullience. Eilidh had accepted the title role with muted enthusiasm, and dutifully attended each rehearsal, but Robert had noticed her smile was less bright and carefree. Instead of going through her lines with him in the bar, as she had over the past couple of years, she and the male lead, Daniel Bell, practised together after the main rehearsals. As a result, Robert was spending a lot of time on his own in the office, listlessly scrolling through the bar's spreadsheets. The Murder Pack had remained unopened in the bottom drawer ever since the meeting with Mirabella.

Any conversation was unusually stilted. Two days after the discovery of Mirabella's body, Eilidh had emerged from the staff bathroom in full make-up – deep purple lipstick and thick black mascara. Taken aback, Robert had blurted out, 'Wow! You look different.'

Eilidh had raised a hand to her face. '*Different?*'

'Errr ... very bold,' Robert had spluttered.

Smiling weakly, Eilidh had mumbled, 'Thanks, Robbie,' before wriggling into her coat and leaving without another word.

Robert could only assume the new awkwardness between them was a sign the other members of the group had decided to drop the investigation. He understood, of course. The whole mood was sombre after the other night. It made sense that Eilidh, Justine and Hammy wanted to move on. Then there was the fact that Mirabella's theories and assumptions seemed even less credible now she was gone. All four members of the Rowley family were dead. Perhaps this was where the story ended and he would simply have to accept he would never know why his father had phoned Mirabella.

Yet, the more he thought about it, the more convinced he became he was missing a crucial piece of the puzzle. The police had already announced there were no suspicious circumstances, but Robert found it impossible to believe that Mirabella took her own life. Yes, she had been distraught, even manic, during much of the short time he'd known her, but she had also been driven by a resolute determination to learn the truth. Surely that was not the mindset of someone who was planning to end it all?

This train of thought repeatedly led to just one conclusion: someone had killed Mirabella Rowley. The idea seemed so outlandish, so terrifying, that Robert barely allowed himself to consider it, yet it kept bubbling up when he least expected it: while pulling pints, walking home, filling the dishwasher, on his morning run. Inevitably, though, it festered most powerfully in the dark recesses of his sleepless nights, until Mirabella's pale and lifeless face loomed from every shadowy corner.

❄

After just over a week of brooding, Robert was standing behind the bar when Hammy peered over his newspaper and suddenly asked, 'Forgetting it then, are we?'

Robert frowned. 'Forgetting what?'

Hammy raised his eyebrows and leaned forwards. 'You know what I'm talking about.'

Robert scanned the room to check no one was listening. It was half-full, with the Bridge Club gathered at the back, by the windows. 'I just assumed, given what happ—'

'Aye, it was a shock,' Hammy interrupted, then took a long swig of beer. 'But you're not telling me you're giving up, are you?'

A week of sleep deprivation and loneliness had taken its toll. Robert felt his face redden as he replied, 'It's not me who's giving up. None of you has said a single word to me about it. I've taken the hint.'

Hammy placed his newspaper on the bar and folded his arms. 'That's what you think?'

'Aye, that's what I think.' Robert stared at the countertop, unable to meet Hammy's eye. He had never argued with him before, and he was finding the experience far from enjoyable.

'We said we'd help—'

'I know what you said ... but now you've changed your mind. It's fine.' Robert checked himself; he hadn't meant to shout. He closed his eyes for a few seconds and said in little more than a whisper, 'It would have been nice for one of you to come and talk to me about it, that's all. I've been...' He had no words to describe his anguish, so he settled for shrugging his shoulders.

Hammy looked at him as if he were speaking a different language. Eventually, he sighed and said, 'Robbie, much as I like you, you can be as thick as a brick sometimes.'

'What do—'

Hammy held up a hand. 'Yes, we've been avoiding you, but only because we were worried.'

'*Worried?*'

Hammy nodded, studying Robert's expression carefully. 'It's not long since your dad died, and there you were, face-to-face with another dead body. Of course we were worried. You've not been yourself since that night. The look on your face told us that much. Justine thought it best that we give you some time and space to ... process it. But we've all been keeping an eye on you. In fact, she's been beside herself with worry.'

Robert felt his cheeks glowing red as he started to come to terms with his own stupidity. 'You mean...'

Hammy picked up his newspaper and ruffled through it. 'When you're ready, we're ready,' he said, without lifting his gaze from the pages.

Robert stared at Hammy, who was feigning interest in an article about the UK's wild boar population. Then he walked around the bar and took a seat on the adjacent stool. Speaking into his lap, he muttered, 'I don't think Mirabella killed herself.'

'Mmmm.' Hammy still didn't look up.

'I'm serious. I think someone knew she was looking into Clara's murder. I think they knew she wouldn't rest until she'd uncovered the truth. Then they—'

'Killed her?' Hammy lowered his newspaper slightly.

'Well, yes,' Robert said, confused at Hammy's underwhelmed reaction.

Hammy nodded. 'Yep, seems about right,' he said. 'Stacks up.'

Robert groaned and slumped forwards onto the countertop. 'You think so too?'

Hammy waited for Robert to sit upright again, then said, 'The same thought had occurred to me and Eilidh. Justine's not so sure. She thinks we're overreacting. And she doesn't want you heading down a dead end. Like I said, she's concerned.'

'Do you think Mirabella could have been right about Dad? Could he have been killed, too? By the same person who killed Mirabella?' Saying it all out loud gave Robert an instant adrenaline rush. He felt his fingertips tingling.

A dark shadow spread across Hammy's face. He clenched Robert's hand and squeezed it gently. 'I think it's possible, even though I'm sorry to say it.'

Robert lowered his voice, barely even whispering. 'McCrae was acting so strangely that night. Stranger than usual, I mean.'

Hammy didn't reply immediately. Instead, he checked over his shoulder for a couple of seconds before turning back to

Robert. 'All I know is there's something funny going on. I agree, McCrae's not right. But we need to tread carefully. He's the boss man, Robbie, so I don't think we should tell the police what we think just yet. Especially given your history with him.'

Robert thought of the Murder Pack and the light it shone on the murder inquiry's deficiencies. It certainly made sense to keep it far from the leader of that investigation and his colleagues for the time being at least.

'So, we're back on?' Hammy asked, failing to disguise an excited grin.

'Eilidh agrees?'

Hammy nodded quickly. 'She's been waiting for you to deploy her on her first undercover assignment.'

Robert smiled, but then his heart started to quicken. 'This could be dangerous.'

'I think it already is,' Hammy replied, his eyes darting from side to side as he took another long swig.

Chapter Twelve

The Ionic was the sort of drinking hole that required an unofficial invitation. The precise nature of that invitation remained a mystery to Robert, though he assumed it was only ever extended to applicants with shaven heads who were in a constant state of simmering aggression. The bar was tucked away from the main drag of the county's main town, halfway down a tired residential street behind the business park. The tall windows at the front were painted black and the door was a metal sheet, more suited to a bunker than a bar. Justine had driven Hammy, Eilidh and Robert the short distance from Findrussie and they were all sitting in her car, just around the corner, watching what seemed to be an almost exclusively male clientele enter and leave.

'Not too many women about,' Eilidh observed from the back seat.

Robert looked at her in the wing mirror. She was dressed in an outfit he had never seen before – a bright blue, tightly fitted top paired with equally figure-hugging jeans and high-heeled boots.

Justine gripped the steering wheel, even though the car was stationary. 'We should go in with her,' she said.

'No,' said Eilidh, arranging her hair into a high ponytail. 'That'll look suspicious.'

They watched a pair of men emerge from the bar for a cigarette. Robert tutted as one of them inexplicably smashed a bottle against the wheelie bin.

'I'm really not sure about this,' said Justine, her knuckles turning white.

'You were the one who found out about Calan,' Hammy reminded her.

'I know,' replied Justine, nodding quickly. 'But this is very ... *real*, isn't it?'

'Look, it's my decision and I'm fine with it.' Eilidh sounded extremely sure of herself. She took a deep breath and looked at Hammy, then listed everything he had told her. 'Don't go to the loo, only order beer, avoid eye-contact with the men in the corner by the dartboard.'

'That's right. It's been years and I was never a regular, but I'd be willing to bet old habits die hard. Remember, though, most of the folk in there are just looking for a quiet, cheap pint.'

Robert turned in his seat to face Hammy, who had been eager to remind him of the price disparity between the Ionic and the Pine Needle ever since they had hatched the plan. 'Your pints are *free*, Hammy.'

'Wouldn't need to be if they weren't so expensive in the first place.'

Justine chuckled. 'I'm sure Robert isn't opposed to charging you, Hammy.'

A slight panic was audible in Hammy's laugh.

'He's here.' Eilidh slid low in her seat as Calan Stuart approached from the opposite side of the street.

He was dressed in a baggy grey tracksuit, a cigarette

dangling from his mouth. He moved with the classic hard man's swagger, accompanied by the trademark sneer that was routinely directed at whichever unfortunate pigeon, dog or human happened to cross his path. His cigarette butt flew over his shoulder and lay smouldering on the pavement as he entered the bar.

'I agree with Justine,' said Robert. 'We should all go in.'

'Robbie, no!' Eilidh began to retouch her lipstick. 'He'll know we're friends. It'll look weird.'

'Fine,' Robert grumbled, the knot tightening in his stomach. 'But at least let me go in with you.' He left the car before Eilidh could protest and wrinkled his nose at the strong stench of weed in the air.

Eilidh hissed through the window, 'We walk in together.'

Hammy gestured towards the bar. 'Go on, Robbie. Get in there first. It's not as bad as all that, I'm telling you.'

Unfortunately, Hammy didn't realise he was the sort of man who never attracted the wrong sort of attention. Robert, on the other hand, suspected he would be a walking target in a place like this. He forced his face into a scowl and shoved his hands in his pockets. Trying to imitate Calan's gait, he made his way across the street, keeping his eyes low to give the impression that he didn't want any trouble.

'Robbie,' Justine hissed, leaning out of the passenger's window. 'Walk normally. You look like you've peed yourself.'

He heard the other two giggling from the back seat, shook his head, and walked briskly towards the entrance, his boots crunching in the frozen snow. Inside, the bar wasn't nearly as bad as he'd imagined. Two large screens, both showing football, adorned the side walls and a faint smell of urine pervaded the space. Otherwise, though, it seemed clean enough. He took a seat on a stool and pretended to watch the game while scanning the room to establish Calan's whereabouts. Thankfully, a few women were dotted throughout the bar, so Eilidh wouldn't be completely out of place. He spotted Calan in the corner by the dartboard, sipping a pint alone.

'What can I get you?' Robert jumped as the bartender slammed his hands down on the countertop.

Robert glanced down and saw all three of the beer taps were Tennent's. 'Err, a pint of Tennent's, please,' he said instinctively, then reminded himself not to be so polite. His nostrils twitched at the sweet smell of perfume as Eilidh leaned over the bar about a metre away from him. He kept his gaze straight ahead but couldn't help watch her in his peripheral vision. She had transformed herself. It wasn't just the outfit; it was the way she was holding herself, the pout, the bored eye-rolls, the insistent tapping of her fingernails on the bar. She was fully invested in the restless, edgy character she was playing. Robert hoped she would remember this was rather more serious than a Findrussie Am Dram Society rehearsal.

Eilidh rested both elbows on the counter, arched her back slightly and asked, 'What does a girl have to do to get a drink in here?'

Robert looked around and saw most eyes were focused firmly on her. His stomach lurched and he had to hold his glass firmly with both hands to stop himself from springing to her defence. He took a small swig of beer while she ordered a gin and tonic, then tensed as she began to gravitate towards Calan.

This part of the plan hadn't been explored in detail. Eilidh had been keen to 'go with the flow' and 'play it by ear', which Robert thought was a terrible idea, but she had insisted. Now he listened intently as she began to talk.

'This seat free?' Her voice was much more gravelly than usual.

A group erupted into a bout of raucous laughter behind Robert, which made it impossible to hear Calan's reply, but

Eilidh wasted no time in taking a seat next to him, and soon they were deep in conversation.

'I'm alone tonight ... arsehole boyfriend, you know how it is...' Robert caught the gist, closed his eyes and prayed that Calan did not suspect anything.

'I cannot believe a wifey like you would put up with an arsehole,' said Calan.

Robert reminded himself this was all part of the plan, but the lecherous tone turned his stomach.

Eilidh snorted, somewhere between a laugh and a yelp. 'Oh, you'd be surprised. Broken my heart more than once, he has. Why else do you think I'm drinking myself mortal?' She took a sip of her drink and hiccupped, as if it were the tenth of the night, rather than the first. 'Nice to have some company now, anyway.' She flashed a broad smile at Calan.

Calan laughed, shifting closer. 'Another?'

'Oh, go on then,' blurted out Eilidh, chuckling. 'Why not, eh?'

'Why not indeed?' Calan said and rushed to the bar.

Robert remained seated on his stool, methodically sipping his beer. Calan stood right next to him to order the drinks. As he waited for the barman, Robert noticed him glancing back at Eilidh, an eager grin on his face. Robert was feeling quite queasy by now.

'Make it a double,' Calan ordered, pointing at the cheapest gin. 'Could be my lucky night.' Suddenly he turned to address Robert. 'Where do you stay, then? I haven't seen you here before.'

Robert felt his hands shaking as he met Calan's eyes a little too quickly, his surprise obvious. 'Err ... Findrussie.'

Calan squinted at his face for a few seconds, then exclaimed, 'You're Bennie's boy. I know you.'

Robert was unsure of what to say, especially as his father had essentially banned Calan from the Pine Needle.

'What brings you here?' Calan asked.

'Hairdresser's,' Robert spluttered, then immediately berated himself.

Fortunately, Calan's attention was diverted by the arrival of the drinks. 'On the tab,' he said to the barman, smirking. The barman nodded briskly and opened and closed the till without recording any transaction. Robert peered behind Calan to Eilidh, who was looking at her phone.

'Keep your hands off her,' said Calan, nudging Robert in the ribs. 'I've got my eye on that one tonight.'

Robert felt his face reddening, but he managed to say, 'So I see.'

Calan stared at him, drinks in hand, his eyes narrow and keen. 'You know her?'

'No,' Robert said and felt his heart begin to thump. Calan had recognised him from the Pine Needle, so he might have recognised Eilidh, too. If so, he would be wondering why they were pretending not to know one another. Robert added, as casually as he could, 'Enjoy yourself, pal.'

'Aye,' said Calan, cocking his head. 'And you.'

Robert didn't dare look up as Calan rejoined Eilidh. The group behind him were becoming increasingly rowdy as they downed ever more shots. He stared into his beer and watched the vibrations in the liquid as the floor began to shake from their jostling and stamping.

'Hope you weren't after a quiet drink,' the barman said with a shrug, then, laughing, disappeared into the back room.

Robert sighed and placed his head in his hands. There were so many places he would rather be than here. The smell, the noise, the boisterousness left him feeling choked. Checking the time on his phone, he glanced up to see how Eilidh was getting on. With a bit of luck, her story about the arsehole boyfriend had encouraged Calan to discuss some of his own past relationships. He seemed the type to try just about anything to secure a younger woman's interest.

Robert blinked at the corner table, thinking for a moment his eyes must be playing tricks on him. But he wasn't seeing things. The table was empty. Eilidh and Calan had gone.

He swivelled round, knocking over his beer.

'Watch yourself!' someone called out.

Robert turned towards the voice. 'Did you see her? The girl with...' He gritted his teeth, forcing himself to think clearly, remain calm.

'Who?' The man glanced at his friends and laughed. 'Someone's had a few too many, I think.'

Robert rushed past them and through the metal door, skidding to a halt on the icy pavement.

'Robbie!' Justine pulled up to the kerb, frowning. 'You all right? Where's Eilidh?'

'She's not with you?' Robert almost shouted as his head continued to spin. 'She's not here?'

'No,' said Justine. 'She hasn't come out. Neither has Calan. We've been watching, haven't we, Hammy?'

Hammy's head appeared in the window, next to Justine's. 'She's probably just in the loo, Robbie. Go back inside and wai—'

'Calan's not in there either.' Robert's voice was so shaky that his words were barely distinguishable. He rubbed his temples and tried with all his might to think clearly. 'What if he's ... *taken* her? What if he knows what we're up to?'

Hammy and Justine exchanged a worried glance.

Robert turned on his heels and ran back into the bar, slamming open the door so it made a thunderous clang against the wall. He ignored the jeers and made straight for the toilets.

'Eilidh!' he hollered, flinging open the cubicle doors. 'Eilidh!' A cold rush of air slipped around the back of his neck. Looking behind him, he saw the corridor led towards a flight of stone steps. He hurled himself down them, two at a time, and almost collided with a brick wall at the bottom, his hands smacking against the hard surface. He groaned and, catching his breath, tried to identify the source of the draught. A door was swinging on its hinges further down the corridor. He pushed himself from the wall and hurtled through the door.

'Eilidh!' he shouted into the darkness of a narrow alleyway as the prickly sensation of desperation stabbed at his chest. 'Eilidh!'

There was a moment of perfect, hollow silence as his eyes located her. To a passer-by, it would have looked like a mound of rubbish covered by a thin dusting of snow. As Robert ran towards her, the world collapsing with each step, he focused on her lips, which were a vivid purple against the white backdrop. They were slightly parted, as if she had been about to call out prior to hitting the ground. Robert heard his own calls for help as if they were coming from someone else. He cradled Eilidh's limp body in his arms, his pulse deafening between his ears.

Chapter Thirteen

Robert handed Justine another tissue, which she accepted shakily before blowing her nose loudly. Hammy was still unable to sit down. Instead, he was staring blankly out of the window. They had been stupid to allow themselves to get tangled up in whatever this was. That much was obvious now. Robert groaned as he remembered the ambulance's arrival, the way the paramedics had lifted her from his arms.

'Will you stop.' Eilidh sat upright in the hospital bed. She could have been addressing any one of them, but she was looking directly at Robert. 'I'm fine. I told you.'

Robert's gaze traced the deep bruise on the side of her face. The doctor had said she'd been lucky: no lasting damage, just a mild concussion.

'Honestly,' she said, rolling her eyes as she leaned back on the pillows. 'My parents will be here soon. You can go. I'll see you tomorrow.'

'Over my dead body,' said Justine, blowing her nose again until the tissue split.

'We should have been there,' said Hammy. 'I know the Ionic ... and the likes of Calan Stuart. What was I thinking?'

Eilidh blew irritably through her teeth. 'I'm fine,' she repeated. 'It's worse than it looks.'

Robert placed both hands on the foot of the bed and hung his head in frustration. 'He dragged you out of the back entrance.'

'I followed him, he didn't *drag* me,' Eilidh corrected.

'Then he punched you in the head.'

'No, he didn't. I slipped and hit it on the kerb.'

'You could have died. And for what?'

His words lingered in the air as he stalked to the chair in the corner and sat down, folding his arms.

'I don't know why you're sulking,' said Eilidh, her eyes twinkling. 'I got what we were looking for.'

Robert stared at her, incredulous. 'You think I care about that? We are *not* talking about *that* now.'

After some time drumming his fingers along the windowsill, Hammy said, 'I suppose it wouldn't hurt to hear. If you're feeling up to it, of course, Eilidh?'

Robert shook his head. As far as he was concerned, the investigation was over. There was no way, no way at all, he was putting any more of his friends in danger. Justine and Hammy hadn't been there when he'd thought he was holding Eilidh's dead body in his arms. They hadn't been there when he'd called her name over and over, thinking he was responsible for her death, that he'd handed her on a plate to that vicious thug. They had arrived only after she'd started to stir. 'Absolutely not. I think we should stop. It's too dangerous. We don't know what we're doing.'

'He didn't attack me, Robbie.' Eilidh seemed positively angry now. She pushed herself up in the bed and held out a hand. 'Come here, will you?'

Reluctantly, Robert eased himself from the chair and sat on the edge of the bed.

'What's this?' she asked, holding her hand in front of his face.

'Err...'

'It's my hand.' She placed it over his. 'Feel that?' she asked.

'What?' Robert shifted uncomfortably on the bed, suddenly acutely aware of how close his body was to hers.

'That's my pulse,' Eilidh continued, smiling. 'Nice and strong, Robbie. I told you, I'm absolutely fine.'

She took his hand in hers and their eyes met. She seemed so sure of herself, so strong. Robert wondered how she managed it. He was a quivering wreck. She gave his hand a quick squeeze, then released it. Robert ignored the suggestive looks exchanged between Hammy and Justine.

'We've come this far,' said Eilidh. 'At least hear me out.'

The strip lighting above them hummed gently as Justine and Hammy shifted closer to the bed. Robert sighed, rubbing his eyes.

'Come off it. You can't be more tired than me.' Eilidh shot him a withering look.

'Fine,' he said, finally relenting. 'What did you find out?'

Eilidh grinned again, sat bolt upright in the bed and lowered her voice. 'He brought the drinks over, but obviously I only pretended to drink mine because ... well, you never know. It was easy enough to get him talking—'

'I bet,' grumbled Robert.

Eilidh shot him a stern glance not to interrupt. 'But he was cagey about his previous relationships. So I asked him straight out whether he'd ever had his heart broken.'

'What did he say?' asked Justine.

'At first, he just encouraged me to drink more. Said that booze was the only way to mend a broken heart. But I told him girls like a man who can show his true feelings – you know, display a bit of vulnerability. That got him to open up.'

'Clara?' asked Robert.

'Not at first. He kept going on about some woman called Caitlin.'

'Caitlin *McLaughlin*?' asked Justine. 'I've seen them together in town.'

'Probably,' said Eilidh. 'Anyway, she's left him, which isn't too much of a surprise. I said what you'd expect me to say – you know, consoled him. Then I asked if there'd been anyone else, when he was younger. Of course it was risky, but he didn't seem to think it was a strange question. He was pretty hammered by then, I suppose. That's when he started talking about a girl from way back.'

'Go on,' said Hammy, stroking his beard.

'He said she was the reason why his life was rubbish. Reckoned he spiralled down the sink hole after her.'

'I suspect other factors may have had a role to play,' said Robert, cynically.

Eilidh cast another reproachful look in his direction before continuing. 'Anyway ... he said she was a different class to him. That was the word he used, "class". Said she led him on, made him think he was the one, you know? They met one summer when her family was visiting friends and had a whirlwind romance. Then she returned for Christmas. It's got to be Clara, hasn't it? Get this, though: he planned on proposing.'

'What!' Justine exclaimed. 'She was only seventeen. The scoundrel would've been in his late twenties.'

'I know,' said Eilidh. 'Plus, I can't see Clara Rowley being seriously interested in someone like Calan Stuart.'

'So did he go through with it?' asked Robert.

'Absolutely. Spent three months' wages on a ring, then popped the question' – Eilidh paused for a second to heighten the tension – 'on New Year's Eve.'

'No!' said Hammy, his eyes wide. 'He's got to be our killer!'

Robert rolled his eyes, 'We don't know that, Hammy.'

'Anyway,' Eilidh cut in, 'he told me she waited until he'd got down on one knee before breaking it off with him. He was getting flustered by then, hot under the collar, and said he needed some air. That's why we went outside.'

'I should have kept an eye on you,' said Robert, quietly.

'No,' replied Eilidh. 'He would've noticed if you'd done that. It wasn't your fault. In fact, it was mine. We were in that alley round the back of the bar and he wouldn't stop talking about how this girl had "played him for a mug". He kept repeating how cold she'd been when she broke it off. Apparently, she even laughed when he said he thought they were serious, as if he'd made a joke. He was really upset ... but he still asked me to go home with him.'

Robert gripped the edge of the bed.

'I thought I could squeeze a bit more information out of him before making my excuses, so I asked for the girl's name. That was a mistake.'

'Why?' Justine asked.

'His eyes changed immediately. All of the pain disappeared and he suddenly seemed as sharp as a fox. I assured him it was no bother, I was just asking, but he wanted to know why I was so interested. I just shook my head, which was when I heard you calling my name. As soon as Calan heard you, he turned to run. I grabbed his arm—'

'For God's sake, Eilidh,' Robert said.

She shrugged. 'It was stupid, I know, but I didn't want him to get away. It was like he had something big to hide. You know the rest. I slipped when he pulled away' – she pointed to her bruises – 'and that's me. Aside from ... no ... I was probably just imagining it. I'd bashed my head, after all. Everything was blurry.'

'What?' cried Justine and Robert in unison.

'Okay, but you're going to think I'm crazy. When I was lying on the ground, I swear I saw Calan just disappear, like a ghost. One moment he was standing by the bins. The next ... *poof.*'

Robert exchanged a worried glance with Justine, who shrugged and patted Eilidh's shin. 'As you said, you'd bumped your head.'

Eilidh giggled. 'You're not wrong. Anyway, luckily I remember everything else clearly.'

They all took a moment to consider what they'd just heard. The mission had achieved more than any of them could have imagined. They'd identified Calan as Clara's mystery boyfriend, something neither the police nor Mirabella had managed to do. And they knew he met her on the night of her death.

'It's undoubtedly a motive,' said Justine, nodding her head solemnly. 'Crime of passion?'

'And he's a known criminal with a history of violence,' added Hammy.

'Problem is,' said Robert, 'we don't have any proof. As far as we know, Clara chucked Calan and that was the last he saw of her. Not everyone who's dumped becomes a murderer.'

'Suspicious though, isn't it?' suggested Justine, surveying the group. 'Is there a DNA test they can do or something? If he killed Clara, his DNA would be all over her, no? I've seen it on TV.'

'She's been buried for over twenty years,' said Hammy.

Robert shook his head. 'Maybe the police could do it, but we can't go to them with this. Especially with McCrae still on the scene.'

'So what *do* we do?' asked Eilidh.

'Keep asking around,' said Hammy. 'We've learned more in one week than Mrs Rowley did in twenty years. And we haven't even started with Felicity Montgomery yet.'

The door burst open and Eilidh's parents rushed into the

room. They hurried to her bedside, their panic-stricken faces serving as a stark reminder of how lucky she'd been.

'What were you doing there, of all places?' Eilidh's mother asked, stroking her daughter's hair.

Eilidh looked past her parents at Robert as he hovered in the doorway and winked. He shook his head but then shot her a weak smile in return.

'Is she in there? Is she okay?'

Robert turned to see Daniel Bell in the waiting area.

'Eilidh? Is she all right?'

Robert blinked, unable to fathom why Daniel would be there. 'I don't think she's up to rehearsing right now,' he said, frowning.

'I know that,' said Daniel irritably, pushing past.

Robert was about to stop him when Justine placed a hand on his shoulder. Through the crack of the closing door, Robert watched Daniel rush to Eilidh's side and kiss her on the lips. The door clicked shut with a soft thud.

'Ah,' he said, flatly.

'Robbie, I've—' began Justine.

'What?' Robert interrupted, determined to sound nonchalant. It was perfectly natural for Eilidh to have a boyfriend, especially one who shared her interests. It was even kind of romantic, given they were playing co-stars in a play. Worried he might seem uptight, he turned away from the door so there was no chance of him eavesdropping on Daniel and Eilidh's conversation. Forcing a smile, he said, 'Right then, I think it's time we all went home.'

Chapter Fourteen

With Burns Night fast approaching, preparations were in full swing. Robert, Justine and some other volunteers were making wreaths on the floor of the village hall, while Eilidh and the band were practising their ceilidh set on the stage. She had expertly concealed her bruising with make-up, although Robert thought he could detect a tiny wince whenever she hit a high note. Daniel was standing in front of the stage, clapping and cheering at the end of each song. Robert knew it was a nice gesture, and Eilidh probably appreciated it, but he couldn't help grimacing every time he heard another heartfelt 'Woop!'

Justine said nothing as she fastened pine cones onto another wire ring, but Robert was well aware that she was checking up on him out of the corner of her eye.

'Another great one,' shouted Daniel, as the latest song came to an end. 'They'll be dancing until dawn.' He leapt onto the stage and embraced Eilidh theatrically.

Robert averted his eyes, wishing he would keep his displays of affection private.

'Damn!' Justine swore sharply beneath her breath. 'Almost sliced my finger off with the scissors.'

'Hold on,' he said, checking the cut wasn't as serious as Justine had made out. 'Put a tissue over it and I'll fetch a plaster.' He jogged across the hall to the kitchen and shivered as soon as he entered. This part of the building was never properly heated. Wrapping his fleece tightly around his chest, he began rummaging through the cupboard under the sink. A curt clearing of a throat behind him caused him to freeze. He swallowed hard, grabbed the box of plasters and turned round, to find himself only inches away from Brian McCrae's scowling face.

'What are you doing here, Brian?' Robert asked, as calmly as he could.

'Nothing wrong with taking an interest in the local arts scene, is there?' He grinned, his teeth reminding Robert of a snarling dog.

'Excuse me, Brian. Justine's cut her finger,' said Robert, shimmying sideways.

'Won't be a moment,' said McCrae, blocking his path.

Robert knew many people would crumble under the intensity of McCrae's stare, perfected over years of policing, but he resisted the urge to look away. 'She's bleeding,' he said weakly.

'I'm sure she'll survive,' replied McCrae, nodding to the table and chairs in the corner of the room.

Robert realised he had no option. He glanced at the doorway but immediately decided it would look very odd if he tried to make a run for it. In any case, McCrae slowly closed the door and checked through the glass to ensure no one was in the corridor. Reluctantly, Robert took a seat at the table, squeezing his legs together to keep warm.

'No money for heating?' McCrae asked, sitting opposite him.

Robert shook his head. 'It would cost a fortune to heat the whole building.'

'I see,' McCrae replied, still not taking his eyes off Robert. 'Speaking of costs, I hear your dad's bar is in a spot of bother.'

'You want to talk about the Pine Needle?'

McCrae let out an unexpected grunt of laughter. 'Why? Did you have another topic in mind, Robert?'

Robert remained silent. He focused on the fact that he was in the village hall's kitchen, not an interrogation room, regardless of how McCrae was behaving. Wondering whether police officers had some special technique that enabled them to detect when someone was lying, he tried to hold his face very still. He had heard somewhere that poker players tried to keep their heart rate as steady as possible, which in turn minimised dilation of the pupils and other tell-tale signs. Unfortunately, he couldn't remember how they achieved this.

'You all right, son?' McCrae asked, leaning forwards.

Robert winced at his use of the word 'son' but still said nothing.

McCrae shrugged and rocked back in his chair. 'Does the name Mirabella Rowley mean anything to you?'

The room seemed to feel even colder at the mention of her name. 'Of course,' said Robert. 'Everyone around here knows that name.'

'True enough,' said McCrae. 'But am I right in thinking you've seen her recently?'

Robert's mind spun in a thousand directions as he searched for the best response. It was pointless to lie: plenty of people had seen a woman fitting Mirabella's description visit Robert in this very hall. 'Err, yes. She came to the Pine Needle's Hogmanay this year.'

'Really?' McCrae raised his eyebrows, as if waiting for further information.

'Y ... yes,' stammered Robert.

'Then you probably know that she killed herself a few days later,' said McCrae.

Robert bit his bottom lip. He knew McCrae had seen him on the night of Mirabella's death. He was trying to catch him out. 'Obviously,' said Robert. Then, without thinking, he added, 'We spoke earlier that night, you and me, near the woods, remember?'

The keenness in McCrae's eyes suddenly turned to blank, menacing darkness. Almost robotically, he said, 'I don't recall.' Robert opened his mouth to protest, but McCrae slammed a hand on the table, cutting him off. 'I don't recall,' he repeated, spitting each word so that droplets sprayed onto Robert's face.

Robert stood shakily, his legs weak. 'I need to get back to Justine.'

'No, you don't.' McCrae stood with him, keeping their eyes level. 'Not just yet. You see, Robert, I think you have something of mine. And I'd like it back.'

Robert was perplexed. What could he possibly have that might belong to McCrae?

'Don't lie to me, Robert Begg,' McCrae growled, his face uncomfortably close now.

'I have no idea—'

McCrae reached into his pocket and Robert flinched, convinced that he was about to brandish a weapon. McCrae merely snorted in derision, shot him a disdainful glance, and brought out his phone. 'I believe you are familiar with this,' he said, showing Robert a screenshot of Mirabella's call log. His point made, McCrae slowly placed the phone back in his pocket and studied Robert with a smug grin.

Robert shook his head, his legs trembling. 'I don't—'

McCrae laughed, although this time it was sharper, more threatening, clearly designed to strip Robert of any lingering confidence. When he had finished, McCrae wiped his eyes and said, 'I never got to know the man well – your dad, I mean – but the apple couldn't have fallen much further from the tree, could it?' He chuckled again. 'He dealt with things straight on. Didn't beat about the bush. He was strong, had conviction, you see? Never squirmed. How the hell did he come to raise *you*?'

An iron-hot spur pierced Robert's chest. He began to shake, his face glowing. 'Don't—'

This only made McCrae laugh even harder. 'You see,' he said, leaning across the table to jab Robert in the solar plexus. 'You can't even tell me what you think of me. Believe me, your dad would've had me—'

'Don't talk about him,' Robert murmured quietly. 'You don't get to talk about him.'

Without warning, Robert found himself pinned against the cupboard, McCrae's sour breath hot on his face. He struggled under his grip, but McCrae shoved him back forcefully, sending the cupboard's contents crashing between the shelves. Robert saw bright, fluttering shapes between his face and McCrae's. His mouth felt sluggish as he tried to protest, leaving him no choice but to listen to McCrae's words, which sounded far away and tinny.

'I'll say what I want about Bennie Begg. I did him wrong, that's true, but he took it like a proper man. Your mother made her choice and we dealt with it like men.'

Robert grimaced and responded in the strongest voice he could manage. 'She didn't stick around with you for longer than a minute, I heard. Why was that, Brian? Did she realise her mistake?' He took a sharp breath, unsure about provoking McCrae further, but the temptation proved too great. 'Perhaps you're not as much of a man as you like to think, eh?'

For a split second, Robert thought he saw a shade of sorrow

hover in McCrae's eyes. Then, just as quickly, he was slammed into the cupboard again. This time, he heard crockery breaking.

'Quiet!' McCrae hissed. 'You ... stay ... quiet.' Robert gulped but managed to maintain eye contact. McCrae was holding him in a vice-like grip and speaking with unnerving precision. The fury he had displayed seconds earlier had subsided to a controlled simmer. 'Mirabella Rowley wanted to give you money.' It was a statement rather than a question.

Robert remained motionless as he tried to calculate how much to reveal. Eventually, he replied, 'Yes, she offered to pay for refurbishments, among other things. She said she felt an affinity to the bar. Her family used to come here on holiday.'

McCrae finally loosened his grip, although he didn't back away. 'And you accepted her offer, did you?'

Robert resisted the urge to blink. 'At first, yes. But then we changed our mind.'

'*We?*'

Robert flinched. 'Yes, myself and the staff at the Pine Needle.'

'Oh yes. How could I forget them? You were all snooping around the woods the other night, weren't you?'

Once again, there was no point in lying. 'We were worried about Hammy.'

'I see,' McCrae replied. Then, very slowly, he leant back against the table. It gave a low creak under his weight. Robert rubbed his head, a dull ache spreading through his skull, and started to make his way towards the door. Without moving, McCrae said evenly: 'If you're hiding something, Robert, I will find out. No good keeping secrets from me, you know.'

Robert turned the door handle, his heart thumping, and whispered under his breath, 'I could say the same to you.'

Chapter Fifteen

'Why on earth would he want to kill Mirabella, Robbie? Seems a bit far-fetched,' said Justine from the passenger seat of Hammy's Jeep, her eyes full of concern. 'Are you suggesting he murdered her then hung her body from the tree to make it look like suicide?'

'I have no idea,' Robert replied sullenly, before sighing apologetically. 'All I know is that he was crazy just now. Reckoned he couldn't remember meeting me that night. He's onto us, I think.'

Hammy glanced at him through the wing-mirror. 'Did he say anything specific?'

'Not really,' Robert admitted. 'But he knew about Mirabella's offer.'

'He could have heard about that from anyone,' Eilidh pointed out. 'She announced it in front of the whole Am Dram Society.'

'He knew about Dad calling Mirabella, too,' Robert persisted.

'She probably had the phone on her when the police arrived,' suggested Eilidh, still trying to be the voice of reason.

'Wonder what he meant by you having something of his, though.'

'Another unanswered question,' mumbled Robert miserably, sinking into his coat collar.

'Aye,' said Hammy as he flicked on the wipers; the snow was falling thick and steady now. 'Doesn't sound like he has a great deal to go on, though. I wouldn't worry yourself. It's not like we're doing anything illegal.'

'It's not *us* doing something illegal that I'm worried about,' said Robert grimly.

'Wow!' Eilidh shrieked in ingenuous delight, her nose pressed against the window.

Kinlogie House loomed into view, its high walls and tall windows shimmering decadently amid the vast, white grounds. The driveway was lined with fire torches that danced dramatically as the snowflakes floated down. Robert agreed the hotel was breathtaking. It was difficult to imagine that such a grand, peaceful place had once been entangled with a gruesome murder.

'Outdoor fires in a snowstorm ... what a terrific idea,' said Hammy sarcastically, turning into the long drive.

'Just keep going,' Justine said. 'Past the house, on the left, you'll see her place.' Her eyes grew wide as they skirted around Kinlogie. 'Oh me, they've spruced it up a bit,' she said, opening her window. 'It looked nothing like this when I worked here.'

'Strange for Felicity to live right next door,' said Eilidh. 'I bet that isn't easy.'

'No,' agreed Justine. 'Lots of sad memories tied up in the house. But that's the way it is sometimes, isn't it? Darkness sticks.'

The four of them shivered as the Jeep crawled past the grand façade. Sure enough, directly opposite, they saw a flicker of light between the trees. Hammy eased the car to a halt and hushed the dogs in the back.

'Remember what I said,' cautioned Justine. 'She's expecting us, but it can take a while to .... make sense of her. You'll see what I mean.'

Robert jumped down from the Jeep while Hammy opened the boot for the dogs. 'They're coming too?'

'Of course,' said Hammy. 'Can't leave them locked in the car like prisoners.'

'Of course,' Robert repeated, smiling. For the briefest of seconds, he thought he saw a beam of light in the grounds. He squinted into the darkness and frowned. Surely they would have noticed had they been followed. There was nowhere to hide on the road to Kinlogie. Then his attention was drawn to the other side of the path and a much fainter, barely discernible glow. He stared into the woods and eventually picked out the silhouette of a rotund woman, dressed in what appeared to be several layers of animal fur.

'Justine? Is that you now?'

Under her breath, Justine whispered, 'Here we go. Just follow my lead.'

'Justine?' The voice, very high and wispy, called again.

Justine made her way forwards. 'No need to panic, Felicity. It's me and my friends.'

Unfortunately, Hammy's dogs chose that moment to throw their heads back and howl to the stars. The fur-clad figure took two shaky steps backwards, the torch trembling in her hand.

'Oh, I say.'

Justine held up a finger to Hammy, who quietened the dogs, patting their heads. 'It's just Hammy's huskies,' she called across the fence. 'They're gentle as they come – all bark, no bite.'

As Robert's eyes adjusted to the darkness, he saw Felicity Montgomery flinch at the word 'bite'.

'Well then,' exclaimed Justine, taking the initiative to approach the fence. 'What do you say to a nice brew, Felicity?'

Felicity's face suddenly lit up. She threw her arms into the air and gestured towards all four of them. 'Goodness, where are my manners? Excuse my befuddlement, I beg you. I just woke up, you see. It's been a strange sort of day.'

Robert suspected the vast majority of Felicity Montgomery's days could be described as strange.

'Come on in, then.' Felicity stood to the side and ushered them through the gate. 'This is no sort of weather to be outdoors.'

They negotiated a path between the branches and into a single-room cabin that would have been the humblest of humble abodes were it not for dozens of elaborately framed portraits that adorned all four walls. A fire-burner crackled in the corner by a small stove upon which a large vat of something with a sweet fragrance was bubbling merrily. Robert started to sweat immediately in the stifling heat and automatically began unbuttoning his coat.

'Mulled cider?' Felicity asked. 'Home-made, like everything here. I'm all about no-waste, you see. You might consider me something of an eco-warrior.'

Robert tried not to stare at her furs, which she was still inexplicably wearing.

'I'll take one if it's going,' replied Eilidh.

'Lovely.' Felicity clapped her hands and bustled about the stove, searching for a mug, then a ladle, then a cinnamon stick. 'Take a seat, please,' she said, waving her arms around the room.

Robert chose what seemed like the safest option: thc end of the four-poster bed. Eilidh opted for the armchair, Hammy the antique rocking-chair and Justine the chaise longue. The dogs piled onto an expensive-looking rug, nuzzling against each other.

Felicity hummed sweetly as she prepared the drinks and eventually took a seat next to Justine. 'So!' she cried far too loudly for such a small space, making Robert jump. 'Justine, introduce me to your friends.'

Displaying a level of obedience Robert had never witnessed before, Justine duly made the introductions, pointing at each of them in turn. Felicity smiled and Robert noted that her teeth were stained purple, presumably from red wine. 'Excellent,' she said. 'Pleasure's all mine.'

The ensuing silence was punctuated only by the dogs' panting and Eilidh slurping her cider until Robert finally blurted out, 'We wanted to ask you some questions.'

Justine laughed a little anxiously. 'Easy goes, Robbie. We've only just got here.'

'No, no...' Felicity waved her arms in the air again. 'I like questions. Go on, please, Robert.'

He saw that Justine was eyeing her nervously, but he pressed on. 'I'm afraid it's a rather delicate matter.'

'Oh?' Felicity leaned forwards, some of the furs falling from her shoulders.

He decided it was best to jump straight to it. The sooner they could get out of this hothouse, the better. 'You were friendly with the Rowley family, I believe. They were staying with you when...'

Felicity brought a hand to her mouth as her emerald-green eyes started to glaze over.

Robert looked at Justine, confused. 'You frightened her,' she mouthed irritably, then shuffled to the other end of the chaise and placed a reassuring hand on Felicity's shoulder. 'It's okay, pet...'

Felicity blinked, once, twice, then gripped the hand firmly. Rather than pulling away, Justine leaned in closer. 'It's me, Justine, and my friends, remember? We came to visit.'

Felicity contemplated Justine for a few seconds as if she were one of her oil paintings before turning towards the rest of the company. 'How lovely,' she exclaimed, then pointed over her shoulder to a well-stocked wine-rack. 'A bottle, Justine? Fetch one, would you?' Justine walked over to the rack, selected a bottle, and uncorked it while Felicity grinned at the rest of them. 'She's always been so much help,' she said, nodding to Justine. 'Cleaned the house for next to nothing, out of the goodness of her heart. Always took such great care of Peter, too.'

Hiding a smirk as Justine rolled her eyes behind Felicity's head, Robert seized his chance: 'Peter?'

'Oh, excuse me.' Felicity turned to Justine. 'I always forget that the younger generation never knew my Peter. He was my husband, dear.'

Her eyelids started to flutter but Justine intervened in the nick of time. 'Why don't you tell us about him?' she suggested. 'It's always nice to be reminded of an old friend.'

'I would like that,' said Felicity, the brightness returning to her eyes. She turned to Eilidh. 'You know, my Peter was quite like your husband.'

Eilidh frowned as she followed Felicity's gaze to Robert. 'No!' she exclaimed as Robert felt himself glowing bright red. 'He's not ... Robert's not...'

Felicity merely chuckled and patted Eilidh's knee. 'No use protesting against the power of passion. Cupid's arrows are potent, you know.'

Robert stared at his knees, sure that his ears were scarlet. He heard Eilidh shuffling in her chair.

Felicity continued, 'My Peter was quiet, sensible. That was one of the reasons why it was so ... difficult when he became unwell. A person's soul is delicate. It's a terrible thing when it has to fight to be seen.' Her voice was deep and resonant now, almost ursine. The dogs began to whine, inclining their heads towards her.

'Come now,' murmured Hammy, rocking almost imperceptibly back and forth.

Robert sagged at the sadness in her voice. He felt he should change the subject, but they may never have a better chance. 'That New Year's Eve with the Rowleys. Did you or Peter see anything unusual?'

Felicity smiled and said, 'I told the police everything I know.'

The dogs began to sniff at her feet, then, tails wagging, jumped up.

'Little wretches,' cried Justine, shooing them away.

Hammy rose to his feet and hollered, 'Sit!' The dogs obeyed instantly and remained rooted to the floor, although they continued to sniff and whine. 'It's like they've picked up a scent,' he said, shaking his head. 'God knows what's got into them.'

'Dogs sense heightened emotion,' said Felicity, as if it were a plain and obvious fact. She cleared her throat and looked directly at Robert, her eyes now pin sharp with clarity. 'What is it you need?'

Robert took a deep breath and looked to Justine for guidance, but she was busy soothing the dogs, so he steeled himself and declared, 'I don't believe Toby Rowley was the murderer. I know that sounds ridiculous, but is there anything you can remember that might suggest Clara was killed by someone else?'

'Mirabella spoke to you.' Felicity said the words flatly. 'Before she died, she must have visited you.'

'Um...' Robert looked to Eilidh, who gave a brief nod of encouragement. 'She thought that someone else might have—'

'There was no "might" about it. She thought it was

inconceivable that Toby could have done it.' Felicity rose to her feet, still holding the wine glass shakily in one hand. Justine stepped over the dogs to refill it and Felicity walked towards one of the more recent portraits. 'This is Peter,' she said, standing before it, 'just after he was diagnosed. He still had the spark in his eye at that stage.' She turned to face Robert again. 'But I had no one to speak to after Clara's murder. By then, Peter was no longer able to hold a conversation. And Mirabella and Anthony were beside themselves, of course. I couldn't get my thoughts in order, but I assumed the police would reach the right conclusion. Certainly, all of the evidence pointed to Toby.'

'It sounds like you're not so sure now, though,' Hammy prompted.

'No, I'm not.' Felicity took a large gulp of wine. 'Mirabella never believed it, and I can understand why. Toby was' – her eyes darted from side to side as she searched for the right word – '*riotous*. He lived a fast life: drank heavily, partied, dabbled with goodness knows what substances. But he was never cruel. Deep down, he was sweet-natured, anyone could see that. When he was a young boy, he used to pick flowers from the garden to say thank-you for having him. So, after the dust settled, I began to question whether he could have done such an evil thing to his sister.'

'But if it wasn't Toby, who do you think it might have been?' asked Robert.

Felicity laughed bitterly. 'If I knew *that*, I'd have told someone long before now. I don't have an answer for you, I'm afraid. My husband died shortly after Clara's murder. Perhaps he sensed the horror of it all and it finished him off, or maybe it was just his time. Either way, I grieved heavily at first. Justine, you remember?'

'Aye,' agreed Justine. 'It was a horrible time for you.'

'But when I sold the house and moved here, I finally had the space to think, and a strange aspect of that visit kept coming to mind, even though I could never make sense of it. Goodness, I haven't shared this with anyone before, not even poor Mirabella.'

The rocking chair creaked as Hammy leaned forwards.

Rather than explaining, Felicity simply pointed to a wooden box, about the size of a laptop, on a side-table next to Eilidh. 'Open it, dear, will you?'

Eilidh carefully picked up the box and opened the lid to reveal a bundle of letters.

'The crest-embossed envelope,' instructed Felicity. 'It should be on the top.'

Eilidh pulled a handwritten invitation card from the envelope.

Felicity waggled a hand in Eilidh's direction. 'Read it. Don't be shy.'

Eilidh looked around the room, took a deep breath and stared at the card. The writing was barely legible. 'Dear Mr and Mrs Anthony Rowley, I trust you and the ... err, *family*? ... are well. The Montgomerys cordially invite you to spend Christmas and Hogmanay with them at Kinlogie. It would be wonderful to see such dear ... I guess that says *friends* ... for what may be my last' – she squinted at the next word before guessing – '*festive* season. Yours faithfully, Peter Montgomery.'

'What's strange about that, Felicity?' asked Justine. 'Peter invited them to stay and they accepted.'

'Yes...' Felicity's eyes were starting to glaze over again. She seemed to be swaying to some unheard melody.

'Mrs Montgomery...' Robert said sharply. 'Mrs Montgomery!'

Justine guided her back to the chaise and raised the wine glass to her lips. 'There you go, pet,' she said gently. 'No need to worry about it now.' She turned to Hammy. 'I think we should leave. It's getting late.'

'No!' Felicity sprang back to her feet, which sent the wine glass flying across the cabin. 'I haven't finished yet.'

'We can come back,' suggested Justine, casting Robert a worried look.

He agreed that Felicity's mood was fluctuating alarmingly, and they would gain nothing by terrorising the woman.

'Look at the invite.' Felicity snatched the card from Eilidh's hands and stared at it, her eyes wild, before showing it to each of them in turn. 'Peter couldn't have written this.' It was as if the truth had only just dawned on her. 'You saw him towards the end, Justine. He couldn't have done this, could he? At the time, I was so annoyed he hadn't consulted me that I didn't even stop to think about—'

'He was too ill to write the invite?' asked Eilidh.

'He had lucid moments, Felicity, remember?' Justine pulled the invite from Felicity's hand, which was now trembling, and studied it closely. 'And you said they were good friends.'

'Maybe,' said Felicity, placing her head in her hands. 'Yes, maybe.'

'Does it look like his handwriting?' asked Hammy, moving in for a better look.

Felicity nodded. 'Yes, I suppose so. Give or take. But his writing changed as his mind deteriorated, so it's hard to tell.' She sniffed. 'As I said, it's a strange detail and probably means nothing. It revisits me often, though. Do you have visitations like that?'

Robert sensed that she was talking directly to him, but when he looked up, he saw that her head was back in her hands and she was rocking slowly back and forth, humming the same tune as before. Justine placed a comforting arm around Felicity's shoulders as she motioned for the others to leave, and they traipsed out into the cold night air, arms folded, frowns deep. But then, as if she had forgotten something, Eilidh ran back into the cabin and called out, 'Mrs Montgomery, if you want, we're having a Burns Night at the hall.'

A sound somewhere between a shriek and a laugh exploded from the centre of the room. 'A party? I love parties! My dear, I would be honoured.'

Eilidh performed an elaborate bow, blushing at the woman's enthusiasm. Robert wondered whether she was aware of the joy she could generate, often unwittingly, among everyone she met.

'Hammy, will you get these dogs away!' called Justine from inside the cabin.

❄

Robert finally broke the silence once they'd rejoined the road back to the Findrussie. 'Any thoughts?'

Hammy, as enthusiastic as Robert had ever seen him, wasted no time in sharing his. 'Aye, a fair few, Robbie. We have succeeded in gaining a significant clue. That letter could be the key to everything..."

'Invitation,' corrected Robert. 'Justine, you knew Peter. Was he capable of writing by that stage?'

'Difficult to say, Robbie. He was already very frail, and shaky most of the time. Then again, who else would have written it?'

'Someone who wanted to lure Clara to her death under false pretences,' speculated Hammy in an uncharacteristically sombre voice.

Robert sighed as they pulled into Findrussie. The snow was showing no sign of abating; every now and then they would be jolted by a loud thud as a clump fell from the trees and landed on the Jeep's roof. 'Calan is still the only person with any sort of motive,' he said, looking out of the window. 'I agree the invitation is intriguing, but I can't put my finger on why.'

'Someone could have snuck in the house, written it and posted it,' said Eilidh. She retrieved the card from her pocket and studied it carefully.

'You *stole* it?' Robert asked, astounded.

'It's potential evidence, Robbie,' she retorted, sitting upright, her eyes wide. 'Could it have been Calan?'

'His heart wasn't broken until New Year's Eve itself, remember,' said Robert, 'whereas the invitation, if it wasn't written by Peter Montgomery, suggests that Clara's murder was premeditated.'

'Aye,' agreed Hammy, then caught Robert's eye in the rear-view mirror. 'Since we're throwing fanciful theories about, it's worth saying that the dogs behaved very strangely around Felicity.'

'Maybe they took issue with the furs,' said Justine.

'She seem all right to you?' Hammy asked Justine quietly. 'What sort of woman is she?'

Justine shook her head, deep in thought. 'She was a good enough employer – more of a friend, really – and she's kind-hearted. Didn't pay enough, mind, and she can be a bit self-centred. You would be too, having lived in that mansion, no?' She chuckled. 'And, like me, she's more of a cat person. Perhaps that explains it.'

'Maybe,' said Hammy as he slowed to a halt alongside a block of flats. 'Justine, that's you then.' Before getting out, she turned towards the mound of thick white fur in the boot and said, 'If only those rascals could talk, eh?'

Chapter Sixteen

After closing the following night, Eilidh, Robert and Justine gathered around a table in the Pine Needle. Eilidh had taken the liberty of drawing caricatures of each suspect and pinning them to the noticeboard that morning.

'Okay,' Robert began. 'We've covered Calan, although some follow-up is needed. Eilidh, have you seen him about?'

'No,' she said. 'He's probably busy with his "job".'

'That's good, but keep your wits about you,' Robert replied, scratching his head. 'I don't want him coming to find you.'

'I'm fine,' said Eilidh, irritably.

'He's the only one with a motive, remember,' added Justine.

'True,' agreed Robert, trying to ignore Eilidh's scowl and looking back at the board. 'It would be good to find out what he was doing at the time of Clara's death. If he has an alibi, then at least we can rule him out.'

'On the other hand, if he killed Clara, he might have framed Toby,' suggested Eilidh. 'Felicity said Toby was well into his drugs. Maybe that's the link to Calan?'

'Maybe...' Robert stood, walked towards the board and added a thick arrow between the cartoons of Toby Rowley and

Calan Stuart. He stepped back. 'Could Calan have dealt Toby a bad dose that left him incoherent and thinking he'd killed his sister?'

'Adds up,' said Justine. 'How do we prove it, though?'

'Not sure.' Robert glanced at the next caricature. 'I think we all agree that Felicity Montgomery seems harmless. And she has no motive to speak of.' His eyes focused on the final picture on the board. 'Then, of course, there's McCrae, who also had no motive to kill Clara, as far as we know. But he seemed flustered when I reminded him we met on the forest road shortly before Mirabella's body was found. You know, the more I think about it, the more convinced I am that she didn't kill herself. If only we could—'

'Sorry I'm late,' shouted Hammy, barging the doors open.

'Where have you been?' asked Justine.

'Night sledging,' Hammy replied, taking a seat at the bar. 'It's freezing outside, but the bairns loved it. They'll be sleeping until midday tomorrow. Got a beer going, Robbie?'

Robert edged away from the board and walked around the bar to pull a pint. Hammy seemed even more excited than usual, his eyes darting from side to side, his hands rubbing together enthusiastically.

'Everything all right, Hammy?' Robert asked.

Hammy grinned. 'Sounded like you were talking about McCrae. Don't let me stop you.'

Robert took a seat next to him. 'He's been behaving suspiciously, but...'

'But...' said Hammy, making a circular motion with his hands. 'Keep going.'

'But he has no motive,' Robert concluded.

'Really?' said Hammy, mysteriously. 'Anything else?' he added.

Robert sighed impatiently. 'Obviously, it would help if we could prove that someone had a reason to kill Mirabella.'

'Bingo!' Hammy shouted triumphantly and started to rummage around in his pocket as he made his way to the centre of the room. He extracted his hand and held a small object in the air for the others to see. Between his rather grubby fingers was a silver ring. His eyes gleamed with satisfaction. 'No need to thank me all at once!'

Eilidh bit her lip and looked at Robert, who bit his lip and looked at Justine, who sighed and said, 'Explain yourself, then.'

'It's evidence,' Hammy exclaimed, lowering the ring and displaying it on his palm. 'Look, will you? Honestly, you'd think I was the only one around here who doesn't need his eyes testing.'

Robert extended his hand so Hammy could drop the ring into it. He traced a forefinger around its edge, then lifted it up to his face.

'Go on,' Hammy urged.

Unsure what Hammy expected him to do next, Robert continued to stare intently at the ring, hoping that some inspiration might hit him. Then Eilidh nudged him in the ribs and whispered, 'Is there an inscription, Robbie?'

Robert blushed and quickly focused on the ring's inner edge.

'Read it aloud,' Justine said, clapping her hands.

Robert squinted at the tiny, ornate lettering. '"Brian + Mirabella 2000",' he recited. 'Hammy, where did you find this?'

'Dogs sniffed it out on the run back tonight, right by where Mirabella was found,' Hammy said. 'Brought it right to me like they knew I'd be interested. Clever scamps.'

Robert was still staring at the inscription. 'Do you think they—'

'Looks like it,' said Eilidh excitedly. 'Question is, what was that ring doing in the woods?'

Something stirred in the back of Robert's mind. He remembered Mirabella's hanging form, swaying gently in the snowflakes, her gnarled, clenched hands, save for just one strangely extended finger.

'You're white as a ghost, Robbie,' Justine said.

Robert's heart began to thump. He held the ring up to the others, 'I think this proves that McCrae killed Mirabella. I didn't think much of it at the time, but her middle finger was pointing straight out ... as if someone had wrenched a ring off it. And Brian accused me of having something of his, remember? Maybe he dropped it while arranging her body to look like suicide and thinks we found it that night. Can anyone remember if Mirabella was wearing a ring before she died?'

They exchanged unsure glances for a few seconds. 'The photos!' Justine exclaimed suddenly. 'Mirabella arrived whilst I was taking Hogmanay pictures, remember? I'm sure I was facing in her direction, I was spinning all over the place. Hang on, let me see...' She busily swiped through the photos on her phone. 'Ah ha!'

'Have you found her?' Robert made a grab for the phone and received a reproachful tut from Justine. 'Sorry,' he said, sheepishly. 'It's just that this is the biggest lead we've had yet. Maybe Dad was onto it, too.'

'You're right, Robbie,' she agreed, handing him the phone politely. 'Well, what's the verdict?'

Robert tried to ignore the caress of Eilidh's deep breaths on the side of his neck as he zoomed in on the unmistakable figure of Mirabella, who was standing in the doorway of the Pine Needle, her left hand covering her mouth. 'I can see it,' Robert said, his own hand shaking as he stared at the silver band on the middle finger. 'It's here, Hammy, look!'

He passed the phone to Hammy, who whistled eagerly. 'Clear as day. It's the same ring, no doubt about it.' Grinning, he patted Robert on the back. 'Great work, son. Bennie always said you were brainier than he ever was. We're one step closer to the truth. He's up there cheering us on, I know it.'

'It's true,' said Justine, beaming, her eyes moist. 'Don't mind me...'

Robert placed an arm around her shoulders, which turned into an impromptu huddle among all four of them.

Eilidh finally pulled away and said, 'So, if Brian killed Mirabella, does that mean he killed Clara, too? And...' She looked towards Robert in horror.

A dark, liquid certainty rushed through his mind before he could respond. He doubled over at the enormity of the realisation, his legs almost giving way beneath him. He gasped for breath, but his lungs seemed to be waterlogged. He felt the others encircling him. Eilidh was shouting something. Was it his name? He couldn't be sure. All he could see was a deep, black tunnel with walls that seemed to be closing in on him. At the end of the tunnel was the loch. So calm. So clear. So innocent. He heard other voices now.

'Pull him in!'

'It's never pretty.'

'You never know, one minute you're fine, the next...'

'Poor Robbie.'

Then the clearest voice of all. 'Cardiac arrest due to drowning. Nothing suspicious here. Shame, I know the family. That's his son, over there.' It was the voice of Brian McCrae.

Brian McCrae, who had presided over the retrieval of his father's body. Brian McCrae, who had told the coroner that there were no suspicious circumstances, that Bennie Begg had drowned, even though he had known the loch better than his own home. Brian McCrae, who had stolen his mother and left her racked with so much guilt and shame that she'd never returned home. Brian McCrae, who had killed another ex-lover, Mirabella Rowley.

'Robbie! Robbie! It's me!'

He realised that Justine was holding his head, a hand on either side of his face.

'I'm here. It's okay, pet.' She rocked him back and forth and he closed his eyes.

Today was a 'P' day. He buried his head deep into Justine's arms and quietly recited, 'Panther, pole-cat, porcupine, porpoise...'

'That's right,' Justine said. 'That's right. Just like when you were wee. Everything's going to be fine.'

Someone dabbed his forehead with a cold cloth and he felt the water rolling down his cheeks. He breathed – once, twice – then managed to collect his thoughts. Pulling himself from Justine's embrace, he looked her in the eye and whispered, 'I'm sure Brian McCrae killed Dad,' as if the walls would shatter at the mere sound of the words. Then he heard Eilidh gasp behind him.

'It's not out of the question, as we said—' Hammy began.

'No,' Robert interrupted, turning to him. 'I'm *certain* of it. Think about it.' He leapt to his feet, strode purposefully to the noticeboard and started scribbling frantically. 'Brian is having an affair with Mirabella and kills her daughter.' He held up a hand to stifle any questions. 'Okay, we don't know *why* he did it ... yet. Maybe he's just sick. Maybe it was an accident. Either way, he frames Toby for the murder and thinks he's got away with it ... for decades ... until Dad stumbles across some crucial piece of information. McCrae learns Dad is onto him...' Robert's voice faltered for a second, but he continued to write, ignoring the brimming tears, before addressing them again. '...So he kills him, too. But then Mirabella returns to Findrussie and starts asking questions. McCrae lures her into the woods on some pretext, murders her and makes it look like suicide.' Robert took a deep breath, light-headed again. 'We've got evidence. There's the ring. And I saw him that evening right next to the woods, for God's sake.'

The fire hissed as Justine, Hammy and Eilidh tried to process Robert's tirade. He had never felt so sure of anything in his whole life, but the pen trembled in his hand as he waited anxiously for a response.

'Oh me,' Justine murmured, without taking her eyes off the board. 'It all seems to make sense, but Brian...' Her voice trailed off as she raised a hand to her mouth.

'We need to take this to someone, Robbie,' Eilidh interjected. 'It's—'

'Horrible,' said Hammy, standing. 'Too horrible for words. I think you're onto something, Robbie. It makes sense to me, too. But we can't tell anyone, Eilidh.'

'What? Why?' asked Eilidh. Robert wondered whether he looked as pale as she did.

'McCrae's only one man,' Hammy explained, twiddling his fingers in deep thought. 'Aye, he's powerful, but he hasn't always been. I'm betting he would have needed some help with all of this. We've no idea how deep this thing goes, how many colleagues he has in his pocket. Any one of them might let him know we're onto him. You know, I'm willing to bet that's why Mirabella never told us about their affair. One of his mates probably tipped him off that she was back in town, and McCrae contacted her to tell her to keep quiet about it. Until he decided she had to be shut up permanently.' A sickening silence filled the Pine Needle. Hammy walked around the bar, picked up a bottle of whisky and poured four large measures. 'We're in this together,' he said. 'If we want to bring justice to anyone, we need indisputable, rock-hard *proof*. It's no good making half-baked accusations, no matter how plausible they seem. He'll be after us before we can say *boo*.'

All four of them stared into their whisky glasses.

'He's already suspicious,' Robert agreed. 'He'll be keeping tabs on us.' He thought back to the beam of light he had seen in the grounds of Kinlogie the night before.

Eilidh looked behind her, her breathing shaky. She held the whisky to her lips and spoke quietly into the glass. 'Then we need to prove it. It's the only way. Hammy's right. I wish we knew what your dad had found out, Robbie.'

Robert nodded. 'We need to talk to Calan again. He was close to Clara; she might have told him something. He might even have seen something ... or someone.'

'You're right,' said Justine weakly. She removed her reading glasses and massaged the bridge of her nose, letting her chin drop almost to her chest.

'You all right, Justine?' Hammy asked.

'Oh me, I'm fine,' she replied, letting out a sigh. 'Just a lot to take in, that's all.'

'You've still got the play to think about, I suppose,' said Hammy.

'Aye.' Justine let out a sad laugh. 'Though that seems like the least of our problems now, doesn't it?'

'We should double check with Felicity, too,' Robert said, although he felt guilty for pressing on. Justine seemed so exhausted. 'Eilidh, have you got that invite?'

She jumped up and retrieved it from her backpack.

'I can't put my finger on it, but something isn't right here,' Robert said, staring at the card.

'Let me have a look,' said Hammy. He took the invitation and peered at it, his eyes bright with concentration. 'Well, I can tell you this much – no laird wrote this,' he said eventually.

'No?' asked Justine, rising to her feet. 'How so?'

'Even I learned it in school.' He pointed to the bottom of the card. 'Here, it's a bit hard to read, but it definitely says, "Yours faithfully". Your friend Felicity's right, Justine. Her husband can't have written this.' He sat back, crossing his arms, as if no further explanation were necessary.

'Hammy!' Justine cried. 'Our nerves are already shot to dust. Will you please tell us what you mean?'

Hammy looked at them with genuine surprise. 'It should read "Yours *sincerely*", shouldn't it? That's what I was taught, anyway. If you name the recipients – like here, "Mr and Mrs Anthony Rowley" – then you use "sincerely". If it's "Sir", "Madam" or "To whom it may concern", you use "faithfully". Now, if humble Hammy Galbreath knows this, you can bet your bottom dollar that Peter Montgomery did too.'

'He did have dementia,' pointed out Eilidh.

'But he was well enough to remember old friends and invite them for Christmas?' Hammy shrugged. 'I suggest we ask Felicity whether she had any courtesy calls from the local detective that December.'

'Okay. So, what's the plan?' asked Robert.

'It's Burns Night tomorrow, so we'll see Felicity then,' said Justine. 'I suppose we should just act as we always do, given that McCrae will be about, too. Eilidh, you sing your heart out. Robert, you serve the drinks, help me with the food and sort the after-party. I'll announce the raffle. Hammy, you'll bring the dogs, will you?'

'Aye, I'll do the sledging, as always,' he said. 'Like you say, we need to act like everything's normal. We can't have him sniffing about any more than he already is.'

'Exactly. No need to give him any kind of a head start. Dress up, look the part, like you're in the mood for a celebration,' Justine said, mustering a chuckle. 'We'll be fine at pretending. We're thespians, after all.'

Beneath the table, she squeezed Robert's hand tightly, and he felt an overwhelming sense of gratitude that these three people, at least, were still by his side.

Chapter Seventeen

The air was spiky, but it felt good against Robert's skin. It was still dark, although the sky already had an orange haze to it, a subtle hue that stretched airily over the mountains. Robert ran faster, his feet pounding against the gravel, his chest heaving with exertion. He imagined finally reaching a place of vivid colour, where all was clear and bright and warm.

The loch emerged, black and shiny below the viewing point. Robert eased to a halt at the top of the path and peered down. Something seemed different. He bent over, resting his hands on his knees, and squinted into the valley. The moonlight was reflecting on the calm water's surface, just as it always did. He closed his eyes and suddenly realised that it wasn't the view that had changed. Instead of deep sadness and aching regret, he was feeling a searing quiver of anger. He fell to his knees but kept his eyes fixed on the water. How had McCrae done it? When had his dad realised he was in grave danger? Robert had read about drowning once. Apparently, it took eight minutes before the human body succumbed completely to the water. Until then, the lungs continued to digest air even as they slowly turned into fleshy bogs. Robert stood, his body trembling. He had wished McCrae out of his life many times before, ever since he was a child, but never like this. The word 'if' began to taunt him: *if* his mother had never cheated on Dad; *if* she had stayed with him; *if* the Begg family had never met Brian McCrae. But all of that was just childish, useless speculation.

'Dad!' he screamed into the darkness.

He didn't cry, either because his eyes were too tired or because he simply had no tears left. He hadn't slept since returning home from the bar. He had gone through the prelims – showered, nibbled on some toast, brushed his teeth – but his mind had refused to shut down. In the end, he had tried to read a few chapters of an old walking memoir he had recently acquired in a second-hand bookshop in Inverness. He had forced his way through the words, moving to the next and the next and the next, willing himself to imagine anything other than frantic splashes and horrific gasping for breath.

The narrator was a Spanish mountaineer who had travelled from bothy to bothy on a route not far from Findrussie. The well-known hook of the story was that he had needed to be rescued from the mountainside, almost losing his life in the process. He had attempted the route in the depths of winter and conditions had been far worse than anticipated, which had caused him to lose his sense of direction. Robert did not approve of such reckless behaviour, but the mountaineer wrote so beautifully about the terrain and its transformative effects that he had started to relax ever so slightly. At one point, the author described lighting a fire in a bothy halfway up the mountain and peering outside to see that a fog had enveloped the building. He thought nothing of it, as he intended to spend the night there, but he was shocked at its opacity: the glen was completely obscured. The passage continued:

The mountains were veiled in a white, thick mist. The feeling of disorientation is often described amid panic, but there was no atmosphere of panic here. This was a cloak of deliberate disguise, the mountains hid from me, very purposefully, and did not feel the need to rush. So, of course, I waited. Yes, because of their majesty, but also because of their total, calm willingness to stop my world as they danced behind the curtains.

Robert had seen such mists descend and knew better than to venture into the hills when they were forecast.

Morning came, but the fog remained. Of course, the mountaineer should have bided his time within the shelter until it lifted, yet he took the fateful decision to proceed up the mountain:

We spend most of our childhood craving fluffy snow; it brings joy, it is fun to play with. On the mountain, I discovered my hatred for the stuff. It engulfed me, even with my snowshoes on. The flotation effect did not work properly, and I exhausted myself, blinded by mist and waist deep in snow. I knew I had to reach the top of the mountain. I am not sure what drove me forwards, other than a primal sense of needing to know: the same urge children have when they rip open Christmas presents early. I knew there was something to be learned; to see. After four hours, maybe more, of furrowing my way through the snow, something extraordinary happened. Imagine being so immersed in fog that you cannot see your hand, your feet, none of your body. It is like you are a phantom, like your body is stolen and replaced only by thoughts. This is what I began to believe had happened. I played conversations in my mind, conversations that had never occurred, fantasy conversations between people I knew, things I regretted not saying, things I wished others had said to me. At that moment, without a body and without reality as I could perceive it, I believed that these conversations could indeed have happened. I began to distrust my memory and questioned everything.

You see, the fog stole not only my senses, not only my body, but also the truth. It sounds unlikely, I know, but that was what happened there, alone, on the mountainside.

Then, without any sort of drama or notice, my head emerged through the fog and I saw the mountain top and the glen. As I pushed forwards, I saw the fog's flattened, oppressive surface continuing to work its magic below my feet. That was when I regained a sense of truth. I had opened the curtain; I had arrived above the mist; and although only a few hours had passed since leaving the bothy, I felt that I had entered a new level of understanding not only about the terrain but about myself. The duplicitous fog had shown me how fragile, how suggestive, the human mind can be and how willing it is to believe anything that is placed in front of it. That was what the fog taught me. I stared at it for a long while atop the peak.

Robert continued to stare at the loch. The birds were beginning to stir, chattering in the trees below. Something about the fog story hung on his mind. He knew that adventure writers needed to make something out of nothing. Who would be interested in a straightforward, uneventful hike up a snowy hillside? But his heart raced when he thought about the ease with which the mountaineer had slipped from reality to become a suggestible phantom, ready to clutch on to anything.

He was about to peel himself away from the view and begin the descent when he saw a figure on the beach. At first, he thought it was a deer, but then he realised it was walking on two legs. When the person reached the water's edge, they knelt to the ground, as if in prayer. The sun was only just beginning to rise, so it was impossible to see who it was, but they seemed to be performing some sort of ritual. They seemed to rock back and forth, and they were fiddling with something in their hands.

Robert fumbled for his phone and scrolled to the camera app, but by the time he held it up to the scene the person was already disappearing into the woods. He zoomed in as much as he could and took a shot of the figure's nondescript coat just before it vanished from view. Peering at the image, he spotted something by the loch. He returned the phone to his pocket and squinted into the distance: it looked like a small cairn.

He charged down the hill, almost leaping rather than running. He knew he was unlikely to catch the mysterious figure, but he had to try. Their behaviour had been strange, to say the least. The clouds were brightening as he sprinted along the track, his breathing erratic as he realised, with a feeling of cold dread, that he was hurtling towards a place he hadn't visited since they'd found his father. He stopped at the edge of the woods, where the path led to the beach. Whoever the person was would be long gone by now. The branches seemed to close ranks around him, warning him to turn back.

He shook his head, his breath sharp in his ribs. He had to face the beach at some point. This was his home. He couldn't let McCrae take that from him. He stared straight ahead and progressed onto the beach path, one foot in front of the other, reminding himself with every step that this was just another way home, nothing special, a route he had taken a thousand times before.

The ground beneath his feet became spongy as he made his way onto the fine white sand. His sigh cut through the morning mist; to Robert, it was a signal. A signal that he had arrived. A signal to McCrae that he was coming, one shaky step at a time, closer to justice. His eyes locked on to the mound by the water's edge. It was indeed a modest pile of black stones, but two shiny objects protruded from them. He made his way towards the cairn, tension forming at the back of his neck. The water was placid, yet unforgiving. Kneeling before the rocks, his eyes widened in surprise. The cairn was serving as a plinth for two whisky glasses – one empty and one full. He bent forwards for a closer look. They seemed expensive, cut crystal, the sort he used for single malts in the bar. He was reluctant to touch the arrangement, as the glasses were precariously balanced on the smooth stones. Instead, he leaned back on his ankles and stared. This was the very spot where his father had been pulled from the water. Beginning to feel the chill of the mist, he shook his head, reached for the full glass, and poured the brown liquid onto the sand. It was an unusually peaty whisky, especially for this area, with a powerful, smoky fragrance. Then he reached for the other glass and shoved both of them deep in the pockets of his fleece.

Letting the cool air massage his face, he turned to leave but stopped in his tracks. He was suddenly filled with a desire to swim. He stood, calm and certain, and removed his clothing, one item at a time, folding each piece carefully and forming in a neat pile. Run-ups never worked well; he knew that from the annual Hogmanay swim. The trick was to pacify the mind, get into a slow rhythm and stick to it. Running alerted the brain to impending danger, whereas a slower pace deceived it into thinking that nothing was out of the ordinary. So, he strode forward as casually as he could. The sand was crisp beneath his toes. The mountains overlooked him, impassive, as always. The icy water lapped around his feet. They prickled, initially repulsed, yet he maintained his rhythm, counting steadily, pushing his knees, his thighs, his hips into the water. He let out a stinging yelp when his chest went under, allowing the water to gush into his mouth. Yet he continued to wade out until his feet began to float and a tingling sensation crept up the back of his legs. He was weightless. There were no burdens here. He was paralysed, yet free. His head drooped forwards into the water and he opened his eyes to see his feet hovering above the bed of the loch.

Then, suddenly, panic. A shout. Splashing. Thrashing. Two arms around his chest. His mouth hanging open, gasping, fighting. Far quicker than he had entered the water, he was dragged out. He let it happen, his limbs limp and sagging.

Hammy's voice sounded broken and distant. 'Come on, Robbie!'

Robert heard the familiar, reassuring sound of the dogs barking.

'Robbie, can you hear me? Say something, for God's sake.'

A sharp pain cut across Robert's cheek. Then again. He blinked and focused upon Hammy's crinkled face and raised hand.

'Can you hear me?'

Robert frowned, unsure why Hammy was so frantic. He flopped his head towards the water, staring at the loch, enjoying the sensation of cool sand against his burning cheek.

'You'll be hypothermic,' Hammy said, removing his coat and wrapping it around Robert's shoulders.

He may have a point, Robert mused, and noticed that his arms and legs were trembling violently.

Strangely, Hammy then removed his belt and started to tie Robert's legs together.

'Hey,' Robert protested, his teeth chattering. 'What—'

'I've got the sledge. Taking it to town for tonight. Come on...' He grabbed Robert's running gear and threw it onto the sledge, then did the same with Robert himself, securing him with some lengths of rope.

'Am I an idiot?' Robert asked.

Hammy chuckled. 'Aye. Not all the time, but right now, aye.' He pulled the ropes tighter. 'All set? Mush!' he shouted to the dogs.

Robert watched the branches flash by in a blur. He closed his eyes for what seemed no more than a moment, enjoying the sensation of being carried home.

'Whoa!' Hammy called, pulling the sledge to a halt. He hurried towards Robert and carried him into the house. 'Burner's on,' he said, setting Robert on the sofa and piling half a dozen blankets on top of him. 'Try to move those toes, Robbie,' he insisted. 'I know you're tiring, but try to focus on that.'

Before Robert could reply, a cup of tea was pressed into his hands. 'Ouch!' he said, scowling.

'It's only tepid,' said Hammy, 'but I guess it feels like the sun to you. Go on then. You need to get some warm fluids inside you.'

One of the dogs rested its chin on Robert's thigh as he watched Hammy boiling the kettle again. It was a few minutes before his legs stopped trembling. He pressed his head into the arm of the sofa and started to feel the dreadful pang of embarrassment. What on earth had he been thinking? 'Oh God,' he said to the ceiling. 'Hammy, I—'

Hammy sat on the armchair and raised his eyebrows. 'Bit of a shock you gave me ... and the dogs, Robbie.'

Robert groaned, pulling the blankets tightly around his body. 'I don't know what to say. The water—'

'I know.' Hammy held up a hand, his eyes kind. 'You don't have to explain.' He tapped the side of his head. 'All sorts going on up here. Sometimes ... well, let's just say the mind bends a bit. It's nothing to worry about. I'm just glad I was around.'

Robert was sure he was blushing, although he couldn't feel his face properly. He remembered the water, how it had called him into it, how he had yearned to lose himself in its depths, inhabit it. 'I saw someone,' he said. 'On my run. From the viewing point.'

'*Someone?*'

'Aye, they were … doing something, fiddling about on the beach, just where Dad…' He didn't need to elaborate.

'Bit early for a beach stroll,' observed Hammy.

'They weren't strolling. They were … I think they were having a dram.'

Hammy stood up and checked Robert's forehead. 'A dram? Do I need to call a doctor after all?'

'No!' Robert shuffled to a seated position. 'I mean it. They left two glasses behind – one full and one empty. Check my fleece. I picked them up.'

Hammy rifled through the pockets, retrieved the two glasses and held them up to the light, as if taken aback that Robert wasn't talking nonsense. Meanwhile, Robert felt a wave of relief that he hadn't imagined them.

'Who would be drinking on the beach before sunrise?' asked Hammy, clinking the glasses together.

'Couldn't see,' said Robert. 'But it's weird, isn't it?'

Hammy's lips pouted from his beard. 'You think it's something to do with your dad?'

'They seemed to be toasting the loch … or maybe they were toasting him.'

Hammy shrugged and placed the glasses on the kitchen table. 'Maybe. No reason to go skinny-dipping, though, was there?' He chuckled and began to put on his coat. 'You all right here for a while? We'll see you later?'

Robert's eyelids were beginning to droop, but he managed a weak nod.

'I've stacked the fire,' Hammy said. 'Keep tucked up for a bit, get some rest. You'll be fine. We need to act like everything is normal tonight, remember. Don't want anyone, especially McCrae, thinking we're onto anything.'

'I know,' Robert replied, dozing off. 'I'll be okay, I promise.'

'Good.'

'Oh, Hammy—' Robert began.

Hammy smiled kindly and tapped his heart. 'Cross my heart. Your secret's safe with me. We've all done a crazy thing or two in our time. No need to dwell on it.'

'Thanks. I wouldn't want to worry Justine.'

'Oh, I know that,' said Hammy with a mock-serious expression. Then he started chuckling again.

As Robert drifted off to sleep, he felt Hammy's hand pat the top of his head then heard the front door close, followed by a faint cry of 'Mush!'

Chapter Eighteen

Burns Night was well underway by the time Robert arrived at the village hall. He heard the sound of dogs barking from behind the building as Hammy drove his sledge along the snowy forest path. A long queue of excited children wrapped in thick coats stretched all the way to the car park.

Inside the hall, Justine was busying herself around the hot-food table. When she saw Robert, she beckoned him over and shoved a serving spoon into his hand. 'Can't keep up with them,' she said. 'We need more haggis. Wait there and try to keep them happy,' she hissed under her breath, 'they're driving me mad.'

Robert took the spoon and smiled at the man at the front of the queue.

'You'd have thought you weren't expecting us,' said the man grumpily in a cut-glass English accent.

Robert tried not to sigh. He was familiar with this sort of 'complaint' from the bar. There was a certain breed of tourist that preferred passive aggression to addressing an issue head-on.

'The haggis is on its way,' Robert replied. 'Not long now. You bought tickets at Kinlogie?'

'What? Oh, yes. Wonderful place. Came specially to see

Burns Night done properly.' The man's eyes flickered over the culinary offerings.

'There'll be an after-party at the Pine Needle,' Robert said, glad to see Justine hurrying back with more haggis. 'I hope you'll join us for a wee dram.'

'*A wee dram*,' the man repeated, attempting to mimic Robert's accent.

Robert grinned and bowed his head, trying not to catch Justine's eye.

'Here you go,' she said, placing a large portion on the man's plate.

He wrinkled his nose, sniffed and said hesitantly, 'Thanks … But does this smell a bit off to you? I can smell citrus. You don't put lemon juice in haggis, do you?'

'Traditional,' sang Justine, giving Robert a nudge. 'Right, Robbie?'

'Oh … yes, traditional,' he agreed, flashing a weak grin.

The man walked away, clearly caught somewhere between disgruntlement and the desire to enjoy an 'authentic' Burns Night.

Robert stared at Justine. 'I smell it too. What on earth is it?'

'Oh, Robbie…' She clapped her hands. 'You wouldn't be asking me to divulge my culinary secrets, would you now?' Then she whispered from the corner of her mouth, 'There's trouble. Stay with me. You'll be fine.'

McCrae had positioned himself in the corner of the room, behind the fold-out tables. He was standing alone, tapping one foot to the music, his arms crossed tightly. His lips were pressed into a tight, straight line, too. Robert felt a jolt of what he could only describe as red, fiery rage. He pictured himself flying towards McCrae, placing his hands around his neck, and squeezing until he begged for mercy. The thought was so visceral that it brought tears to his eyes.

'Just act normally,' Justine cautioned, placing a hand over his. 'We knew he'd be here. There's no point causing a scene.'

Robert took a deep breath and focused on serving the food, although he kept a keen eye on McCrae. Thankfully, the detective didn't seem to be paying them any attention at all. In fact, he seemed to be scanning the room for someone else, his eyes moving in quick, furtive glances.

'Who's he looking for?' Robert asked under his breath.

Justine looked up, tilting her eyes over her glasses. 'No clue,' she said. 'The man has a unique ability to suck the joy from any room, I can say that much.'

Robert helped her clear away the plates and fold the tables once the supper was finished. The evening seemed to be going well, especially among the Kinlogie crowd, who were ordering single malts at an alarming rate. Eilidh waved at Robert from the stage and he waved back enthusiastically until he spotted Daniel Bell shooting him a less-than-friendly glare from the side of the room. He awkwardly turned the wave into a head-scratch and pretended to bend down to tie a shoelace. When he stood up, he found himself face to face with Felicity Montgomery.

'Felicity! I mean ... Lady Montgomery...'

'Felicity, please.' She smiled and Robert fought the urge to stare at her exuberantly applied red lipstick. 'You're not dancing?' The band had just launched into a Gay Gordons. As he struggled to think of a suitable excuse, Felicity kicked him lightly in the shin. 'Come now. You wouldn't leave me alone for a dance like this?'

'Um, no, no, I wouldn't,' Robert stammered.

Eilidh ran down the steps of the stage to meet Daniel for her break. Felicity followed Robert's gaze knowingly. 'Let's show him,' she said. 'It's not my first rodeo, you know.'

With that, she dragged him into position and began kicking her feet more energetically than anyone else on the dance floor.

Then she linked arms with immense force, almost sending him flying. Her dynamism seemed to catch like wildfire as everyone around them started cheering and bouncing ever more energetically. The sound of stamping feet and squeals of delight rose up to the rafters. Over the music, she shouted, 'I enjoyed having you as my guest the other night.'

They were twirling next to Eilidh and Daniel now. As Daniel turned, he threw Robert what seemed like a very forced smile.

'Robbie,' Eilidh called, giggling, before the pair spun away.

'You shouldn't worry,' shouted Felicity.

'What?' cried Robert over the music.

'I said you shouldn't worry. She likes *you*. Trust a woman's intuition. That boy's what they call a "stopping station", trust me. It's you she wants. Anyone can see it.'

Unfortunately, the music stopped just as she bellowed the last two sentences. A few people turned their heads out of vague interest and Robert looked around, praying that Daniel was not one of them. However, he was standing barely a metre away, glowering at the pair of them. Eilidh tugged at his arm. 'Ignore that,' she said light-heartedly, though Robert could hear the anxiety in her voice.

'Oh God,' whispered Robert.

'Ah,' said Felicity, her eyes widening. 'It seems I have rather overstepped the mark.'

'Outside.' Robert stared as Daniel stepped towards him, his chin jutting forwards and two small red circles forming on each cheek.

'Daniel...' Eilidh began.

'No!' Daniel shouted, his face already a deep scarlet. 'We'll settle this man to man. Outside, Begg.' He prodded Robert in the chest and squinted at him menacingly. A few dramatic gasps emanated from the crowd.

'Um...' Robert looked at Eilidh, who shrugged, rather unhelpfully, he thought. 'I don't think that will be necessary...'

'Fight him,' urged Felicity, stamping on the ground excitedly. Robert frowned at her as she sprang from foot to foot and started chanting, 'Fight! Fight! Fight!'

Justine placed an arm around Felicity in a bid to calm her down and shot Robert an apologetic look.

Robert let out an exasperated sigh. 'Look, Daniel, there's nothing between—' Mid-sentence, he spotted McCrae's face immediately behind Daniel's shoulder. He was wearing the same sneer as when he had cornered him in the kitchen, the sneer that signalled Robert was weak, useless, would never stand his ground.

'Fine,' said Robert, shrugging. If Daniel wanted to make a spectacle of both of them, then he was welcome to it. Stepping aside, so Daniel could lead the way, he said, 'Let's go outside then.'

'Robbie, what are you doing?' Eilidh tried to pull Daniel back, but he shook her off. She looked to Justine. 'Will you say something?'

'Now, Robbie...' Justine began.

'No!' Robert shouted, feeling like he was rapidly losing his grasp on reality. He had no clue how to fight and, judging by the nervous twitch Daniel had developed in the last few moments, his opponent didn't either. Still, neither of them seemed close to backing down, especially as the tourists were now echoing Felicity's chant of 'Fight! Fight!'

'Let's go,' said Daniel, a note of disbelief vibrating in his voice. He headed straight for the door to the car park, his fists clenched by his sides.

Robert followed as the guests parted, watching with intense interest. He heard the man who had complained about the haggis whispering excitedly to his friends. Justine shouted his name a couple of times, but Robert ignored her, furiously trying to remember any useful moves he had seen on TV.

Daniel almost slipped on the icy ground but Robert caught him before he fell backwards. Daniel shook him off, which led to an awkward exchange of apologies and muffled swearing. Robert backed away and waited patiently while Daniel brushed the snow from his coat. The onlookers slowly began to return to the hall, clearly unwilling to brave the cold for this half-hearted showdown.

'Go on then,' the man from the food table shouted, tilting his wine glass towards them. 'Someone throw a punch. Let's make this interesting.'

Robert shook his head. He wasn't keen to provide the evening's entertainment for a drunk tourist. Eilidh was standing by Justine, a hand on either side of her face, as if she could not believe what she was witnessing. McCrae was nowhere to be seen. Felicity was still clapping her hands and shouting, 'You show him, Robert. How chivalrous ... a duel. Who'd have thought it?'

'Felicity, quiet,' Justine hissed.

Robert raised his eyes to Daniel's. The anger McCrae had incited in him was ebbing away. This was a stupid idea. One or both of them could really injure themselves on the hard ground. And anyway, it was ludicrous to fight over Eilidh. She'd already made her choice. He shook his head and said, 'Look, Daniel, there's nothing between me and Eilidh, I swear.' He turned to look at her and rolled his eyes in what he hoped was a jovial manner. 'Honestly. She's just an employee, nothing more. Felicity had her wires crossed, that's all.'

Eilidh let out a loud sigh, which Robert interpreted as relief.

'I don't believe you,' Daniel attempted to shout, but his teeth were chattering, which somewhat ruined the effect.

Robert took a step towards him and held his arms

outstretched in what he hoped Daniel would interpret as a gesture of surrender. 'As I say, she's an employee, that's it. I don't think about her in that way at all. I'm happy for the both of you. Seriously.'

Daniel looked between Eilidh and Robert with the expression of a confused deer in the headlights. Then he shook his head and started to laugh. 'You know, I think I've probably had a bit too much beer.'

Robert relaxed and cracked a smile himself. 'Nothing to worry about,' he said, though his voice was a bit stiff, and held out a hand. 'We can shake on it. No more ... duels, okay?' Daniel laughed again and seized the offered hand.

'Unbelievable.' Eilidh stalked back to the hall, her shoulders hunched.

'Eilidh!' Daniel made to follow her, almost slipping again. 'Eilidh, I'm—'

She rounded on him, her face ablaze. 'Do *not* follow me,' she shouted. 'What do you think I am? Some piece of meat to fight over? Did you think to ask me? Or do you not trust me?'

'Eilidh,' Robert began. 'He just thought—'

'And you can shut up too!' The look she gave him caused Robert's chest to tighten. She seemed genuinely hurt. Her face was creased with anger, but her eyes were sad and wide. 'Why would you care?' she asked. 'I'm "just an employee". Nothing more. Isn't that right?'

Robert gulped, trying to think of something useful to say.

'Save it, *boss*,' she said, sarcastically. 'I'm going home.' She stormed away with Daniel following in hot pursuit.

Robert remained rooted to the spot, trying to process what had just happened. He'd been reasonable, hadn't he? He'd diffused a potentially violent situation caused by Daniel's jealousy. So why was Eilidh so furious? He shook his head. The stress of potential financial ruin, not to mention investigating a string of murders, was more than enough already. He didn't need Daniel Bell accusing him of stealing his girlfriend, too. He watched the wispy clouds scudding across the night sky like a misty distress signal. Then he heard a long, blaring screech.

Time seemed to slow to a crawl over the next few seconds. First, the car park was bathed in a dazzling blaze of white light. Then there was a yelp of surprise, then a scream, then a skid. But the sound that reverberated through Robert's skull was a sickening crunch. He had never heard anything like it before. It reminded him of a twig snapping, only much thicker and far more brutal. Then further screams began to echo around the car park.

Robert rolled onto his back and only then realised he was lying on the ground. His hands felt numb against the ice. He groaned, blinking uselessly, and wondered if he was waking up from a strange dream. Someone was weeping. He could hear the sobs clearly, high-pitched but groggy, interspersed with wet gasps. He eased himself onto his side and squinted into the darkness. Somehow, he had ended up at the far end of the car park, under the kitchen vent. He groaned again as a great wave of confusion washed over him.

Forcing himself to breathe steadily, he slowly pushed himself to a crouch, using the fence as support. Sirens sounded in the distance. He stared at the figures bustling about in front of him and tried to put the pieces together. A mass of orange hair was hunched over a body on the ground. 'Justine,' he mouthed, but his voice was muted, as if he'd been struck dumb in a nightmare. He cleared his throat and tried again. 'Justine. Who's...' His vision blurred as a sense of dark panic set in. Eilidh had gone back into the hall, hadn't she? The screech, the sound of skidding wheels on ice, the bright lights had all come later, hadn't they? He staggered forwards, straining to see who was lying on the ground. 'Justine,' he said again, this time gaining her attention. Her mascara was smudged all the way down her cheeks. Her eyes were red and wet. She shook her head, her mouth hanging open.

Robert just about managed to maintain his balance as a rush of relief knocked him backwards. It wasn't Eilidh. But then the full horror of the scene came into sharp relief. Felicity Montgomery was lying splayed on the ground, her body contorted at an impossible angle, a garish, surprised smile still etched on her lips.

Bodies began to tumble from the hall. Murmurs grew louder and more panicked.

'Oh my God!'

'She's not...'

'Looks that way.'

'I heard a crash.'

'The ice...'

'Where's the driver?'

Hammy and the dogs arrived from the track. Justine flinched at their barks, visibly shaking. 'What happened?' he called, jumping from the sledge. 'The kids said something about...' He took in the whole scene until his gaze finally fell upon Felicity. 'Oi,' he whispered. The dogs pulled against their harnesses, sniffing at the ground, dragging the sledge towards the lifeless body. Justine whimpered in distress, covering her face with both hands.

'Keep those dogs under control, will you,' shouted McCrae. 'Get them out of here.' He showed his badge to the paramedics who were rushing from their ambulance. Then he turned his attention to Hammy, Justine and Robert. 'Meeting again next to a body,' he said darkly. 'Seems we're forming an unfortunate habit, here.'

Robert clenched his fists and staggered towards McCrae. His legs were moving erratically beneath him and he fell forwards, only to be saved for the second time that day by Hammy's powerful arms.

'Robbie,' Hammy whispered into his ear, holding him upright. 'Remember, don't give him what he wants. He's fishing. Now, let's get you looked at.' He waved over one of the paramedics.

Robert pushed Hammy away from him, his head spinning. 'Who did this?' he demanded. Then, pointing at McCrae, he shouted: 'Go on then, Brian. Tell us.' He gestured to the guests who had now gathered in the car park. McCrae merely looked at him blankly. 'I said, "Who did this?"' He wriggled free from Hammy's grasp and again lunged clumsily for McCrae, his body heavy and awkward. He got to within inches of the detective's face before the paramedic caught him by the arms. Still leaning forwards, he hissed, 'I know it was you, Brian. I know what you've done. I know you're behind all of this.'

McCrae's eyes seemed to blacken before he nodded to the paramedic. 'Check him over and take him somewhere to calm down. The Pine Needle will be empty. He's the owner. The boy's upset, understandably. This is one tragedy too many for the whole community.'

'I'll prove it,' yelled Robert as he was dragged away. 'You won't get away with this.' He twisted around to hold McCrae's gaze.

'Your interest in this case is very much noted, Mr Begg,' Brian called after him. 'Thank you for alerting me to your concerns.'

Chapter Nineteen

Robert stared at his phone. He'd sent Eilidh at least fifteen messages and left her three voicemails. She had not replied to the messages, but the ticks indicated she had at least seen them, which was the most important thing. Still, he would have felt much happier if she were here with them. He didn't consider Daniel Bell much of a bodyguard.

Hammy carried three steaming mugs into the living room. Justine was sitting silently in the corner of his enormous sofa, twiddling her fingers, staring into the space in front of her. The smell of her special haggis – that strong, citrusy odour – seemed to have seeped into her clothes. It made Robert's belly rumble as he realised he hadn't eaten anything since the morning.

'Baked fresh today.' Hammy placed a knobbly cake on the coffee table. 'Not the bonniest thing in the world. Delicious, though.'

Robert took a slice and bit into it miserably. 'I didn't know you baked.'

'I find it relaxing,' said Hammy. One of the dogs stirred next to the fire and grunted loudly. Hammy smiled. 'If they wake up, they'll demolish it. Eat up.'

Robert chewed mechanically. A high-pitched buzz had been sounding in his ears ever since the incident in the car park. Justine remained silent. Neither Robert nor Hammy knew quite what to say to her. She hadn't seemed too close to Felicity, but the psychological impact of being so close to the crash, of seeing the body fly through the air like some limp fish, must have been terrible.

It seemed that Justine herself had only narrowly escaped the oncoming vehicle, which had sped around the side of the hall and ploughed into Felicity before she had a chance to move. According to Justine, Robert had thrown himself out of the way in the nick of time. The car had then careered onto the main road. It had all happened far too quickly for anyone to note down the registration number.

'He's picking them off one by one,' said Robert. 'Anyone who can link him to Clara's murder. He must have known we'd spoken to Felicity. I saw that light in the grounds. It was McCrae, I'm sure of it.'

Hammy stared into the fire. 'Aye, seems that way.'

Justine sniffed. 'She was right next to me. I could have dragged her out of the way.'

'No, Justine,' Hammy said sternly. 'You can't think like that.'

Robert shook his head. 'Hammy, this is our fault, isn't it? If we hadn't visited Felicity, brought her into all this, she'd still be alive.'

Justine turned grimly towards the two of them. 'I need something stronger than tea, Hammy.'

Hammy fetched a bottle of whisky from the kitchen and poured three large glasses. 'I wonder who he used,' he said. 'Where do you find someone who's willing to mow down an old lady?'

Robert pursed his lips, annoyed the thought hadn't occurred to him earlier. 'What about Calan Stuart?' he suggested. 'He could be working for McCrae. That might explain why we haven't seen him since the Ionic.'

'The local hard man,' Hammy agreed, taking another slice of cake. 'Not a bad shout. I bet a friend in the police would be very appealing to a character like Calan.'

'It doesn't matter,' Justine cried suddenly, wiping a tear from her cheek. 'What do details matter, Hammy? Another woman is dead.'

Robert stood and began pacing the floor. 'You heard what he said. He's "noted my interest". He'll be coming after us.'

'Thanks to you.' Justine spoke very clearly. There was a severity in her eyes that Robert had never witnessed before. Different from the dramatic sternness she employed while directing, this was both chillingly cold and disappointed.

'Justine...' Hammy began.

'No, Hammy. It has to be said. I know it's been difficult for you, Robert, but your outburst tonight has put all our lives in danger. McCrae probably knows we spoke to Mirabella. He might even know we spoke to Felicity. But now he knows for sure that you *suspect* him. I told you to behave normally ... and what did you do?'

Robert was astonished. 'I'm not the one you need to blame, Justine.'

'Really?' She wiped her eyes with the back of her hand. 'You think not? Because here was me thinking we were helping you solve your little mystery out of the goodness of our hearts, and now we're walking targets thanks to your big mouth.'

'Come on now.' Hammy looked cautiously at Justine. 'Let's not get overexcited.'

'I've worked tirelessly at your dad's bar for years, going above and beyond. Practically raised you when Bennie couldn't cope on his own. Believe me, I wouldn't have had it any other way. I never once asked for a favour in return. I love you, Robert

Begg, as if you're my own, but, by God, I never thought I'd have to lay down my life on account of your ... stupidity.'

'I won't let that happen,' Robert cried, raising his voice as a deep panic grew in his belly. He wasn't cut out for this sort of pressure. No wonder he'd cracked earlier. How could he be expected to protect them, make all the right decisions? They looked up to him, he knew it. But only because of his dad. McCrae was right: Robert himself was a weakling in comparison.

'How can you promise that?' Justine asked. Her lips wobbled as she held Robert's gaze. 'You can't even protect yourself, let alone anyone else.'

'Justine,' Hammy said quietly. 'We all agreed. Robbie never forced us to do anything. Remember, it's for Bennie, too.'

'That was before half the village became potential murder victims,' Justine cried. She downed her whisky, her hand shaking, and slammed the glass back down on the table. Her eyes were brimming with tears. Hammy cast Robert a worried look. Neither of them had ever seen her like this before. She leaned forwards, hanging her head between her knees, and expelled all the air from her lungs with a loud whooshing noise. Robert was about to leap over to help when she looked up, her eyes dry. 'You're right,' she said, calmly. She looked at Robert. 'Rant over. I'm sorry. But I still think you weren't smart tonight. Far from it.'

Robert had to admit that everything she'd said was true. He should have kept his mouth shut. He had been selfish, blinded by his own pain. He'd played straight into McCrae's hands and called his bluff. And now they were all in danger. A hard lump of guilt formed in his stomach.

'It's scary, I'll give you that for free,' said Hammy carefully, placing a hand on Robert's shoulder. 'But Justine, what you've just said is precisely why we can't give up. We'll be sitting ducks if we do nothing. We have to keep going. We have to prove McCrae's our killer.'

She glanced from Robert to Hammy and back again. 'I know,' she said. Frowning, she smacked her lips and looked at her glass. 'What is this, Hammy? Bunnahabhain?'

'Aye. I've got more local stuff if you'd prefer.'

'No.' Justine smiled. 'I like it.'

Robert sighed with relief; she seemed back to her old self. He didn't think he could hold himself together if she fell apart, too.

'You two want to stay tonight?' Hammy asked. 'I can make the beds up.'

It sounded like an excellent idea to Robert. 'I'll help you,' he said, giving one of the dogs a ruffle on the neck as it stirred. Three of the others were already eyeing the cake that Justine was cutting into hungrily.

'They must be as tired as me,' Hammy said with an ostentatious yawn. 'They'd usually be fighting you for that, Justine. They never show me such courtesy.'

Justine chuckled and mumbled something about having the magic touch.

'Come on then,' said Hammy, still yawning uncontrollably. 'It's been a long night and I reckon we've got a few more coming.'

Chapter Twenty

Robert had been staring at the spreadsheet for over an hour. The bar's accounts were even worse than he'd feared. A sombre atmosphere had descended upon Findrussie in the wake of Mirabella's death, and now a hit-and-run driver was on the loose. Who knew when someone would next fancy a drink at the local bar? He punched yet more projections into the boxes, but they were so ambitious, so unrealistic, that it was barely worth it. Groaning, he pushed the keyboard to one side and rested his forehead on the desk.

'That bad, is it?'

Robert jumped as Eilidh appeared in the doorway. He scrambled to turn off the screen but then realised there was no point. He would have to tell her sooner or later. Sheepishly, he said, 'Thanks for turning up for your shift. And, yes, it's very, very bad.'

She didn't reply immediately. Instead, she stood with her arms folded, her eyes narrowed. Finally, she said coolly, 'I'm your employee. Of course I turned up.'

'Eilidh, you know you're not ... *just* an employee. I just said that to—'

'Then what am I?' Her arms remained folded, but she cocked her head to one side. She wasn't going to let him off that easily.

Robert felt his face burning red. He hated conversations like this. Surely it was obvious what everyone was to everyone else? Did it have to be constantly discussed and defined? Eilidh showed no signs of backing down, though. 'You're a ... friend. You're *my* friend. Actually, you're my only friend under the age of fifty-five, so count that as an honour.'

She continued to watch him for a few long seconds. 'Fine,' she said eventually, with the barest hint of a smile. 'Fine. And thank you.'

He was now thoroughly confused, though pleased that he seemed to have said something right, for once.

She perched on the arm of his chair and nodded at the screen. 'I know we're "friends", but I'd also like to register my interest in remaining your employee.'

'Ah.' He leaned back in the chair. 'It's a mess,' he said miserably. 'There are hardly any customers. Haven't been since Hogmanay.'

Eilidh studied the figures, running her finger down the screen, which he wished she wouldn't do, though he realised this was hardly the best time to mention it. She turned to him, grinning. 'Good news or bad news, boss?'

He rolled his eyes. 'Bad.'

'Well, you're right. These accounts are going south and fast, Mr Begg.'

He sighed. 'So, what's the good news?'

'The good news is that I'm going to save the day.'

He laughed. 'Eilidh, if you think you can fiddle those numbers, you're welcome to try.'

She put a hand to her chest, as if amid a dramatic

monologue. 'I could lend you the mystical, alluring, unquenchable pull of my musical talents for a few more nights.'

He shook his head, unable to suppress a smile. 'I can't afford any more music nights, Eilidh. The band costs more than we make in drinks.'

She pretended to knock him on the head. 'Hello? Anyone in there? Listen to what I said. What if I can *lend* you the nights? I'll sing for free. I'll be here anyway and I could strip down the accompaniment and ask the band to work for drinks and dinner. You know it works ... people always turn up for live music.'

Robert was overwhelmed by the gesture. 'You'd do that? You think you could persuade them to play for free?'

'Not for free. For drinks and dinner. But also for the good of Findrussie. Don't underestimate the power of this little bar, Robbie. Everyone will do their bit to protect it.'

He didn't know what to say. The plan would keep the bar ticking over for another month, at least. 'Thank you, Eilidh.'

'What are friends for?' She shrugged and stood, knocking the mouse and accidentally shutting down the spreadsheet to reveal the computer's web browser. 'What's this? Anthony Rowley? Clara's father?'

He sighed. 'I thought it was worth doing some research. At this point, I'm willing to look anywhere for evidence against McCrae.'

'Find anything?' Eilidh asked, scanning the search results with interest.

Robert sat up straight and took control of the mouse. 'Most of the hits are archived newspaper articles about Clara's murder. Plus some shorter pieces about his suicide. He killed himself the following July, seven months after Clara's murder, shortly after Toby had hanged himself.'

'That's terrible,' Eilidh said. 'Poor Mirabella.'

'Yes,' agreed Robert. 'Unimaginable, really. No wonder she never gave up trying to identify the real killer.'

'What's this one?' Eilidh pointed at a headline: VANESSA KING SPOTTED WITH SECRET LOVER. 'What's that got to do with Anthony?'

'No idea.' Robert clicked on the link, which took them to an old tabloid article. Vanessa King seemed to be some sort of minor celebrity. She sported a deep fake tan and hair extensions down to her waist. The photograph showed her leaving a nightclub in the arms of a rather dishevelled companion. The caption identified him as Anthony Rowley.

'Says it was 1998,' said Eilidh.

Robert scrolled down the page. 'Seems he was having an affair,' he said. 'I thought Felicity said the Rowleys had a happy marriage?'

'Doesn't look like it to me,' replied Eilidh. 'Search "Anthony Rowley lover".'

Robert quickly typed the words and a deluge of images appeared on the screen. Every picture had a similar theme: a young, highly made-up woman in high heels leaving a glamorous nightspot with Anthony Rowley in tow.

'My God,' said Eilidh. 'He was out with a different girl every night. These were published in the tabloids. Mirabella must have known.'

'Certainly would have been hard to miss,' said Robert. He clicked on an image of the Rowley family posing in front of Kinlogie House. It looked idyllic: the quintessential happy-family photograph. Mirabella was smiling pertly at the camera, her hair pulled into a tight ponytail, her hands clenched tightly at her waist. The two children were standing at her feet. Clara looked to be about six or seven. She was grinning widely and her head was tilted, as if she were about to laugh out loud. Anthony was standing next to his wife, an arm around her waist, a hand upon his son's shoulder. He projected an image of power.

'Who's that?' asked Robert, pointing to a young, pretty, blonde woman. She was kneeling a few steps away from the family, as if she thought she was out of shot, and pointing, seemingly in the hope of encouraging Clara to look at the camera.

'Doesn't say,' said Eilidh, leaning into the screen. 'She seems to know them, though.'

Robert stood to stretch his legs. Thinking about the Rowleys was making his head hurt. There was something about old photographs that always seemed so melancholy, so prophetic. The way their faces stared frozen in time unsettled him. It felt like the camera knew what would befall them. 'So, Mirabella knew that her husband was having multiple affairs,' Robert said.

Eilidh grimaced as she clicked through some of the more drunken and debauched images.

'Might explain why Mirabella fell into the arms of McCrae,' Robert began. He opened the drawer and took out Mirabella's ring. Twiddling it between his fingers, he asked, 'How long do you think you'd need to be with someone before you bought them a ring?'

Eilidh flashed a grim smile. 'Don't ask me. Daniel's not even bought me a burger yet.'

Robert bit his lip, trying to keep his face as neutral as possible. 'Hasn't he?'

'No!' Eilidh giggled. 'There's no need to look so terrified, though. We're fine ... thanks to you, actually. Daniel got the wrong idea, that's all. But you set him on the right track.' She looked at him from under her eyebrows. 'Convinced him me and you aren't—'

'Good,' interrupted Robert, attempting to sound as casual as possible. 'So, anyway, the ring?'

Eilidh shook her head. 'That's something you get someone when it's really serious. I'd say years.' She took the ring from his hand and held it in her palm. 'As good as a proposal, in my book, isn't it?'

'That's what I thought,' mused Robert, looking back at the screen.

'What is it?'

Robert rubbed his temples. He was sure he was missing something. 'We don't know how long McCrae and Mirabella were seeing each other,' he said. 'For some reason, I've been thinking it started shortly before Clara's murder, but...'

'The ring suggests otherwise,' said Eilidh.

'Exactly. As you say, it signifies long-term commitment. I wonder if McCrae ever visited her in London in the years leading up to Clara's murder?'

'It's possible. Why do you ask?'

'If we're going to prove McCrae's a killer, then we need to understand his motivations,' said Robert. 'We're chasing about in circles here. I think we need to move into the Rowleys' territory. Try to find someone who knew them before Clara was killed, someone who might remember McCrae.'

'You mean a trip to London?' Eilidh did her best to remain professional, but her eyes lit up at the prospect.

'Better than sitting here doing nothing while we wait for McCrae to set his henchman on us.'

Eilidh wrapped her arms around herself.

Robert noticed a slight tremble in her lips at the mention of Calan Stuart. 'I wouldn't let him...' he began, but as much as he wanted to promise her that everything would be fine, he couldn't lie to her. He leaned back on the chair and stared at the keyboard. 'Eilidh, I'm so sorry. You shouldn't have to be dealing with this. I've put you in danger and—'

'Stop,' Eilidh said firmly, placing a finger to his lips. Her hand smelled of orange blossom and nail polish. He didn't pull away. Tentatively, he raised his eyes to meet hers. Her face was serious, her eyes clear. He sensed a thousand unspoken words working their way through his body ... and through hers. 'I want to help,' she said simply. 'You don't need to apologise.' She withdrew her finger and he realised he'd been holding his breath. A great, embarrassing cascade of air escaped from his chest. Eilidh was already searching for her rucksack in the rear of the office. She slipped the straps over her shoulders, zipped up her coat, and said, 'We'll need some people to stay here. We can't have all the Pine Needles jumping ship and heading to London.'

'The Pine Needles?' Robert laughed.

'Has a ring to it, don't you think?' said Eilidh with a wink. 'We're an exclusive club now.'

Robert thought he understood what she was trying to say. 'Of course, you have the play to think about. You stay here. I'll go with—'

'No!' she blurted out. Robert thought he detected a sudden flush to her cheeks. 'I'm coming. I meant Hammy and Justine should stay here ... in case of further developments.'

'Oh, right,' he said, again marvelling at his unique talent for misunderstanding. 'I guess that will be fine. Justine can manage here. But won't she mind you missing rehearsals?'

'Robbie, we're investigating *four* murders, most likely committed by the most powerful man in Findrussie.'

'Yes, but ... the play...' He didn't want to cause Justine any more stress than he had already.

'If you don't want me—' Eilidh started.

'I do!' shouted Robert, then immediately regretted the outburst as an uncomfortable silence settled between them. He cleared his throat. 'I'll book the tickets tonight.'

Eilidh pursed her lips and moved awkwardly from foot to foot. 'Right,' she said flatly.

'Good,' said Robert, turning away from her as he felt his ears starting to burn.

'Good,' she repeated, hurrying out of the office. Just before she disappeared, she called over her shoulder, 'Email me some of those pictures, will you?'

Then she was gone.

Robert stared at the images of Anthony Rowley for a few seconds before opening a new tab. He knew it was ridiculous, given the circumstances, but he felt a tiny glimmer of excitement as he typed 'Train tickets – Inverness to London' into the search box.

Chapter Twenty-One

It took all of Robert's strength not to tell Eilidh to remove her feet from the seat opposite. A script was resting on her knees and she was mouthing through her lines, raising the occasional arm to indicate some heightened emotion or other. Robert watched her furtively for a while, then, worried he must seem creepy, returned to his book. The Spanish mountaineer was dragging himself along the bottom of a narrow crevice. Things were not looking good for him – both of his legs were broken – but he maintained a kind of rugged optimism, keeping his eyes to the sky, in the knowledge that nothing worth fighting for is easy. The writing was slightly melodramatic, but Robert appreciated the sentiment. He looked out of the window as the scenery became progressively flatter and greener.

'No good?'

'Hmmm?' He raised his eyes to Eilidh, who was watching him with a smile.

'Your book. No good?'

'Oh!' he said. 'No, it's fine. How are the lines going?'

Eilidh rolled her eyes, leaned forward conspiratorially and spoke in a guilty, hushed tone. 'Between you and me, I'm not sure that this play is one of Justine's best ideas. It's very violent and upsetting. Not really our standard Findrussie Am Dram material.'

'That's good, though, isn't it?' suggested Robert. 'Something for you to get your teeth into for a change.'

Eilidh sat back and bit her lip. 'It's just so ... dark,' she said. 'With everything that's been going on, I think people need a bit of cheering up.'

Robert remembered how excited Justine had been about her choice. She must have spent ages researching it, plotting new and innovative ways to tell the story. She'd be hoping that everyone would find the decision surprising but stimulating. Robert knew that, deep down, she placed a great deal of weight on the approval of others, despite her bravado. The success of this year's play would be more important to her than ever.

'We can't ask her to change it now, Eilidh,' he said loyally.

'I'm not saying that.' She shivered, as if her skin were itchy. 'Rehearsals have been a bit ... intense, that's all. She has very strong feelings about this particular play. She won't settle for anything less than perfection. Especially where I'm concerned. I think she could probably recite all of Medea's lines herself.'

'It's something for her to focus on,' Robert said. 'A distraction from ... well, all this.' He waved a hand in the air.

'I know. I just hope it's well received ... for Justine's sake. The dress rehearsal's coming up soon. She's invited the high school and teenagers are never the easiest audience. I know that from bitter experience.'

'You'll be great,' said Robert. 'You always are.'

'Since we're on the subject of the play,' said Eilidh, leaning under the table to rifle through her bag. 'Um, if Daniel asks, can you not mention this trip? I've told him I'm visiting music colleges.'

'He doesn't know we're together?' Robert heard his voice rise a notch.

Eilidh re-emerged from under the table and raised an eyebrow. 'No, he doesn't. I didn't think it would go down too well.'

Robert sighed. 'I suppose not.'

❄

Robert had found a private hostel room in Clapham, just a ten-minute train journey from the Rowleys' old family home. It was tiny, with two single beds separated by a narrow gap. The only saving grace was that it had an en suite bathroom.

'How much did you say you paid for this?' asked Eilidh from the doorway, eyeing the room suspiciously and wrinkling her nose.

Robert placed his suitcase on one of the beds and began unpacking before realising that there was no wardrobe. 'Too much,' he said. 'Welcome to London.'

Eilidh chuckled. 'Suppose I'd better get used to it.'

'Oh?'

She was still hovering by the door, fidgeting. 'I may have lied to Daniel about music colleges this time, but I can't stay in Findrussie forever. Not if I want to ... well, *make it*.' She giggled, but Robert could tell she was serious.

He tried to arrange his features into a supportive expression. 'Good job we're here then,' he said. 'Gives you a chance to get a feel for the place.'

Eilidh smiled, but seemed a little hurt. Sensing a need to change the subject, Robert pulled a folded sheet of A3 paper from his suitcase and smoothed it out on the bed.

'What's that?'

'Our investigation board,' he said, handing her a marker pen before sticking the sheet onto the wall with Blu-tack. 'I thought it would be useful to keep track of everything while we're here, since we can't meet at the bar.'

'Great idea,' said Eilidh enthusiastically. She popped open the pen and immediately jumped up on his bed to write. 'Okay,' she said as she scribbled. 'The time is...'

'Ten o'clock.'

'Ten p.m. ... And tomorrow we go to...'

'Wimbledon Park Road,' Robert read from his notes. 'They lived at Number Eleven. The house is still there, I believe.'

'Right. So we'll just quiz the neighbours, that sort of thing?'

Robert felt a sudden twinge of panic. This was a ridiculous idea: they had no idea if any of the Rowleys' old neighbours still even lived there. Still, it was too late to turn back now. 'I'd like to find out whether anyone remembers McCrae. You know, if they saw him visiting the house while Anthony was away with work.'

Eilidh folded her arms thoughtfully. 'It would also be good to ask about the family dynamic. Learn something about what they were really like with each other, when they weren't posing for happy-family photographs.' She suddenly jumped down from the bed and pulled a sheet of A4 from her bag. 'Talking of which ... we need to track down the mystery woman.'

Robert looked at the printout, and specifically at the young blonde woman who was kneeling just to the left of the Rowley family. 'It might be nothing, but I agree. It'd be good to know who she is. If she was a friend of the family, she might have some valuable information.'

Eilidh jumped back on the bed and started writing again, saying each word out loud. 'Ring. Invite. McCrae. Anything else?'

'Whisky,' he said. 'On the beach. I don't know if it's connected, but...'

'Worth noting,' said Eilidh, her face tight with

concentration. 'Then there are the dogs. Remember, Hammy said they were acting strangely around Felicity.'

'And Calan,' said Robert grimly. 'He seemed to have something to hide. And he was dumped by Clara just before she died.'

'There.' Eilidh stepped back to admire her handiwork. 'Still a tangle, isn't it?'

'If we can just find a way to prove that McCrae murdered Clara, then we stand a chance of linking him with the other murders, too,' said Robert. 'We already have the ring, but there must be something else that connects him to the Rowleys.'

Eilidh yawned loudly. 'We'll find it. But now, it's pyjama time. And you know what they say?'

'What's that?' asked Robert, searching for his toothbrush.

'Lucky to live another day when you're hunted by McCrae,' Eilidh sang.

'Clever,' said Robert, rolling his eyes as he walked to the bathroom.

'Well, it's not *not* true,' cried Eilidh as he closed the door.

Chapter Twenty-Two

Wimbledon Park Road reminded Robert of a film set. Nothing seemed quite real as they wandered past house after extravagant house. Strangest of all was that hardly any of the properties showed any sign of life. Shiny cars stood on the driveways like ornaments; the gardens were eerily still, well kept, yet somehow sterile.

'Why don't any of them have house numbers?' Eilidh asked, her head bent over her phone, following the blue route.

'I suppose the sort of people who live here don't want to be found,' suggested Robert.

'I'm sure the postie's delighted about that,' mumbled Eilidh.

'I don't think we need to worry,' said Robert, holding up another family portrait, this one taken in front of their London home. 'It hasn't changed much at all.'

'No,' agreed Eilidh, gazing up at the enormous villa. 'That's their place all right.'

The house loomed over them, its windows like gaping black eyes in the smooth white walls. Robert had a strange longing to hear laughter, the sound of children playing, but there was nothing save for the grunt of car exhausts from an adjacent road. For all its grandeur, he had a sense that this house was held together by sadness. Suffering permeated every brick. He placed his hands on his hips and scanned the equally magnificent properties on either side of the Rowley residence. 'Which one first?'

Eilidh took a deep breath. 'Yellow door.'

'Okay. Why?' asked Robert, intrigued.

'I like yellow.'

Unfortunately, the yellow door proved fruitless. After four attempts to work out the intercom system, a woman eventually started shouting angrily from an upstairs window.

'Rude,' Eilidh shouted back as Robert tugged her down the driveway and towards the other house.

On closer inspection, this one was less kempt than the others on the street. The paving was uneven, the window frames cracked and spongy. Thankfully, it also had a conventional doorbell, though Eilidh pressed it with apprehension. After a minute, they heard shuffling from within. Robert held his breath and realised he had given no thought to how he might introduce himself. He could hardly open with 'Hello. We're investigating a series of murders.' Anyone sensible would slam the door in his face.

An elderly man opened the door while supporting himself precariously with a walking stick. Eilidh grinned at Robert. He knew what she was thinking: good sign – he's probably lived here for years. Yet, Robert shifted uncomfortably, his mouth growing dry. He had absolutely no idea what to say.

Thankfully, Eilidh jumped in. 'Hi! Sorry to bother you. I'm Rebecca and this is my friend Paul. We're looking for Mirabella Rowley. Is this the right address?'

She had adopted a flawless English accent. Robert tried his

best not to let the surprise show on his face, though his hands were sweating. He hoped she didn't expect him to do any acting.

The old man studied Eilidh closely and sniffed the air. 'Apple cake?' he said.

'*Apple cake?*' Eilidh repeated mildly, her lips still curved in a warm smile.

'And cinnamon,' the man added, earnestly. 'No surprise. It's Thursday, after all. Next door but one always bakes apple and cinnamon cakes on a Thursday.' He winked at Robert. 'I might get a slice if I'm lucky.' Robert felt a deep pang of guilt. Lying to this gentle soul was a rotten business. He reached for Eilidh's arm, about to put a stop to it, when the man said, 'Mirabella, you say? Poor, poor things...' He shuffled on the spot, turned and disappeared into the hallway with a painful-looking limp, leaving the door wide open.

Eilidh peeked through the doorway. 'Um, Mr...'

'Stougely,' the man shouted from somewhere in the recesses of his home. 'Dr Leonard Stougely.'

'Nothing wrong with his hearing at least,' said Robert, beneath his breath.

'Nothing at all, young man,' Dr Stougely responded. 'Please, come in, will you? I'm catching the draught.'

Eilidh glanced at Robert and stepped through the doorway. Robert followed, closing the door behind them. The decor was eclectic, at best: pictures of birds covered every inch of the long hallway's walls; ornate but threadbare furniture occupied every nook and cranny; the loud tick of a dusty grandfather clock echoed from the creaky wooden floorboards.

'Tea?' Dr Stougely re-emerged from the rear of the house, a delicate china tea set balanced unsteadily on a tray in his free hand. 'We should go into the sitting room.'

Eilidh rushed forwards to rescue the tray while Robert pushed open some double doors that led into a dilapidated, though very grand, room. Two enormous sofas were facing each other before a blackened, stone fireplace. Dr Stougely took a seat with a soft grunt and pointed towards the hearth. 'I wish I could light it for you, but we're in a smoke-free zone. I've been warned one too many times.'

Eilidh began to pour the tea. 'So, Dr Stougely, you're still in touch with Mirabella, I presume?'

Robert was impressed. It was a clever approach. She was trying to determine just how well Leonard knew Mirabella by pretending that they hadn't heard about her death. He assumed that any of her close contacts would have been notified.

'I'm sorry to be the bearer of bad news,' Leonard said soberly, 'but Mirabella passed away a few weeks ago.' He tapped his teacup to indicate that he would like more tea. Then, raising his impressively bushy eyebrows, he added, 'But both of you knew that already, didn't you?'

'What?' Robert jumped, spilling tea over his trousers.

Leonard chuckled warmly. 'Please, don't be alarmed. It's just that I recognised you, Mr Begg. I may be old but I'm still good with faces. Most doctors are.' He fumbled in his back pocket, produced a phone and started swiping rapidly. A few seconds later, he held it up to them: the screen showed a photo of Robert and his father standing proudly in front of the Pine Needle. It was the image they used on the website. 'Mirabella sent it to me when she left for Findrussie. She was very excited about meeting you, Robert.'

Robert saw Eilidh had turned a deep shade of pink. He placed his teacup and saucer on the table. 'I'm so sorry, Dr Stougely. I think we should go.'

'*Go?*' Leonard seemed shocked. 'Why would you want to go

now? You've travelled all this way, after all. I expect you have some questions for me.' He smiled at Eilidh. 'I appreciate your efforts with respect to the accent, my dear, but I'd ask you to speak with your own voice. I'd find that much more endearing.'

Robert shot Eilidh a helpless glance. She was biting her lip. 'All right,' she said carefully, no trace of her English accent remaining. 'So ... what do you know?'

Leonard sat back in his chair as his eyes suddenly filled with moisture. 'I know I lived next door to the most enduring sadness any human could contemplate. Whoever killed poor Clara brought a curse upon that family until only Mirabella was left standing. She never gave up hope of finding her daughter's killer. She never once thought it was Toby. It was her life's work to attain justice for her family.'

'That's why we're here,' said Robert. 'We don't think Toby Rowley did it, either. In fact, we think we know who did.' He leaned forwards, his heart thumping. 'Did you ever see Mirabella with another man, Dr Stougely? Did she have any visitors ... from Findrussie ... before Clara's murder?'

Leonard sighed, as if slightly bored. 'You mean Brian McCrae?'

Robert spluttered, 'Yes! How do you—'

'I've thought the same thing myself,' Leonard interrupted. 'Let me guess: she kept their affair a secret from you?'

'Yes,' said Eilidh. 'We only found out about it after she died.'

Leonard tutted. 'I told her not to keep anything secret, but that was Mirabella. She was a woman of principle and intense pride until the very end. Even though she was investigating her daughter's murder and the framing of her son for it – the two tragedies that led to her husband's suicide – she never confessed to that affair. I'm sure it was ancient history, as far as she was concerned.'

'But you saw Brian McCrae here in London?' Robert persisted.

'No, I did not,' said Leonard firmly. 'And you should be aware that Mirabella thought he was incompetent, nothing more. She was angry he refused to investigate the case further, but she never accused him of killing Clara.'

'And what do you think?' Eilidh asked, placing a calming hand on Robert's shoulder. He took a deep breath, forcing himself to pull through the anger that flared every time McCrae's name was mentioned.

Leonard took a shaky sip of tea and eyed both of them carefully, as if considering how much to share. Then, looking at the ceiling, he said, 'I suppose it's all water under the bridge now. I think Toby was an easy – and reasonable – target.' He bowed his head. 'I was the Rowleys' neighbour from the moment they moved here. I knew Toby as a little boy. He was the sweetest thing. But then he began to unravel, go off the rails, not long after he went to secondary school. Laura really had her work cut out with him. I often heard them on the drive—'

'Mirabella, not Laura,' corrected Eilidh, gently. 'Don't worry – I'm always mixing up names, too.'

'Ah...' Leonard looked to the ceiling again. 'It seems that Mirabella left out something else. I told you she was a proud woman. Laura was the Rowleys' au pair. She was trying to make it in show business, I believe. Laura Stanley.' His eyes misted over slightly as he stared into the middle distance. 'She was beautiful, young, fun ... more than a match for Mirabella. For any woman, really.'

Eilidh let out a sad laugh. 'Another of Anthony's conquests?'

'I'm afraid so,' Leonard replied. 'Mirabella turned a blind eye to his affairs, for the most part. People held her in high esteem for how she handled it. She almost never wavered, never commented, always behaved as if nothing were happening. Laura was the exception. Probably because she was exceptional.'

Eilidh rummaged around in her coat pocket and pulled out the portrait of the family standing in front of Kinlogie House. She pointed at the young blonde woman. 'Is this her?'

Leonard smiled. 'Yes, that's her. I always thought she had the patience of a saint, the way she dealt with those children. We chatted often ... although Mirabella never knew that. She asked if I'd be her doctor. I was in private practice back then, and obviously there was no way she could afford my fees on an au pair's salary. But as I say, I knew how much she did for those children, so I saw her for free.'

Eilidh tilted her head slightly and Robert realised they were both thinking the same thing – it didn't sound like the most innocent of arrangements – but he figured it was none of their business and tried to steer the conversation back to the Rowleys. 'And you're sure she was having an affair with Anthony?'

Leonard's eyes sharpened and Robert could have sworn he saw the trace of a wince. 'Certain. It lasted longer than the others, and Mirabella could hardly ignore it when it was happening under her own roof. They argued a lot around that time. I could hear them in the garden. I suppose they could raise their voices there without the children hearing.'

'I'd be raging too,' said Eilidh.

'It was the one affair that really affected Mirabella,' continued Leonard, 'but you have to understand her marriage to Anthony was never a love match. I'm not saying it was entirely love*less*, but it was a combination of convenience, mutual respect and financial security that kept them together. Plus the children, of course. That was why Mirabella never put her foot down and sacked Laura: she could work miracles with Toby. Even before bigger demons reared their ugly heads, he had tantrums, panic attacks. They left him petrified, rooted to the spot. Laura was the only one who knew how to calm him down. I think she used a counting exercise, a soothing technique she'd learned at drama school.'

'Where is she now?' asked Robert. 'Maybe she saw McCrae somewhere? Maybe she heard Mirabella talking to him on the phone.'

Leonard shook his head. 'No. She disappeared long before Clara was murdered. Seven or eight years before, I'd say.'

'*Disappeared?*' asked Eilidh.

Leonard held himself very still and closed his eyes for a moment. 'People like to talk,' he said. 'And the people around here are no exception. Laura was young and vibrant, full of hopes and dreams, but I think she eventually realised they would never materialise. She started to cling ever tighter to Anthony, probably convinced herself that she would replace Mirabella one day. That was never going to happen. He was a philanderer but loyal to his wife, in his own way. Some say...' His voiced trailed away.

'What?' Eilidh prompted, sitting forwards.

Leonard gripped the arms of his chair and craned his neck, as if he were listening to something neither Eilidh nor Robert could hear. 'She became a nuisance. There were rumours that she went crazy. Some say she lost her mind in a fit of passion, obsession, love, whatever you want to call it, and just took off one night, never to be seen again. Others say that Anthony *resolved* the problem himself.'

Robert frowned, thinking he must have misunderstood. 'Are you suggesting that Anthony killed Laura?'

'People like to speculate,' said Leonard, stifling a yawn. 'Rumours. Smoke and mirrors, fog and dust. It's difficult to know what to believe these days.'

Eilidh shot Robert a look, which he understood to mean that

they had outstayed their welcome. As he stood, he caught Leonard's eye. 'If you don't think McCrae killed Clara, who did? And do you believe that Mirabella really took her own life?'

Leonard spoke through half-opened lips, his head tilting backwards and his eyes closing as he drifted off to sleep. 'Patience, Robert Begg. The truth will out eventually.'

Chapter Twenty-Three

Back in the hostel, Robert and Eilidh lay sprawled on their beds, scribbling notes, staring at the ceiling, occasionally jumping up to add something to the sheet of A3 on the wall.

'No trace of her whatsoever after 1985,' said Robert, his voice tired and frustrated. He tossed his laptop at the pillow. 'All I can find is a biography for a show she did at something called the Guildhall.'

'It's a drama school,' said Eilidh. 'Quite a prestigious one, actually. She must have been good.'

Robert retrieved the laptop and beckoned her towards the screen. 'Here, look. It says she played Linda Loman in their big summer production of *Death of a Salesman* as well as various roles with the school's touring company the previous year.'

'She's absolutely gorgeous,' said Eilidh, studying the headshot closely. 'Maybe she changed her name. Actors do that all the time.'

'Maybe...' said Robert, plumping the thin pillow as best he could. 'Is this a waste of time? We don't even know if she'd be any help.'

'Worth keeping in mind, though,' said Eilidh. She rolled

onto her side and grinned up at him. 'But now I'm going to crack open the wine. Want some?'

Robert checked his watch. It was already 9 p.m. He had envisioned them exploring the sights of London together, but they had returned to the hostel straight after the meeting with Dr Stougely and hadn't left the room since. Eilidh had dropped a few hints about a change of scene to clear their heads, but he had ignored her. Now, as he looked at the meagre results of five hours' searching, he realised what an idiot he'd been.

Eilidh unscrewed the bottle and fished two plastic cups from her rucksack. 'Cheers!' she said, handing him a brimming cup. Then she sighed heavily, crossed her legs and stretched her back until she was sitting upright. 'No more we can do tonight,' she said. 'We have another potential lead. That's something.'

'We're no closer to finding anything solid on McCrae, though.' Robert winced at how whiny his voice sounded. He gulped down a large mouthful of wine. 'What are we going to tell Hammy and Justine?'

Eilidh stared at him and took a deep breath, as if she were trying to decide whether to tell him something or not. He slumped back into his pillow, hoping that whatever it was would not make him feel any worse.

'Do you think...' she began tentatively, then took a sip of wine. 'Do you think ... maybe ... the reason why we can't find anything on McCrae is because ... well, because he didn't do it? And by that I mean *any* of it.'

'But the ring,' pleaded Robert, scarcely able to believe what he was hearing. 'And he's been at every scene of death.'

'He's a detective,' said Eilidh, firmly. 'And there's a big difference between having a secret affair with someone and killing them.'

'How do you explain Mirabella's death, then? Suicide? Really? And what about Felicity? Was that just a coincidence?'

He didn't want to argue, but he felt his temper rising. If they weren't looking for evidence against McCrae, what were they doing? He turned away from her and looked at the sheet on the wall. Everything still pointed to McCrae. Every path still led to him. He felt a hand on his shoulder and flinched.

'I'm not saying it was a coincidence,' Eilidh said, her voice soothing. 'Of course, someone has something to hide. I'm just saying that we could consider other options.'

Robert pulled away and jabbed a finger repeatedly at his father's name. Then he rounded on Eilidh, raising his voice. 'He killed my dad! Or have you forgotten that?' Eilidh recoiled and Robert forced himself to take a long, shaky breath. She seemed hurt, or maybe even fearful. He rocked back onto the bed and closed his eyes. 'Eilidh, I'm sorry. I didn't mean to shout.'

The silence was too long and too deep. Finally, he opened his eyes to find Eilidh perched on the end of his bed.

'I didn't mean...' he began. 'It's just so complicated. And scary.'

She nodded, although her eyes were still wide. Eventually, she moved closer and placed a hesitant hand on his knee. 'I know,' she said. 'But Robbie, remember that we only *think* he killed Bennie. We don't know for sure. It could have been an accident. You've come up with a strong theory, I'm not denying that, and I'm certainly not saying we should write off McCrae just yet, but nothing's definite. I just want you ... *us* to tread carefully, that's all.'

Robert was dismayed. Although he knew deep down that Eilidh was on his side, her words felt like a sharp, slithering betrayal. His lower lip began to tremble and the words began to spill from his mouth – words he must have thought in some dark moment between sleep and consciousness but had never expressed before. 'You'll think I'm mad, Eilidh, but there was a part of me that was glad about McCrae and my dad. I remember on the day' – he shuddered but pressed on – 'the day he died, I couldn't bring myself to believe it was an accident. How could he have died like that? It seemed so senseless. So meaningless. I wanted to find a reason for it. There had to be some meaning, something to cling on to. Does that make any sense? I suppose I'm saying that I needed something – some*one* – to blame.' He clasped his hands tightly around his knees and drew them to his chest. 'So I was happy when McCrae came along. He gave me ... direction.'

He waited for Eilidh to tell him he was talking nonsense. She had every right to be angry with him. After all, the whole investigation had been his idea. He should have been a strong leader, rational, clear-minded. That latest outburst proved he was anything but.

'I don't think you're mad,' she said. Her hand was still resting on his knee. He liked the way it felt – protective and warm. 'You're just searching for a reason. It's what humans do. We want a narrative, not chaos. At least if there's a story, we feel like we have some semblance of control. It's like your thing with the animals.'

Robert wiped his eyes and glanced down at her. She wasn't mocking him. Her face was kind ... and beautiful. 'My lists?'

'Yes,' she said. 'They work because they place you in control of something. It makes sense to me. Funnily enough, that's what Justine's play is about, too. And do you remember Dr Stougely mentioned that Toby used to do a similar thing? We all do whatever we can to make the pieces fit. I suppose it's like tidying up the world to try to make it less scary.'

Robert laughed sardonically. 'It's not exactly working out for me at the moment.'

Eilidh shot him a look but then wriggled between his hip and the wall. Her body was soft and warm against his side. She gazed up at the large sheet of paper. 'It's fine to want to take control of this. It's good. But it's important to make sure we don't get tunnel vision. Your history with McCrae ... well, you're—'

'Biased,' he admitted. 'I hope you're not saying that I have to like him.'

'God, no!' said Eilidh, reaching over for her wine. 'I'm not saying that at all. I can't stand the man, either.' She gestured violently and the wine sloshed over his stomach. 'Whoops,' she said, grabbing a tissue and starting to dab at his shirt.

'It's fine...' he insisted.

'It'll come out. Trust me, I'm good at this sort of thing.'

Her face was inches from his, the wine sweet on her breath, tiny flecks of mascara just beneath her lower eyelashes. Without thinking, he raised a hand and touched her cheek. She didn't pull away. They held each other's eyes for a few seconds. His heart was pounding within his chest, his fingertips tingling.

Later, he would try to attribute it to the effects of the wine, or perhaps the heated words they had exchanged earlier in the evening. In the moment, though, he made no attempt to rationalise it. Her lips were uncertain at first. He focused on his breathing, afraid that he would do something wrong. But then she pressed her forehead against his, so her eyes were impossibly close. Her arms wrapped around his neck and their bodies pressed together. She fumbled beneath his shirt and he wriggled out of it as she buried her head into his chest. Then they kissed again, more forcefully this time, urgently.

He was vaguely aware of his phone vibrating on the bedside table. He tried to ignore it but it was insistent.

Eventually, it was Eilidh who said, 'Answer it. It could be important.'

She eased herself away reluctantly and Robert reached for the phone. He had missed five calls and even more messages. 'It's Justine,' he said, his chest beginning to tighten.

'Oh no,' whispered Eilidh. She moved behind him to look over his shoulder. He opened an attachment and a photo of the Pine Needle appeared on the screen. The front of the building had been smeared in great slashes of red paint, dripping around the timber in garish swirls. It looked like the bar was bleeding.

'Zoom in,' said Eilidh. 'It says something.'

Robert, his fingers shaking, enlarged the image. Crude but bold letters stretched from the roof to the decking. They spelled out: ROBERT BEGG AND FRIENDS. STOP. OR DIE.

The phone vibrated again in his hand. He swiped the answer button and said, 'Justine, I've just seen—'

'Oh, Robbie, it's such a mess. An absolute mess. Hammy's helping, but—' Her voice was high and frenzied.

'Hammy's okay, then?' Robert relaxed ever so slightly.

'Well, as okay as any of us can be,' Justine wailed from the phone. 'It's happening. We're being watched, Robbie.'

'*Watched?*' Robert turned to Eilidh, who was already packing up their things.

'I was only gone an hour. I locked up to fetch some groceries. When I got back I saw the paint. Someone is watching us ... closely. They knew I'd left the bar, Robbie...'

He heard Hammy consoling her in the background. He massaged the bridge of his nose, struggling to think. 'Did you see anyone, Justine? Anyone at all?'

'I would have mentioned if I had, wouldn't I?' she shrieked uncontrollably.

Robert pulled his ear away from the speaker. 'Okay, we'll try to get a train right now,' he said.

It sounded like Hammy was struggling to grab Justine's phone from her, then he came on the line. 'All right, Robbie?' Even he seemed uncharacteristically flustered. 'Look, Justine's really upset ... and I can understand why. I think she'd appreciate it if you could make it back up here—'

'He'd better be leaving now!' Justine cried in the background.

'We're on our way,' said Robert, hanging up.

Eilidh looked up from her own phone. 'There's a sleeper to Inverness at ten to midnight. We'll make it if we hurry.'

Robert's mind felt as if it were splitting into two. He could barely comprehend what had happened only minutes earlier. The atmosphere had changed so dramatically that he felt faint. He grabbed his bag and began to stuff his clothes into it. Suddenly realising, with some embarrassment, that he was still topless, he turned his back to Eilidh and pulled on his damp shirt, which still smelled faintly of wine. Meanwhile, she was peeling the sheet of A3 from the wall and folding it neatly before placing it in her rucksack. Neither of them tried to make eye contact, which Robert took to be a bad sign.

❄

The journey home didn't provide much in the way of conversation. Eilidh snoozed opposite Robert with her head resting on her rucksack. His eyes accidentally fell upon her face a couple of times, and he was transported back to the hostel room. He could still feel the touch of her hands on either side of his face, her breath against his lips. He shook his head and just about managed to suppress an embarrassed groan. He had always prided himself on being a decent person. He may never have been the funniest, the brightest, the coolest, but he had always thought his heart was in the right place. Justine had instilled that in him. So, how could he have let this happen? Clearly, Eilidh had confused a desire to comfort him with a more primal sort of desire. He should have spotted it at the time. And now they were hurtling through the night, back towards Findrussie, with an unsavoury secret that would only cause upset to others. Just like McCrae and his mother all those years ago. The thought made him shiver.

Unable to sleep, he reached for his book and sank low in his seat. The overhead light cast a flickering beam over the pages, which made the words dance and skip. He was nearing the end: the Spanish mountaineer had been rescued from the summit and was now exploring less perilous corners of the local area, keeping to the low routes, taking in the manses and the stately homes. Robert was surprised to read that he had visited the 'tiny, beguiling ward of Findrussie'. He sat bolt upright, excited to learn what the author had made of his home. The adventurers in these books often wrote of the mountains that surrounded his village, but rarely of Findrussie itself.

Nestled in the foothills of three – perhaps four – mountains, and with a loch set unobtrusively as its centrepiece, though majestic and alluring as it stretches below the mountains, Findrussie struck me as a curious place. I stayed for two days in one of the area's most easily accessible bothies, in the grounds of a great house named Kinlogie. Here I had one of those meetings that is impossible to understand and equally impossible to forget. This happens when travelling, I find. The characters you meet stick to you, though it is only a veneer. Thereafter, your memory scratches at it; you ruminate upon their words, question their motives, their meanings. This was one such character. It was an unlikely exchange.

It was late – or rather very early – when I started to make my way back to the bothy, after some beers at the local pub...

The bothy must have been the Ryvune; the pub, the Pine Needle.

Robert hesitated for a moment before turning the page, then

let out an enormous yawn. He closed the book, finally feeling the indomitable pull of sleep. He must have given into it, as he dreamed the loch was filled with red paint. As he swam further into it, the liquid became thicker, more viscous, until he was unable to move his limbs at all. He struggled for breath and felt the acrid, oily fluid pour into his mouth, fill the crevices of his throat, seep into the walls of his lungs. He tried to flail his arms, but it was useless. He was drawn down, deep into the chemical depths.

'Robbie!' Eilidh was standing above him, shaking his shoulder.

He squinted at her, his mouth hanging open. 'You're snoring like a trumpet,' she said, her lips forming into a smile.

'Oh!' he said, hastily, wiping the dribble from his chin.

'Sexy,' she murmured.

Robert hunched over, thinking that it was far, far too soon to be making jokes about their grave misdemeanour. Eilidh snuggled back into her chair, covered herself with her coat and closed her eyes.

Chapter Twenty-Four

Hammy was scrubbing at the front of the bar methodically, his breath billowing in great swirls around his face with the exertion.

'Sorry, Hammy, could you just run me through it one more time?' Robert asked.

He had allowed himself barely five minutes at home to drop his off bag before racing to the Pine Needle to help with the clean-up. Justine had greeted him in better spirits than Robert had expected. She was also wearing far more make-up than usual. The dress rehearsal was that night, and she was currently rehearsing with a patient, though rather exasperated, Eilidh inside the bar.

'I told you. This is not how Hammy Galbreath operates. I'm not the sort to sit back and wait for the Grim Reaper to start banging on my door.'

'No, I got that. You said you went to find Calan?' Robert sat down on the bench and reached for one of the dogs for comfort. He could really do without members of the team – what had Eilidh called them, the Pine Needles? – going off-piste, especially as everything seemed to be hanging in a precarious balance.

'Aye. I thought I'd squeeze the truth out of him, one way or another. Ask him straight out if he's working for McCrae, you know.'

'All right, so ... what did he say?' Robert suspected that Calan was hardly likely to confess to anything.

Hammy stopped scrubbing and wiped his brow, eyeing Robert seriously. 'Well, that's the thing. I went to the Ionic. You remember the barmaid there?'

'I suppose,' said Robert, preferring not to be reminded of his one and only evening in the bar.

'That's Fiona,' said Hammy. 'Known her for a while. Done a bit of carpentry for her now and again. Nice lassie.'

'Okay...'

'Well, she told me that Calan hasn't been in for weeks. Interestingly, she remembered the last day she saw him. Said there was a particularly rowdy crowd in, plus what she described as an unusual fella.' Hammy did a little dance with his hands.

'There was a rowdy group when we were there,' said Robert. 'Wait ... was I the unusual fella?'

'No need to focus on that.' Hammy smiled and cleared his throat. 'Anyway, Fiona said that there was no sign of him after that. No word, no news. He's usually in there every day, Robbie.'

'Yes, that was obvious when I met him,' said Robert, staring at the soapy water trickling onto the decking. 'Does she have any clue where he's gone?'

'None.' Hammy turned and got back to scrubbing. 'That's why I did some digging.'

Robert tried to maintain a calm expression but couldn't quash a sense of rising panic. '*Digging?*'

'Aye, digging. That's what we're doing here, isn't it?' He nodded at the fading red words. 'If we're being threatened for doing something, I figure we might as well do it properly.'

'I suppose,' said Robert weakly as Hammy threw him a sponge. He took the hint and began to scrub away his own name. 'So, what did you dig up?'

'Well, you know the back of the Mountain Brewery, opposite the Ionic, give or take, in the business park?'

The brewery was a roaring success. 'Liam and Sammy's place?' They had been a few years ahead of Robert in high school. Now he served their beer in the Pine Needle.

'Exactly. Well, remember a few winters back, when the roads were blocked with snow?'

'Yes, the drifts were massive. We had no end of supply issues.'

'That's right. Liam was in a huge panic because they couldn't deliver any orders to the Pine Needle or the two hotels on this side of town, so—'

'You stepped in and transported the kegs by sledge.' Robert laughed at the memory.

'It was great fun.' Hammy chuckled, his eyes crinkling. 'Now, as you know, Robbie, I'm not one to cash in a favour. You get out of this life what you put in. I live by that, always have.'

'I know,' said Robert. 'I'm sure they were grateful, though.'

'You bet they were,' said Hammy, prodding the sponge towards Robert's chest. 'So, last night, I asked Liam if I could have a look at his security footage from the brewery. Told him I'd mislaid my wallet and wanted to see if someone had picked my pocket outside the Ionic. There's a camera on the back fence. I thought it might show the entrance.'

Robert stopped scrubbing and turned to Hammy, suddenly more interested in what he had to say. 'And does it?'

'It does. He even sent me the videos.' Hammy made a great

show of retrieving his phone from his back pocket. He had clearly been building up to this.

Robert could scarcely contain his excitement as they waited for the video to load. After what seemed like an age, the file finally opened and Hammy passed him the phone.

'It's two a.m. The day after you met Calan,' said Hammy. 'Keep watching.'

Robert squinted at the screen as Calan arrived at the Ionic and disappeared inside.

'You can fast-forward this bit,' advised Hammy. 'Go ahead about half an hour.'

Robert scrolled through the video until Calan re-emerged from the bar, looking decidedly wobbly. He lit a cigarette, then a dark figure in a hooded coat approached him from the side alley. They moved like a blackbird, with a feathery motion, twitchy and alert.

'Who's that?' asked Robert.

'No idea. Watch carefully, though.'

It seemed as if Calan knew the hooded figure, judging by the way he waved as they approached, and they exchanged a few words.

'I can't make out the face.' Robert paused the video and zoomed in. 'But I'd swear this is the same person I saw on the beach that morning. Same coat. They're not very tall, whoever they are,' he added, feeling his heart sink slightly. Brian McCrae would have towered over Calan.

Robert started the video again and before long the pair on the screen were in a heated discussion. The hooded figure seemed to be trying to lead Calan away, but he was resisting.

'Here we go,' said Hammy softly.

At first glance, it looked as if Calan simply stumbled and fell drunkenly into the hooded figure. 'Wait! What just happened?' Robert shouted, sliding the cursor back and adjusting the playback to slow motion. This time, just prior to the stumble, he saw the hooded figure jabbing something into Calan's arm. It was a deft movement, only noticeable if you were looking for something suspicious. Then, with what seemed to be considerable difficulty, the hooded figure dragged Calan away from the bar and out of shot.

'Was he *injected* with something?' asked Robert in astonishment.

'Looks like it to me,' Hammy replied. 'I was all for taking this to the police ... but it's hard to know who to trust these days, isn't it? It's obviously not McCrae, though.'

'Doesn't mean he doesn't have something to do with it,' snapped Robert, rather more petulantly than he would have liked.

'Aye, true,' conceded Hammy. 'But the laddie's been missing for two weeks now. My feeling is we need to do the right thing.'

Robert clenched his fists, hoping that the tension would kickstart his brain. 'We don't *know* he's in danger.'

Hammy shot Robert a look that told him to reconsider. Robert sighed. Deep down, he knew Hammy was right.

'I suppose we could let Liam know. Maybe direct his attention to this particular tape. Make it sound like you thought you saw a security breach that might concern the brewery and suggest he should call the police.'

'Not a bad idea,' said Hammy, more cheerfully. He returned to scrubbing the red, frothy mess on the wall. 'Of course, given what we've just seen, I think we can say it's likely Calan wasn't responsible for *this*.'

Robert hung his head. He didn't know what to think any more.

Hammy gripped his shoulder and shook him gently. 'It's all right, Robbie. We'll sort it out soon enough. We'll be okay as long as we stick together.'

'Can you email me that video?' asked Robbie. The mystery figure's bird-like movements were still fluttering uncomfortably in his mind's eye.

Hammy whistled pleasantly enough as he continued to scrub, but Robert sensed a sudden undercurrent of awkwardness between them. Then he realised what he'd done ... or rather failed to do.

'Errr ... good work, Hammy,' he muttered, guiltily.

Hammy saluted Robert with the sponge still in his hand. 'You're welcome,' he said, beaming.

❄

For Robert, the dress rehearsal was a welcome break from his whirring thoughts. He stood in the wings, relieved that his part required no more than his usual jeans and a jumper. In fact, in line with Justine's modern adaptation, most of the company were wearing their normal clothes. Eilidh was sitting cross-legged on the floor, frantically flicking through the script. Daniel was nowhere to be seen. Robert had heard them sharing a heated exchange in the car park a couple of hours earlier. He'd tried not to eavesdrop as he felt it was their business. That said, if Daniel had found out about the ... *incident* in London, maybe it was Robert's business, too.

'Ugh! This feedback...' Eilidh cried, turning the script from side to side. 'I'm so nervous, I can barely read it.'

'Let's have a look,' said Robert, although he doubted any last-minute guidance would be of much use now.

Eilidh shook the script in the air, hissing, 'More peeling? What does that even mean? *Peeling?*'

Robert knelt beside her and squinted at the handwritten note. 'Could it say *feeling?*' he suggested, easing the script from her hand. It was clear Eilidh was suffering some sort of pre-show jitters. The hall had already started to fill with the excited chatter of teenagers.

'Oh God, I can't remember anything!' wailed Eilidh, miserably, her hands on either side of her head. 'This was a mistake. There's so much going on. I should have pulled out.'

Robert wanted to say he was confident she would do a stellar job, which was true, and he would be cheering her on from the wings (also true), and it wasn't as if this were a life-or-death situation (unfortunately, not necessarily true). However, as was usually the case when he was faced with an emotionally charged situation, words evaded him.

He started to whisper, 'Viper, vulture, vicuña...'

Eilidh looked up and smiled gently. 'Vampire bat?'

'Vole,' Robert added.

She giggled and stretched her arms to the ceiling. 'Thanks, Robbie,' she said.

'You'll break your leg,' Robert offered.

Eilidh laughed and pushed herself from the floor. 'It's "break *a* leg",' she corrected, peeping through the curtains. 'Things are filling up out there. Oh!'

'What is it?' Robert jumped up, immediately by her side.

'Brian's here. See – there, right in the middle.'

Sure enough, McCrae was incongruously surrounded by a crowd of restless schoolchildren, sitting with his arms firmly folded, as if afraid of catching some horrible disease. He seemed to be scanning the hall at regular intervals.

'What's he doing?' asked Robert.

'No idea.' Eilidh began to limber up on the spot, jumping from side to side and rotating her arms in a circular motion. 'But at least this means you can keep an eye on him.'

'I'm pretty confident he's not just come to take in the show.'

Eilidh sighed and bent down to touch her toes. 'No point panicking about it, though. There's not much he can do from the middle of the audience. Anyway, Hammy said the person in the video was far too short—' She stopped suddenly and glanced up to see the look of resignation on Robert's face. 'I know, I know, that doesn't mean he's not behind it...' she mumbled.

Robert would have protested, but the lights suddenly dimmed.

Eilidh placed her hands on his shoulders. 'We'll sort this.'

'See you later...' He turned to leave and jumped as Daniel stepped out of the darkness. How long had he been there?

'Robert.' Daniel was staring at the stage, avoiding eye contact.

Robert cleared his throat and inadvertently mimicked the stilted tone: 'Daniel...' Eilidh was deep in concentration now, practising her first few lines, apparently oblivious to the rising tension between the two men.

The hall fell into a hushed silence as the opening music began to play. Robert stood to one side to allow Daniel to take his place in the wings. Then, not wanting to cause any more of a scene, he crept down the wooden stairs to the side of the stage and made for the kitchen, which the actors were using as a makeshift dressing-room.

'Robert – your face,' said Ruth McLuckie, seizing him as soon as he walked through the door. She plonked him onto a stool and hurriedly dabbed his face with a sponge. 'You should have come to see me long before now.'

Justine had insisted that every cast member must wear face powder to combat what she called 'shiny forehead syndrome'. Robert fought the urge to scratch his cheeks and remove floury, dry substance.

'There...' said Ruth lovingly. She took a step back to admire her handiwork. 'Not bad at all, if I do say so myself.'

'Thanks,' said Robert, unsure whether he was supposed to keep his face still while the make-up dried. He settled upon pursing his lips into something that resembled a smile but did not crinkle the corners of his mouth.

Ruth folded her arms and looked at him with an expression that Robert had recently noticed among people who were about to launch into a heartfelt enquiry into his well-being. He was wondering how he could politely excuse himself when Ruth announced, 'You're an easier customer than most of the men. A couple took some real convincing. But they need to understand that this is the *theatre*. Justine likes to do things properly.'

Relieved that she wasn't about to ask any deep and searching questions, Robert relaxed a little. 'Everyone looks great, Ruth.'

'Oh, I take it all back, you know. What I said about this play being too serious. Justine's even talking about going to Edinburgh.'

'Really?' Robert was surprised she hadn't discussed such an ambitious plan with him. He made a mental note to pay her more attention. He knew he must have seemed quite distant over the last few weeks.

'Exciting, isn't it? Although, between you and me' – Ruth leaned in conspiratorially – 'I'm not too sure about Daniel Bell. I know it's unfair to compare anyone to Eilidh – she's a star, that's obvious – but his mind really hasn't been on the show at all. Justine's been fretting about him remembering his lines – it's all she can talk about. And, you know, I spent half an hour trying to scrub some red dye off his hands today. He told me it was food colouring. I thought, "Why would you be baking today of all days?" Anyway, I couldn't let him go on stage looking like he had blood on his hands. That'd be confusing for the audience. They notice every detail, you know?'

Robert stared at her. The powder already felt thicker, pastier. He gripped the side of the stool and swayed a little, suddenly dizzy.

'Robbie? Are you all right? Can I get you some water? You look a bit—'

'I'm fine,' he managed. He let out a breath and rose a bit too quickly.

Ruth skipped back in surprise. 'Edinburgh's only an idea,' she began. 'Nothing's confirmed.'

Robert frowned at her, trying to get his thoughts in order. 'It's not that,' he said hesitantly, forcing the words from his mouth. 'I just forgot to have lunch. I've got some food in my bag. Thanks, Ruth.'

'You can't eat in costume,' Ruth shouted after him as he made his way out of the kitchen and towards the main hall.

Red stains on Daniel's hands. Red paint on the bar. Daniel had every reason to dislike Robert. On Burns Night, he had disappeared shortly before Felicity was killed. And he was short enough to be the hooded figure in the video. Robert pushed open the doors to the main hall and quickly stepped into the darkened room. A few faces turned to stare at him.

Eilidh was onstage, lamenting the fact that her husband, Jason, was leaving her. Robert pressed himself into the back wall and watched for a moment. He had always known she was a talented performer, but the role of Medea – a woman fuelled by jealousy, passion and burning anger – gave her an opportunity to show what she was really made of. There was no other word for it: she was sensational. She delivered the monologue – which could easily have seemed long and drawn out – as if in intimate conversation with the audience. There was no hint of overacting. She spoke with quiet strength, her eyes conveying Medea's innermost thoughts and emotions.

He scanned the audience of students. They were surprisingly enraptured, give or take a few malcontents in the last few rows. Hammy, who was sitting right at the back, periodically kicked the chair of the boy in front every time he leaned over to chat to his friend. Unbelievably, he'd brought the dogs with him. In the darkness, they looked like an enormous, deep-pile rug at his feet. Robert shimmied along the row of seats, trying his best not to cause a scene.

'Hammy!' he hissed.

Again, a few faces turned his way, including Hammy's, whose lips were already pursed to say 'shhh'. When he saw it was Robert, he waved him to the neighbouring seat. 'Shouldn't you be backstage?' he whispered. 'Aren't you breaking the brick wall?'

Robert frowned. 'Do you mean the *fourth* wall?'

'Maybe. Been trying to show a bit of interest in the theatre, for Justine's sake. There's a lot of interesting terminology, it turns out. What's going on?'

'Can we talk outside?' Robert was acutely aware that the teachers were shooting them exasperated looks.

'But Eilidh's—'

'It's important, Hammy,' said Robert, hoping that the gravity of his discovery was coming across in his voice. 'Please!'

'All right,' said Hammy. He patted the dogs on the head and tapped the arm of the boy in front. 'Look after them, will you?' The boy opened his mouth to protest, but Hammy placed a firm hand on his shoulder. 'Be back shortly,' he whispered, before sneaking out of the back door with Robert.

Robert took Hammy's arm and led him to the car park. They had no time to waste. Daniel would be onstage for most of the next ninety minutes, but then he would be free to do whatever he wanted. Judging by the message he had scrawled on the Pine Needle, that was not an appealing prospect.

'It's Daniel Bell!' Robert felt the words explode from him. He realised his hands were shaking and shoved them in his pockets. 'He wrote the message on the bar. He's the hooded figure. He's the one who's been killing people.'

'How do you know that?' asked Hammy, placing two strong hands on Robert's shoulders.

Robert closed his eyes and tried to compose himself. Hammy was right. It was no good shouting allegations into thin air. And, now he came to think about it properly, having red stained hands certainly didn't prove Daniel had murdered anyone. He blew through his lips, suddenly embarrassed. 'I don't know anything Hammy, never mind. All these new leads and occurrences ... I'm losing it. One minute I'm certain it's McCrae, the next ... Daniel!' He laughed at how ludicrous he sounded. 'I'd just love to know for *sure* ... Who's behind all this?'

'I have the same question.' The voice came from the alley around the back of the hall, followed by a waft of cigarette smoke. Brian McCrae emerged from the shadows. He looked far more fatigued than usual; the circles beneath his eyes were a deep purple. 'Maybe you'd like to share your theories?'

'You're crazy if you think I'm telling you anything,' said Robert as he started to lead Hammy away.

Hammy put up minimal resistance before sighing and following Robert towards the Pine Needle. 'Maybe a talk isn;t a terrible idea,' he began.

'No way,' Robert hissed, looking over his shoulder to check where McCrae was.

Just before they crossed the road, McCrae called, 'Your father was a stubborn bastard too, Robert.' Then Robert heard him whisper under his breath, 'Didn't do him any good, either.'

Robert had heard of people snapping with anger, although he had never experienced it himself. Now, though, it was almost as if he heard the sound – like the twang of an elastic band or the cork popping out of a bottle of champagne. The sensation was very pure and physical between his ears. And the decision to charge at McCrae was an easy one to make. It was like he was ten years old again. His legs propelled him with the wild, untamed motion of a child running without thought or care. He leapt into the air, tackled McCrae onto the car park pavement and held the lapels of his coat in his fists. Then he emitted a brutal, ferocious howl.

He felt Hammy's powerful hands pull him from the ground and prise his fingers from McCrae's chest. He tried to throw himself back towards the detective, but Hammy held him firmly. 'Easy,' he said. 'For God's sake, Robbie. Easy!'

McCrae spat on the ground next to him and coughed, doubled over on all fours. Robert watched him with disgust, still seething with anger between Hammy's arms. Why did he stop him? He didn't need protecting. When would people realise that he was not a child? Eventually, McCrae met his eyes. As Robert opened his mouth to tell him exactly what he thought of him, the detective held up a shaky hand. 'Save it,' he said, his head hanging low. 'I know this is my fault. I've caused this.'

'What?' Robert spat the word, although he could feel his anger abating as the much more familiar combination of embarrassment and shame started to take its place. He pulled away from Hammy, who remained close by, though he made no attempt to restrain him this time.

Brian looked between the two of them, then at the hall, and said, 'We've got a bit of time. What do you say to a dram?'

'Sounds grand,' said Hammy, already halfway across the road. 'Robbie, fetch the dogs, will you?'

❄

Hammy and McCrae were exchanging terse yet polite small talk when Robert arrived at the Pine Needle. It all seemed so civilised that Robert wondered whether Hammy had forgotten who McCrae was. He unlocked the door, directed them to a table in front of the fire and poured three large glasses of whisky. He had considered recording their conversation on his phone, but then remembered that the detective would be adept at spotting such trickery. He took a seat opposite McCrae and tried to recall the last time he had seen him in the bar. It must have been over eighteen years ago, when his mother had still been his mother and life had still seemed easy.

'There.' He slid one of the glasses towards McCrae in the unfriendliest way he could muster. McCrae caught it easily between his forefinger and thumb and tipped it back to Robert with a raised eyebrow. Robert slumped into the back of his chair, folding his arms, painfully aware that he was behaving like a moody teenager.

'Out with it, then,' said Hammy, clinking his glass against the tabletop.

Brian sighed and took a large swig of whisky, then looked directly at Robert. He was about to start speaking when he thought better of it and took another swig, rolling his eyes to the ceiling. Finally, he began: 'I'm not one for speeches, but ... Robert, I know I've been goading you. I'm not proud of it and it's not befitting of my role as servant and protector of the public.' He broke off and shifted uneasily in his chair. 'God, this is difficult.'

Robert continued to frown at him. This was hardly the revelation he had been waiting for. 'I don't understand what you're trying to say,' he said brusquely.

McCrae sighed again and shook his head. Again, Robert noticed how tired he looked – ragged, even. 'No, I don't suppose you would. It's always been difficult between us, hasn't it, laddie ... I mean, Robert. It was never going to be easy. I'm not good with kids.'

'I'm not a kid,' said Robert, looking to Hammy for support.

Hammy responded by pushing out his bottom lip as if to say, 'Give the man a chance, for crying out loud.'

Grudgingly, Robert added, 'You're right, though. It could never have been easy between us ... obviously.'

Hammy poured himself and McCrae another dram as Robert studied McCrae's face. For the first time ever, he thought he detected a slither of vulnerability. But he warned himself not to be taken in: this man was highly trained in extracting information from people, which meant he must be a good actor. It would take more than a drink by the fire to make Robert trust him. As far as he was concerned, McCrae was still their most likely suspect.

'I am sorry about all that, Robert. For what it's worth, I meant what I said before: I always respected your dad.'

Robert squirmed in his chair. It was odd to hear Brian McCrae praising his dad in the Pine Needle. He listened carefully to the crackling wood and tried to imagine what his father would say in response. Clearing his throat, he said, 'As you said, it's history. More to the point, it's not why we're here, is it?' McCrae's head jerked up and Robert was pleased to see that his blunt tone had clearly hit home. 'You said I have something of yours?' He hoped the detective hadn't noticed how tightly he was gripping his glass.

McCrae sat back and contemplated Robert with an expression that seemed surprisingly close to pride. Was he about to admit that they'd outsmarted him? Was he about to confess to killing Mirabella, not to mention Clara and Felicity? Could it be that easy?

Instead, McCrae said, 'I believe so. May I have it back?'

'Have what?' Robert wanted to hear the word. It was their main piece of evidence against him, after all.

There was a long silence, punctuated only by the dogs yawning and the fire crackling.

Eventually, McCrae said, 'You're going to make me say it, aren't you? Okay. The ring. Mirabella's ring.' He sighed, shakily placing his glass on the table. 'I know I should have just asked you for it. My behaviour towards you that day in the village hall was inexcusable. It's no defence, but I was in a panic, you see. If anyone found out ... well, that'd be me done.'

'Because they'd know you killed her, you mean,' said Robert quietly. His heart was fluttering as the tension rose between them.

'What?' McCrae threw himself against the back of his chair with such force that he almost toppled over. 'What did you say?'

'You killed her,' said Robert, simply. 'Like you killed my dad, like you killed Felicity.' He wasn't going to let him get away with it. He looked at Hammy, who gave a sharp, nervous nod. They were both ready for him to make a run for it. They both knew the bar like the back of their hand; they'd be onto him in a flash, whichever way he went.

Suddenly, in what Robert assumed must have been a fit of insanity, McCrae started to chuckle. It began as a slow, throaty rumble, then grew into a wild, spluttering guffaw. Before long, he was slapping his thighs and doubled over, gasping for breath. 'Say that again!' he cried, his eyes brimming with tears. 'You think I killed ... *how many people*? Why on earth would you think that?'

Robert opened his mouth to explain his theory, but Hammy cut in. 'I guess it's not true, then. You didn't kill Robbie's dad? Or Felicity?'

'Bennie? Felicity? Is that what you've been thinking?' This set McCrae off again.

Robert looked to Hammy as the laughter finally started to subside. Hammy merely shrugged and stared at McCrac with interest.

'Sorry!' said McCrae, snorting as he took a sip of whisky, which seemed to calm him down and enabled him to regain his composure. 'Let me just check I understand this correctly. You think I've been running around town killing – what are we saying – *three* people?'

'And Clara Rowley,' Hammy offered, which prompted an exasperated glance from Robert. He had to admit, if McCrae was behind the murders, he was putting on the most extraordinary show.

'Well, I'm sorry to disappoint you,' said McCrae, with yet another snort of laughter. He slapped the table so hard that it wobbled. 'But I've never killed anyone in my life. I can't think why you'd conclude—'

'It's not so stupid,' interrupted Robert, even though he was beginning to feel very stupid indeed. 'I saw you that night by the woods, remember. Then Hammy's dogs found the ring with your name on it. I put two and two together and came to the conclusion that you must have killed Mirabella during an argument or something. It's hardly inconceivable, given your history.'

All the laughter suddenly drained from McCrae's eyes. In a low voice, he said, 'You're right about us having history. It was ... well, stupid's the word. Shame I didn't realise it at the time, given that I made exactly the same mistake a few years later with your mother.'

Hammy let out a sound halfway between a hum and a groan, which Robert took as an attempt to mollify him.

McCrae continued, 'The Rowleys came here most summers as well as some winters. She always drank alone. That was how we got talking. She was unhappy in her marriage, although that's no excuse, of course. Never is, I know that much now. We met here, actually.' He turned to the armchairs by the back wall. 'Right there. Two years before Clara was killed.' He shook his head. 'When we charged Toby ... well, you can imagine. She could never bring herself to believe it. Could never forgive me, either. Didn't want anything to do with me from then on.'

'But none of that explains why you were in the woods with her a few weeks ago.' Robert watched McCrae carefully, ready for any misstep.

'Aye, I can see why that would've looked strange to you,' he conceded. 'You noticed the cut on my face, didn't you? The rip in my trousers? I received a call from Mirabella that night. Totally out of the blue. She said she wanted to meet me in the woods. She walked in the dark, you know? For years after Clara was killed, she returned to Findrussie and walked in the woods, just searching and searching for ... God knows what. She was convinced I'd missed something, that the area held some sort of "secret" that would lead to her daughter's killer. Near the spot where Mirabella was found...' McCrae blinked awkwardly as tears filled his eyes. 'That was where we used to meet. As you know, it's secluded, but not completely off the beaten track. Easy enough to access.' He stopped speaking for a moment and began to search his pockets.

Hammy handed him a napkin.

'Thank you,' McCrae said, blowing his nose. 'I wasn't going to go. As I said, we hadn't spoken in decades. I couldn't see what good would come of it. But then I found myself wanting to see her. I can't explain it to you. It's nice, isn't it? To feel wanted. That was what I thought, anyway.' He took a deep breath and steadied himself. 'I'm not proud of what happened next. We got into a fight. She had this idea – this fantasy – that she was closer than ever to bringing Clara's killer to justice. She said she had new evidence. Afterwards, of course, I found the call from your dad on her phone, but I've no clue why he called her, Robert. I told her that she had to move on, as best she could, that the case was closed more than twenty years ago. She couldn't take it. You met her. She was passionate.' He gave a small, sad laugh. 'She was probably a bit drunk, too. She began to throw some punches. I didn't fight back at first, but then she really went for me, you know? That's when she reminded me about the ring. She screamed that she was still wearing it after all these years – not out of love, but to remind her never to give up seeking the truth. Those were her exact words. That's all I was to her: a reminder of her pain.

'I was still thinking rationally at that point. I thought if she returned the ring to me, she'd be free from me, free from the memories, free from the crazy theories. So I asked for it back. But she said no. That made me angry. I grabbed her hand and tried to wrench it off her finger. There was a snapping sound. Oh, God...' He stared into the fire as a single tear worked its way down the creases in his cheek. 'I broke her finger. It was bent backwards, but the ring was still on it. She screamed, called me every name under the sun. I panicked, ran away. It was still light enough for her to make her way home. I thought she'd be fine, so I left her there. I left her alone and ran.'

Robert looked at his hands as he pieced together what he had just heard. 'And that's when I saw you?'

'Aye.' McCrae sounded choked. 'I know I must have looked very strange. Then, later that night, when I got the call about her body, I couldn't comprehend it. I'll be living with that for the rest of my life.'

Hammy interjected, 'But the ring *wasn't* on her finger when she was found. Which was good for you, as it would've given you away. I bet no one knew the lead investigator in Clara's murder case was in an illicit relationship with the girl's mother.'

McCrae nodded grimly, the fire flickering in his wet eyes. 'I never thought this would be me. You hear about corrupt police officers ... I never thought I'd be one of them. Trying to conceal evidence ... it's shameful.'

'But you didn't conceal it,' Hammy reminded him.

McCrae raised an eyebrow at Robert. 'No, I didn't, but somebody did. When I saw you hanging about in the woods, I thought you must have taken it, though I couldn't figure out why. You do have it, don't you?'

'Aye, we do,' said Hammy, 'but only because the dogs found it in the woods a few weeks later. Someone else must have pulled it off her finger after she died. But why would they do that if the only person it could incriminate was you?'

'Search me,' said McCrae.

The three of them took another sip and allowed a silence to settle.

Robert stared into the fire. 'It's not like it even would have helped you,' he said eventually. 'Your DNA must have been all over her – especially under her fingernails, given that scratch on your face.'

McCrae put his head in his hands and moaned. 'It seemed to be a suicide. I was so sure of it. I included details of her mental health and family history in my report to the coroner's office, and stated that there were no suspicious circumstances. They opened an inquest, of course, but with no next of kin, and a note from her GP that she had been having suicidal thoughts for years, they didn't even recommend a post-mortem. She was cremated.'

Robert stared at him. 'So, you admit that you covered it up.'

'I thought she'd killed herself!' McCrae insisted, his voice cracking into what sounded like a hundred shards of glass. 'But then Felicity Montgomery was murdered and I realised my mistake. Coincidences like that simply don't happen in a place like this. It was because of me that Mirabella's killer was free. I'll have that on my conscience for the rest of my days. And there might be more to come: there's a missing person's report on Calan Stuart, too.' He eyed Robert. 'Let me guess, you established some sort of link between him and Clara. Was he the mystery boyfriend?'

Robert looked at Hammy, who shrugged. There was clearly

no point hiding anything from McCrae any more. 'That's right. He proposed to her on the night of her murder. He freaked out when her name was mentioned.'

'Three dead, one missing, all with some sort of connection to Clara Rowley,' McCrae said. 'And what was it you said about a hooded figure, back at the village hall? You mentioned Daniel Bell.' He sounded far from convinced. Robert was about to explain when McCrae let out a loud sneeze. Recovering himself, he said, 'Sorry, I'm allergic to dogs.' One of Hammy's huskies was pawing at his lap.

'You should have said.' Hammy directed all of the dogs to sit at the far end of the bar. They moved obediently at the sound of their master's voice, wagging their tails happily.

'It's okay,' said McCrae. 'I work around police dogs all the time. They love me for some reason. It got so bad that I was issued with a special citrus spray to keep them away. Nasty stuff. Sorry, Robert, you were saying...'

He was just about to begin for the second time when they all heard a sudden commotion from the other side of the road.

'The play can't have finished yet, could it?' asked Hammy, standing to get a better look.

Robert made straight for the door, a feeling of unease bubbling in his gut. Sure enough, a large crowd was gathering in the car park of the village hall. 'Something's happened,' he said. 'Quick!'

Chapter Twenty-Five

The chorus of crying schoolchildren was one of the most dismal things Robert had ever heard. He knew that something must be terribly wrong as soon as he reached the car park. Teachers were comforting their students while simultaneously trying to contact the coach company on their mobiles. They clearly wanted to get out of Findrussie as soon as was humanly possible.

Robert pushed his way through the crowd and tried to identify the source of the commotion. The lights were on in the auditorium but the curtains were still open, framing a giant chariot emblazoned with sun rays – the vehicle in which Medea escapes from Corinth after murdering her children as a final act of revenge for her husband's infidelity. It should have been hovering about two metres in the air. Instead, it lay shattered in two pieces on the stage. It was only when Robert moved closer that he saw the legs sticking out from the side. At first, his mind would not make sense of the mess. It was as if an enormous, injured spider was crouching on the stage, its depleted limbs sticking out at odd angles. Then, in a horrible realisation, his brain began to process the information it was receiving from his eyes. The first pair of legs were stocky, short: Daniel's. The second pair were longer, slender: Eilidh's. Robert's knees buckled and he fell to the ground, but everything else was moving in slow motion. He heard McCrae calling for assistance on his radio. The sound of an ambulance screeched to a halt outside the hall.

'Help,' Robert said. 'We've got to get it off her.' He crawled towards the sheets of plywood and twisted metal. 'She can't move under there.' He felt someone dragging him back. He kicked out at them. What were they doing? He had to rescue Eilidh. She was trapped. Why was no one helping him? He heard someone repeating his name over and over, trying to calm him. Why were they doing that? Why were they focusing on him rather than Eilidh. 'Help her,' he repeated. 'Get it off her.'

His mind seemed to disintegrate into a garish kaleidoscope of what he had seen and heard over the last hour: red-stained fingernails, Ruth McLuckie's lips mouthing 'Edinburgh', 'Fetch the dogs, will you?', 'She walked in the dark', 'Three dead, one missing', 'Then she was cremated'. He closed his eyes and attempted to shake himself back to reality but a wave of nausea rushed over him. Perhaps this was it. Perhaps life would be like this from now on, locked in a horrifying merry-go-round of fragmented phrases and visions. He opened his mouth and gasped for air. Curiously, he tasted the acrid tang of lemons at the back of his throat but immediately dismissed it as just one of the ways in which his mind was playing tricks on him, along with visions of two hands kneading red cake batter, a spinning ring and a forlorn figure hanging stiffly from the branch of a tree.

❄

'Focus on the positives.'

Robert glared at Hammy as if he were mad. As far as he

could see, there were no positives. It was as if reality had slipped through the cracks of his existence. The scene in his kitchen attested to that: Hammy and McCrae were sitting on the sofa, a new noticeboard was pinned above the fireplace and Justine was standing in his dad's old dressing-gown, her hair wrapped in a towel. She had been in the wings when the chariot had crashed to the stage and had been covered in sawdust and debris. Her face, devoid of any make-up for the first time Robert could remember, looked older and sterner than usual. The dogs had been banished to Robert's bedroom on account of McCrae's allergy.

Robert began to pour the tea. 'Really struggling to think of any, Hammy.'

'They're not dead,' Hammy pointed out, calmly.

Justine cut in before Robert could answer. 'I think what Hammy means to say is that Eilidh and Daniel are going to be fine.' She shot Hammy a look. 'They were lucky. It could have been a lot worse.'

'True enough,' said McCrae. 'They're questioning Daniel as we speak. We'll have some answers about the paint soon enough.'

'And Eilidh's got no more than a mild concussion,' said Justine gently. 'If you'd seen it happen, though...'

'The ropes must have slipped as soon as she stepped on the thing,' said McCrae. 'The safety clips weren't attached. From what I hear, the chariot smashed straight into Daniel, and Eilidh was thrown underneath it. They were both knocked unconscious but no bones broken, amazingly.'

Robert tried to block out the graphic details as he brought the mugs of tea over to the coffee table.

'The clips were checked and double checked,' insisted Justine, a little heatedly.

McCrae shook his head. 'They weren't attached, according to my team.'

'So someone sabotaged the set,' added Robert.

McCrae nodded briskly and stood to sketch an aerial view of the village hall on the noticeboard. 'We must assume the intent was to kill,' he said. 'The perpetrator cut the ropes, bypassed the safety device. They can't have envisaged the victims escaping with mild injuries. If the chariot was checked at six-thirty, which Justine has confirmed, they had a two-hour window in which to tamper with the ropes.' He tapped the newly drawn image with the marker pen. 'They could have entered the backstage area from either the kitchen corridor or the fire escape at the rear of the building.'

Robert hated to admit it, but McCrae was proving highly adept at summarising the incident.

'What do you think, Robbie?' Hammy asked.

Robert noticed McCrae shift a little uncomfortably. Perhaps he resented Hammy's conception of the group hierarchy. 'If we think it was Daniel, then he would have had access to the backstage area throughout that time.'

'That's yet to be confirmed,' said McCrae. 'He's got an alibi for Calan's abduction, though. He's not the person in the hood. He was staying at his mum's house at the time. It's watertight. And he wasn't the hit-and-run driver who killed Felicity. There's CCTV footage of him emerging from the village hall with Eilidh shortly after it happened.'

'Both of those pieces of information would have been quite useful before,' said Robert sourly, taking the pen from McCrae. 'But he's still our main suspect for the message on the bar.' He flipped over the sheet to reveal an old spider diagram the Pine Needles had drawn. An uncomfortable silence descended on the group as they all read the title: 'REASONS MCCRAE HAD TO

KILL CLARA ROWLEY'. 'Ah,' said Robert, blushing furiously. 'We thought ... well, we weren't entirely sure—'

'You have to admit, you were suspicious as muck,' said Hammy. 'Being a detective, I'm sure you'll appreciate—'

To Robert's surprise, McCrae laughed. 'Look, I see where you were going with that particular ... line of enquiry. I probably would have thought something similar myself. I'm just grateful you've shared what you have with me now. We might actually start getting somewhere.'

'Won't your superiors mind?' asked Justine. 'It's good to have the help, don't get me wrong, but isn't it a bit ... unorthodox?'

McCrae observed the group carefully, looking at each of them individually, before folding his arms. 'They don't know,' he admitted. 'I'll tell them about Mirabella, what I did, and that'll be me. I won't work for the force again. But I was counting on you lot to keep quiet about it until we've identified the killer. I reckon we can solve this case and finally discover who really murdered Clara.' He bowed his head. 'The more I think about it, the more convinced I am that I got it wrong all those years ago. I'd like to make amends for that ... while I still can.'

Robert took a gulp of tea, hardly believing the events of the last few hours, least of all that they now seemed to be working in tandem with Brian McCrae. But he had to admit that he was a useful addition to the Pine Needles team. He had information that they never could have accessed on their own, and he seemed open to their theories. 'Fine by me,' he said, feeling like a great weight had suddenly been lifted from his shoulders.

McCrae made an indistinct, gruff sound and extended a hand. Rather awkwardly, Robert grasped it and they shook hands. Despite his discomfort, he had the strong impression that they had just shared a significant moment. Meeting McCrae's eyes, he said, with new confidence, 'So, what's next?'

'The most important thing is that Eilidh and Daniel are safe,' said McCrae. 'We've stationed police guards at the hospital. So we can concentrate on listing everything we know about our killer. It's called profiling.'

Hammy sat up very straight, clearly elated at the prospect of working with a real detective.

'I think we all agree that the killer of Mirabella Rowley and Felicity Montgomery is the same person who murdered Clara Rowley, so they are likely to be at least forty years of age. They were also clever enough to frame Toby Rowley, so they probably had an idea of his history with drugs. And they seem to have lured the Rowleys to Findrussie by writing a false invite under the guise of Peter Montgomery, which indicates they had access to Kinlogie House at the time, or at least succeeded in breaking into the property. All of that seems pretty clear. As for the rest of it ... well, we're entering the realms of speculation.'

Robert exchanged quick glances with Hammy and Justine before all three of them looked expectantly at McCrae, urging him to continue.

'Let's assume Bennie somehow found out who really killed Clara. What I want to know is why he chose to call Mirabella, rather than tell anyone else. Perhaps he was trying to protect those around him. He might have known it was a dangerous secret to share with anyone in Findrussie.'

Robert noticed that McCrae's hand was trembling as he turned back to the noticeboard and wrote the word 'Strong'.

'The killer was strong enough to hoist Mirabella up a tree, to make us think it was a suicide. Although we should remember Mirabella was injured at the time, so she would not have been able to put up much of a struggle. As for the hit-and-run driver who killed Felicity, we only have footage from the security camera at the rear of village hall – the one that recorded Eilidh and Daniel leaving the building. The other camera, at the front, was faulty. After the incident, the driver reversed out of the car park and onto the main road, which has no traffic cameras for miles. They could have dumped the car anywhere. Frustrating, I know, but it does suggest that our killer knows the area well. Dare I say, they're probably local.'

'Can we go back to the person in the hood?' asked Justine. She seemed impressed by McCrae's efficiency, whereas Robert was still finding it hard to remember they were all now on the same team.

'Total mystery,' admitted the detective. 'As is Calan Stuart's whereabouts.' His phone buzzed and he took the call with the marker pen still in his hand.

Robert stared at the noticeboard and tried to think of anything he could add. His mind drifted back to the image of the smiling au pair, Laura Stanley, but she seemed a non-starter. A few holiday visits with the family more than thirty years ago hardly made her a local. And she'd left the Rowley household years before Clara's murder, so it wasn't as if she could have gained access to Kinlogie to forge the invitation.

'That was my colleague, calling from the hospital,' said McCrae. 'They questioned Daniel about the vandalism of your bar. We've got a confession.'

Robert's stomach flipped.

Justine cried, 'Daniel Bell! I never would have thought...'

Hammy mumbled in a very deep and wise voice, 'It's always the quiet ones. I've said so before.'

McCrae smiled and held up his hands. 'He doesn't have anything to do with the murders, though,' he reminded them. 'Seems he suspected Eilidh was caught up in something unsavoury ... involving you, Robert ... and wanted her to stop.

Intuition tells me he was motivated by jealousy, rather than anything else.'

'But he did write that message on the bar?' Justine asked.

'Seems like it. But only because he felt his girlfriend's attention had been diverted ... well, elsewhere.' McCrae shuffled on the spot in an uncharacteristic display of awkwardness. He glanced at Robert.

'I see,' said Hammy, clearly enjoying every second of Robert's embarrassment.

'So!' Robert clapped his hands in a bid to change the subject. 'We're looking for someone over forty who knows the area. Not exactly a short list.'

'Starting with Calan seems a good bet,' suggested Hammy, positively beaming as he sat back in his chair proudly, crossing his legs.

'I agree,' said McCrae. 'Not least because his car has just turned up in the woods fifteen miles from the village hall.' He held up his phone. 'Hot off the press. There's a dent on the bonnet consistent with the collision with Felicity Montgomery.'

'What?' cried Robert. 'But he's been missing for weeks. That doesn't make any sense.'

'I know,' said McCrae. He scratched his chin and swayed backwards and forwards, deep in thought. 'Can you think of anything that might lead us to his current whereabouts? Anyone he might be involved with? Any clue to his assailant's identity? His address has been checked regularly, he's not been home, but we've got to assume he's still in the area.'

Robert closed his eyes and tried to recall his exchange with Calan at the Ionic. He hadn't said anything out of the ordinary. But there was something unusual about that night. He could almost touch it; a niggle in the back of his mind. 'Ah!' He jumped up and punched the air, then looked at Hammy and Justine. 'Do you remember, in the hospital, we thought Eilidh was talking nonsense because of the painkillers. But do you remember what she said?'

'Not really,' admitted Justine, looking a little concerned.

'She said she saw Calan *disappear*. Like a ghost. Remember?'

'That's right,' said Hammy. 'I was worried she'd gone in the head.'

'Robbie, Calan's not a ghost,' said Justine, the worry on her face intensifying. 'You've spoken to him yourself.'

'I know that.' Robert laughed. 'But think about what Eilidh might really have seen. It was dark. Look...' He got out his phone and found the footage from the brewery. 'The hooded figure drags Calan to the very same spot in the alley, next to the Ionic. What if there's something there?'

'Like what?' Hammy asked.

'What if Eilidh saw Calan disappear into some sort of hideaway? Maybe a cellar?'

'The old whisky stores are down there, I know that much,' said McCrae. 'Drug users have been using them for years. They're a convenient, secluded spot for them to shoot up.'

'Or a convenient spot to hide if someone suddenly starts quizzing you about the ex-girlfriend you murdered. Think about it.' Robert felt his eyes widen as the theory unfurled in his mind. 'Everyone knew Mirabella was back in town. She hardly kept a low profile. Calan hears about it, panics, murders her too and thinks he's got away with it when it's reported as a suicide. But then Eilidh suddenly turns up at The Ionic and seems strangely interested in Clara. That's when he does his disappearing act. Then, later that night, as a bit of insurance, he returns to the bar and stages his own abduction. He knows it'll be recorded on the brewery's security camera. After all, the police are hardly likely to pin a couple of murders on him if he's a victim. He decides to keep tabs on Eilidh once she's released from hospital and follows us to Felicity's cabin. Then, he learns that Felicity will be at the Burns Night supper and hatches a plan to kill her. The car park is usually quiet, so he's probably waiting for her to come out alone. But that doesn't happen. The car park is full of people because of my fight with Daniel. Calan panics again and opts for a quick hit and run. Then he speeds away and dumps the car in the forest in that hope that nobody will ever find it.'

'If it were me, I'd have used a stolen vehicle,' mused Hammy.

'Well, we know he's not the sharpest tool in the shed,' replied Robert, eyeing McCrae to gauge his reaction, then looking away. He didn't want anyone to think he was seeking his approval. 'And he knew didn't have much time to act. Felicity could remember something at any moment.'

McCrae took a step back and ran his eyes over the noticeboard. 'He's certainly about the right age, and the profile fits him nicely,' he murmured. 'Okay. I suggest we check out those whisky stores.'

'You're not going to call for ... back-up?' asked Justine, looking slightly sheepish.

'And tell them what? This information appeared to me in a dream? They'll know something's up if I call them in. It's down to us, I'm afraid. We're in this together.'

Robert was sure that McCrae had intended his final comment to sound encouraging, but his smile still looked like a snarl from where Robert was standing. Nevertheless, there was no denying that his input had been useful over the last couple of hours, which made what they were about to do next marginally less terrifying.

Chapter Twenty-Six

The Pine Needles – minus Eilidh, plus McCrae – stood in the dark alleyway next to the Ionic, looking at three enormous bins. Two of the three were wedged into the snow, but it looked like the third had been wheeled in and out frequently, judging by the tracks in the sludge. McCrae pointed to it, holding a finger to his lips, and gestured for Robert to help him move it. Robert stepped forward and pulled his gloves tightly up his wrists. He glanced at Hammy and Justine, who were huddling together in the corner. Justine was holding her hands to her face, seemingly to suppress a terrified scream. Robert gave her a thumbs-up, forcing himself to appear confident, then placed his hands on the bin. It gave a low creak and McCrae blew through his lips, then signalled with his eyes to be careful. They slid it gently to the side to reveal a deep, stone stairway.

Robert could scarcely imagine anything more frightening than descending those stairs to meet a violent serial killer. His torch wobbled in his hand as he took his first, tentative step. McCrae was a few paces ahead of him, striding assertively with the sort of poise that only years of police training could hone. His back was ramrod straight, yet relaxed; he seemed ready for aggression. Robert tried to loosen his own shoulders, but that only earned him a cautionary glance from McCrae as the contents of his pockets rattled.

A thick, wooden door awaited them at the foot of the stairs. The air smelled damp and musty, as if it had remained in precisely the same spot for decades. The door was ancient, too. Its hinges were iron, and it was shaped in a sort of Gothic arch. Robert thought it was a shame it was hidden down here, behind some rubbish bins. McCrae looked at him, and he quickly realised the conundrum. If the door was unlocked, they could burst through and overpower Calan. However, if it was locked, trying to open it would only alert him to their presence. Robert didn't fancy meeting a well-prepared, and potentially well-armed, criminal face to face. He looked up the stairs, where a sliver of moonlight was gleaming off the moisture on the steps, making them shimmer. Then he turned back to the door and shone his torch on the handle – an iron press-paddle. McCrae, who had his back against the wall, nodded for him to try it. Robert found himself praying that McCrae had kept up with his combat training, even though it must have been many years since he'd last had to deal with this sort of situation. Then, just as he was about to press down on the latch, the door shook violently. He fell backwards, into McCrae. The torch smashed on the floor and he scrambled about in the darkness. McCrae grabbed his collar and steadied him, then whispered, 'Quiet,' into his ear.

'Help! Is someone there? For fuck's sake, help me. I'm in here!' Then there was an excruciating screech, like something being dragged violently across the floor.

Robert, completely taken aback, looked up at McCrae, who was wearing a similarly confused expression. The voice sounded like Calan Stuart's. They heard another loud crash and the sound of a struggle.

Then, from somewhere further away, Calan shouted, 'Please. For fuck's sake. They'll kill me. They've locked me up. She's coming back, I know it.'

McCrae replied in a firm voice that Robert had never heard him use before: 'Police! It's the police here! Open this door!'

A short silence followed, then Robert thought he heard a strangled gasp before Calan pleaded: 'They're here. Get me out, *please*.' His voice sounded far removed from the last time Robert had spoken to him – higher-pitched, with the helpless tremor of a terrified child.

McCrae fumbled about in his pocket before looking at Robert. 'Where's my phone?'

'I don't know,' shouted Robert over the intensifying screams from within. 'Someone must be in there with him. We need to help him.' He hammered on the door, ignoring the pain that shot through his fist. 'Calan! Calan, is that you? Who's in there with you?'

'The English wom—' His response suddenly turned into a strangled scream. 'No! Who are you? What do you want? Oh God, let me out. What do you want? I'll do anything. No, no, *please*!'

'Robbie?' Hammy appeared at the top of the stairs with Justine. 'What's happening down there?'

There was no time to reply. McCrae counted firmly, 'One, two, three,' then booted the door. 'Again,' he said.

Robert stared at the thick iron hinges, convinced that it was pointless. Nevertheless, he kicked against the wood. The door shifted slightly, but the hinges held. The screams had turned into hopeless, vaporous whimpers.

'Hammy, help us!' Robert shouted. He and Justine were already halfway down the stairs.

The three men shoved against the door in sync with

McCrae's rhythm: one, two, three; one, two, three. The door groaned and finally the top hinge split away from the frame.

'Calan! Calan!' shouted Robert. 'Do you hear that? We're almost in.'

As if in response, another high-pitched scream echoed from beyond the door. This time there was a breathiness to it, a rasp tethering its edges. It was a noise drained of all colour and life. It sounded like a surrender.

'Calan!' Robert shouted again. 'Calan!'

They continued to barge against the door with a panicked, solemn energy. McCrae threw his whole body against it, twisting his shoulder like a boulder. Finally, with a terrible groan, the door lurched to one side.

McCrae took the lead, keeping flat against the dank, stone walls, gesturing for the others to stay close behind. The stench was immediate – thick, hot and sour. Then Robert saw McCrae's shoulders sag. His eyes were still adjusting to the grey light within the whisky store, but he knew, deep down, that the silence indicated something really bad had happened. That they had been moments too late.

Calan Stuart was sitting on a flimsy wooden chair, his arms tied behind his back, his ankles bound to the chair legs. He was astonishingly thin. His ribs protruded in sickening desperation, as if the bones themselves were begging for sustenance. His mouth was slack and wet. Even in the darkness, Robert could see the saliva dripping down his chin. He felt like he was prying into a deeply private moment. This was not how anyone would want to be remembered. McCrae ran to the chair and placed two fingers against Calan's neck. He raised his eyes to Robert and nodded grimly, confirming what they both already knew.

Robert's eyes were drawn to Calan's chest, which was red raw and covered with puncture marks. It looked as if someone had torn into him, tried to rip him apart in a frenzied attack.

The blood that had spilled from his emaciated body was almost black. Then Robert heard a dripping sound and realised that fresh blood was still leaking from him. His vision blurred and he found himself on all fours, retching. Then he heard footsteps from the far side of the room and rolled pathetically onto his side.

McCrae was scanning the store with his torch, presumably to ensure that the killer had fled. Robert felt incredibly stupid: he had been too busy throwing up his guts to think about whether they were in immediate danger. The murderer might be hiding no more than a few feet away, watching their every move, drinking in their fear. The beam illuminated two old, rotten whisky barrels on either side of a mob and bucket in the corner. That explained the stench.

'Christ, they kept him a prisoner here,' murmured the detective. He swore loudly and kicked one of the barrels with a deafening thud. 'Minutes!' he shouted. 'No, seconds. We were seconds too late. How the hell did they escape?' He shone his torch to the rear of the store. 'Stay here,' he said.

'Brian...' Robert began.

'Keep back,' said McCrae, firmly, as he headed into the darkest recesses of the room. From what Robert could make out, a number of whisky casks had been arranged into a small pyramid under a low, stone archway.

'Hammy, Justine, don't follow me,' Robert whispered. 'Get out of here.'

'What? No!' Hammy protested. 'Come back here.'

Robert ignored him and followed McCrae into the shadows, under the archway. The detective held up a hand, signalling for Robert to slow down. His head was cocked to one side. Robert did the same, listening for any noise that might divulge the murderer's hiding place.

'No use hiding!' shouted McCrae suddenly. 'My team is on

the way. I'd give myself up if I were you. It'll be much better for you.'

Robert held his breath, wishing with all his heart that McCrae had changed his mind and alerted his colleagues after all. The detective extended an arm to hold him back and advanced into another room. The air was icy now. Robert's chest reacted to it, his lungs shrivelling as he kept his breaths shallow, silent.

At that moment, a barrel crashed to the floor at Robert's feet, causing both him and McCrae to topple over. Robert's forearm hit the ground with excruciating force. Then he heard the sound of footsteps, heavy and slow in the cold air. The rhythm seemed vaguely familiar: a drag, then a pull, then a shuffle; a drag, then a pull, then a shuffle.

'Stairs,' he said, looking up from the floor and seeing a faint shaft of moonlight beyond the arch. 'There.' He pushed himself to his feet and winced at the sharp pain in his knee. McCrae held out a hand and Robert helped him up. The hooded figure was already at the top of the stairs. Robert flung himself after the silhouette as it shuffled into the darkness outside. Then the door was slammed in his face, almost causing him to fall backwards.

'Watch yourself!' shouted McCrae from the foot of the stairs.

Robert pressed his hands against the door and it flew open immediately with a great rush of fresh air.

'See them?' asked McCrae. He had already caught up with Robert and was now running ahead, scanning the area with his torch.

To Robert's surprise, he found himself standing on a disused railway line that the council had recently converted into a cycle path. An engine revved behind him and he turned to see a car hurtling towards them. 'Who are you?' he hollered into the windscreen, desperately trying to see the face behind the wheel. 'Who are you?'

The car began to decelerate, as if in response to the question. Robert stood his ground, but his heart was hammering behind his breastbone. The headlights made it impossible to see who was driving. Then the driver floored the accelerator again so that the wheels spun on the frozen ground. Robert threw himself to one side and felt an icy gust of wind as the car sped past, missing him by inches. For a moment, he imagined what the impact would have felt like. He would have sprawled across the bonnet, his forehead pressed against the windscreen, but at least he would have seen who was sitting in the driver's seat. As it was, he was no closer to identifying the hooded figure than he'd ever been.

'Robert?' McCrae's face peered over him, his brow folded and creased. 'Can you hear me?'

Robert nodded, but decided that he wasn't yet ready to stand. The ground seemed quite appropriate for the time being. 'So, it wasn't Calan,' he said quietly, a bitter taste in his mouth. 'I thought he'd gone into hiding because—'

'No,' said McCrae gruffly. He fumbled in his pockets again, then patted himself down. 'Where is my bloody phone?'

Robert heard a crunch of snow and saw Hammy and Justine walking arm in arm beneath the moonlit trees.

'It's here,' said Hammy, handing the phone to McCrae. 'You left it in the Jeep.'

'Thanks,' said McCrae as he took the phone and started dialling. His face was grey with concentration.

'Who are you calling?' asked Justine. She was shivering, her eyes watery and glazed.

Robert rose unsteadily to his feet, enveloped her in his arms, and led her back towards the car. He never should have placed her – nor Hammy – in such danger. Their proximity to a violent murder was more than he could bear.

Chapter Twenty-Seven

'How long did they say?' Eilidh propped herself up on an elbow, looking over the loch.

The beach was deserted, which was unusual for such a beautiful day, although unsurprising. The details of Calan's murder had trickled through the community, leaving the residents with little else to contemplate, and something new to fear. Robert looked to the mountains in the hope that they might provide some answers, allay the frenetic buzz that had taken up seemingly permanent residence between his ears. They seemed taller, more still, today, as if they'd imposed a barrier between the ugliness occurring in the valley and their own ancient beauty.

'Well, the video footage was taken a few hours after we saw him in the Ionic, so Brian thinks probably since then. Almost three weeks. Calan used to store his gear in the cellar, apparently. He did the murderer a favour by keeping it a secret. Not even the owners of the Ionic knew about it. They thought it had been filled in when the railway was closed. Now at least we know the hooded figure is our killer.'

'And you saw them here, too?' Eilidh glanced awkwardly at

the trees behind them, the neck brace still restricting her movement.

'Maybe. They poured a couple of drams. God knows what they were doing.'

'Have you spoken to Brian since you found Calan?' She turned back to face him.

'Suspended with immediate effect. He's certain he's facing dismissal on the grounds of gross misconduct. His boss thinks Calan's murder is unrelated to both of the Rowley deaths, Felicity and the ... *incident* at the dress rehearsal. So, the killer is...'

There was no reassuring way to finish the sentence. Eilidh understood: the killer was still very much alive, well and at liberty. They could not afford to relax.

'I saw Calan's mum in town,' said Eilidh, her eyes settling on the water again. 'She's just an old lady. She was so confused.'

Robert didn't know what to say. He'd heard a few awful rumours about Jayne Stuart, a woman who usually kept herself to herself, wandering the streets after a few too many drinks. She had apparently started following folk as they walked by and shouting incoherent, rambling questions at them. She'd even accused a few of her friends.

'It's grief,' said Robert. 'It's brutal.'

'I know,' said Eilidh. 'I know.'

Robert rested his forehead on his knees and drew a deep breath. 'I heard them running away.'

'You couldn't have stopped them, Robbie.'

'That's not what I mean. Their footsteps sounded familiar ... as if I'd heard them before.'

'How can you recognise footsteps?' asked Eilidh.

'You can't, I suppose. Still...'

'Everything must have happened so quickly,' said Eilidh.

'And your memory can play tricks on you sometimes. It's probably difficult to remember everything clearly.'

'You're right,' he said, although he wasn't sure if he agreed with her or was just exhausted from hearing the fleeing footsteps over and over again in his mind. 'Have you spoken to Daniel?' He tried – and failed – to make the question sound casual.

Eilidh let out a ragged laugh and looked at Robert in disbelief. '*That's* the most important thing, is it?'

He joined in with her laughter. For a few seconds, it seemed as if they were the only two people in the world. The laughter was liberating and they surrendered to it, allowing the tears to dampen their eyelashes. 'Sorry,' he said as he wiped his eyes. 'I just...'

'I know,' she said, fanning her face to cool it down. 'As you're so interested, yes, I have. He's obviously an idiot, but he is sorry. He sent me flowers, actually.'

'Oh?' Robert held his breath.

Eilidh slapped him on the thigh. 'It was a nice thing to do. And he owed me an apology ... as well as you. He said he couldn't think of what else to do.'

'Of course. I understand. A death threat was the only sensible solution—'

'Shut up!' Eilidh giggled again, then let the sound melt into silence. 'For what it's worth, we're done now ... Daniel and me. It wouldn't have worked anyway, not with me going to London.'

'No,' said Robert. His jaw tightened and he looked at his boots, which were half-smothered with damp sand. 'Probably for the best.'

Eilidh stood up suddenly, patted her jeans dry and shook herself, ruffling her hair. 'Shift's about to start.'

Robert leaned back on his elbows and hung his head backwards. The sky was an odd, off-white colour. He found it difficult to think about something as trivial as work when so much was still at stake. Ever since the night in the whisky store, he had been studying people's faces, interrogating their expressions, trying to read their body language. He also knew that he had developed a hunch as he walked, as if shielding himself from an unexpected strike. In the back of his mind, the wet, sinewy mess that had once been Calan Stuart's chest continued to fester. It was insidious, the way the image lingered then suddenly rose to the surface when least expected.

'Are you coming?' Eilidh asked.

Robert looked out onto the loch once more, then followed her down the forest path.

❄

Robert wouldn't have said he was pleased to find McCrae waiting at the bar. He had claimed a spot by the fire, opposite Hammy, who was reading a newspaper with his feet resting on a stool, although his eyes periodically peered over the top as he cast small, eager glances at the detective. Justine nodded towards them as Robert approached the bar, rolling her eyes. 'Been here since morning,' she said. 'Waiting for you, I think. Hammy's on the edge of his seat.'

Robert grabbed some dirty glasses from the countertop and took them into the kitchen. He felt a sudden need to pretend that everything was normal, that the only thing he had to worry about was the bar's imminent financial collapse. Justine followed, a pile of plates balanced in her arms.

'Has he said anything about the other night?' Robert asked in a hushed tone. He eased the kitchen door closed.

'No,' Justine replied. She checked the door and continued, 'He'll be in serious trouble, mind. Not surprised he's keen on a drink or three.'

Robert sighed and began filling the dishwasher. 'Doesn't seem real,' he said, ramming a wine glass between two plates. 'I keep thinking it's not real.'

The glass was wedged at an awkward angle. He wiggled it until it shattered, swore loudly and allowed Justine to intervene. She checked his hand for any injury, then, satisfied he'd escaped unscathed, patiently began to pick the shards from the dishwasher. 'I'm just about keeping above water myself, Robbie,' she said without looking up. 'Stick together, that's what I say. You lean on me, I lean on you. It's all we can do."

Eilidh opened the door slowly and poked her head into the kitchen.

Justine dropped the pieces of glass into the sink and let out a squeal as she hurried over to embrace her. 'Eilidh!' she said. 'When I think about what—'

Eilidh shared a smile with Robert as Justine embraced her as best she could around the neck brace. 'It's okay, Justine. The doctors said I'm fine. Just got to wear this bloody thing for a while. I'm so sorry the play was cancelled.'

Justine pulled away from her and held her cheeks between her hands. 'Look at me,' she said, her eyes wide and tearful. 'There is nothing – *nothing* – more important to me than your safety. A play's just a play; this is real life. You have as many shots as you like at a play; you get only one at life.'

Eilidh struggled to tie her hair back and smiled. 'At least we performed it once. Well, *almost* once,' she said. 'It's as if whoever cut the ropes wanted us to get right to the end.'

Justine removed her glasses, which had steamed up. 'I wouldn't want to give them any credit, but every cloud, as they say.' She grasped Eilidh's hands. 'I thought your final monologue was magnificent, Eilidh. You captured her triumph, her vitriol, her joy. It was precisely as I imagined it.'

Robert noticed Eilidh turn a deep shade of red as she

continued to wrestle with her ponytail. 'Thanks,' she said. 'Actually, I was thinking about using that speech for an audition.'

She was interrupted by the kitchen door swinging open. McCrae braced himself against the door frame while Hammy stood in close attendance. McCrae was wearing his characteristic frown, though his lips were curled into what Robert thought was meant to be a smile. 'I've been waiting for you out there, you know?'

'Waiting for what?' The exasperation in Robert's voice was wholly unintentional, but a shade of disappointment passed over McCrae's face, his lips drooping. Robert opened his mouth to apologise, but McCrae interrupted.

'I've got an update from my old team. Still got a friend or two, despite ... well, you know.'

'What is it?' Robert could have kicked himself for sounding so dismissive. It was just so difficult to accept that Brian McCrae was on their side. 'Have they found Calan's killer?'

'No. I remembered the car's number plate and passed it on to them, but they can't trace it.'

'How did you manage that?' spluttered Robert, astonished that anyone could commit a string of numbers and letters to memory while a car was accelerating towards them.

McCrae scowled. 'I am ... *was* a detective, you know,' he said simply. 'Second nature.'

'So, what's the news?' asked Justine.

'As I say, the number plate is a dead end – no MOT, no tax, no insurance, it's useless to us. My news is about the police investigation. It's not looking good, I'm afraid. With no other leads, they're dancing in the dark. They're treating Calan's murder as an isolated, drug-related incident. They're convinced Felicity Montgomery was the victim of a road-traffic accident. The coroner has already recorded Mirabella's death as a suicide.

And finally' – he looked sympathetically towards Robert – 'your father's death has long been considered an accidental drowning.'

'What?' Robert's mouth hung open in disbelief. 'Why are they not connecting the dots? What are they thinking, that all of these deaths are coincidences?'

McCrae shrugged and looked at the kitchen floor. 'The woman who's taken my spot, she's good, but she'll be taking things steadily. It'd be a tall order to convince a team to get onboard with a multiple-murder theory with so little evidence to go on. I know where she's coming from, if I'm honest.'

'Can't you persuade her?' asked Robert, incredulous.

McCrae let out a grisly laugh and shook his head. 'I'm public enemy number one, remember,' he said. 'Even if I told them what we know, or think we know – we have no solid proof, as yet – they'd never take me seriously. I'm lucky I've not been locked up.'

A jolt of something between excitement and terror twitched deep within Robert's gut. 'So, we're on our own,' he said. 'Whoever killed Calan will be coming for us, and the police aren't even looking for them.'

'You're not wrong,' said McCrae grimly. 'But remember, nothing much has changed. The killer was after us then and they're still after us now. They'll be frustrated, mind.'

'Why's that?' asked Eilidh.

'Because they're slipping up,' said McCrae. 'Eilidh, you should be dead, for a start. Then there was the whisky store, which seemed like a rushed job.'

'That's the one thing that doesn't make any sense to me,' mused Eilidh. 'They had no qualms about killing Mirabella and Felicity – or trying to kill me – so why did they wait to kill Calan? Why did they keep him alive in that cellar for weeks on end? What's different about him?'

Robert had been thinking the same thing himself, especially as Calan would have been the easiest target, given the insalubrious company he kept. 'The killer used Calan's car to hit Felicity,' he said slowly, looking at McCrae. 'You said it was found in the forest, right? Maybe that explains it.'

'What?' asked Justine. She was massaging her temples in deep, slow circles.

'I'm trying to put myself in the killer's shoes,' said Robert, pacing up and down. 'They literally think they've got away with murder for over twenty years. Then my dad somehow uncovers their dark secret ... although *how* is still a mystery. He tries to contact Mirabella, she contacts us, and we start looking into Clara's murder again. So, the killer is forced to take her out, along with anyone else who might be getting too close to the truth. However, at some point, they're going to need to frame somebody. Just as they did with Toby. That's the only sure-fire way to stop people digging.'

'Calan was a pretty good choice,' agreed Eilidh. 'He had a ready-made motive – Clara rejected him on the night she was killed – and it's not much of a stretch to imagine him snapping.'

'Precisely,' said Robert. 'I'd be willing to bet that the killer wanted the police to find his car. Maybe they were planning to get him to sign a confession before staging another suicide.'

'But they killed him,' said Hammy. 'We were there. We heard it happen.'

'That's true,' murmured McCrae. He took a deep breath; his eyes were bloodshot and strained. 'But if we'd managed to question him, he might have been able to identify his kidnapper – the killer. Even if he didn't know their name, he probably would have given us a bloody good description. They had to kill him as soon as they realised we'd tracked him down.'

'But how did they know we were coming?' asked Robert. 'The killer was already in there with him when we arrived.'

McCrae observed them all keenly, his eyes little more than slits. 'As I said, nothing much has changed. We've all got to be careful. I mean it. I'm counting myself as a target, too. The killer is watching us. They're good at that. Ruthless, too. And we've angered them now. The stakes have never been higher.'

A few dark moments of silence followed. Robert felt his throat tighten as he remembered they had been at his home just before driving to the whisky store. It was surrounded by trees and not much else. How often had the killer hidden behind those dark branches, studying his movements? How well did they know his routines, his daily rituals? The sense of darkness encroaching on him and the people he loved was becoming unbearable.

'We need to find them,' said Robert. His voice sounded reedy and distant. 'We must.'

❄

None of them had planned to stay behind after closing time, but as the customers began to drift away and the wind began to howl, neither Robert, nor Justine, nor Eilidh, nor Hammy, nor McCrae showed any inclination to leave the bar. Hammy settled the dogs in the office. Sitting on a stool, Robert worked on his laptop, moving the cursor over the previous month's takings and flinching occasionally whenever Justine snored in the armchair by the fire. Eilidh typed on her own laptop opposite him, the glow of the screen illuminating the dark circles under her eyes. McCrae scrolled on his phone in a seat next to the main window. He was researching the Rowleys again but had failed to uncover any new information. After emerging from the office, Hammy sat with his feet up, arms folded, eyes weary but alert. Every so often he did a circuit of the bar, checked outside, rattled the front doors, scanned the kitchen.

Robert rested his head against the countertop, then reached underneath, selecting the nearest bottle. There was no need to look at the label: everything under there was top quality, reserved for friends and family. He raised it silently to the room, so as not to wake Justine.

'Count me in,' she called groggily from the armchair. 'Make it a double, will you?'

Robert looked up, surprised she was awake. Perhaps they were all experiencing the same half-baked sleep that had afflicted Robert himself ever since his dad had died. Sometimes, in the depths of the night, he struggled to know if his eyes were closed or he was just staring blankly into the darkness. He poured a glass and carried it over. Justine seized it eagerly and took a determined sip. None of them had ever been tee-total, but Robert had noticed that their alcohol intake had taken a sharp upward curve over recent weeks. However, he knew that it was probably not the best time to chastise Justine ... or anybody else. If a wee dram was what they needed to get through this, he could live with that.

'Islay?' she asked.

'What's that?' Robert blinked down at her.

'The whisky. Islay?' She smiled dreamily, her eyes drifting between sleep and wakefulness. 'My favourite.'

'Good,' said Robert. He grabbed a blanket from the box next to the fire and placed it over her. 'Get some rest just now, Justine.'

After distributing the rest of the drinks, including a decent measure for himself, Robert looked around the bar, his hands on his hips. He couldn't face looking at the finances again. Instead, he opened his book and wriggled into the window seat – where he had read as a child, hunched over. There were only a few pages left. The Spanish mountaineer was still reflecting on his time in the village.

> *Sometimes a chance meeting has a great impact upon a person. These lands are nothing without the people who inhabit them; to escape company is to acknowledge the significance of companionship. The woman I met in the tiny village of Findrussie remains with me to this day. She was running. Not unusual in itself, but peculiar because she was not wearing running shoes, nor shorts, nor was her hair tied back. It flowed behind her in great, voluminous waves, illuminated by the moonlight. She did not see me immediately. She was wringing her hands with a sort of frantic intensity. I did not mean to watch her; certainly, I did not wish to startle her. But the way she moved, the way her eyes reflected the moon, unblinking, she was a sight to behold. I had never fully understood the meaning of that phrase ... until that moment.*
>
> *After a while, her eyes came to rest on me. Of course, I was concerned that she would be terrified. A lone woman can never be certain whether a man means her harm or not. I thought that the best course of action was to wave. Have you ever seen a hare freeze, its ears piqued, its eyes blank in contemplation? Time stops for the hare in those moments. This woman reminded me of just such a hare. Then she broke her stillness. I believe she made a conscious decision to speak to me. The smooth veil that had shrouded her face suddenly evaporated. Now she seemed distressed, breathless.*
>
> *'Thank goodness!' she said in what even I recognised as an English accent.*

It was only then that I realised her hands were covered in blood. The front of her dress, too. The dark liquid described a great 'V' on her torso. I remember wondering whether the freckles on her face were also, in reality, specks of blood.

'Thank goodness you're here,' she repeated.

I asked if she was all right, then pointed to the big house behind us, through the trees. I told her I would take her there, tried to reassure her that they would be able to call for help.

'No!' she shouted, beginning to shake.

I immediately recognised this as a sign of shock. I offered her my coat to place around her shoulders and suggested we should walk towards the main road, thinking this would put her mind at ease and that we could eventually find help. She agreed.

We walked mostly in silence. A wide path leads from the great house to the village. It is well lit and lined with tall trees. She seemed quite capable of walking, at least, so my concern that she had sustained some sort of serious injury abated. Nevertheless, I felt obliged to escort her to a friendly, less isolated place. However, she stopped dead on the path as soon as we heard the sound of drunken singing. I told her not to be scared, insisted that we should press on and find her somewhere safe to stay. To my surprise, she started to giggle. But the sound was not light and airy. It was as black as charcoal.

Then she said, 'I will always be safe. I've arranged that much, at least. Don't worry about me. Nothing can harm you if you don't exist. I have a friend. He'll take care of me. He'll take care of everything. His help gave me courage – the courage to survive. The will to win. He supports me. Says he always will. Do you think I'm weak?' She held my gaze.

I gave an honest answer. 'I think you're hurt, not weak.'

This made her smile, which pleased me. She replied, 'I have never been weak. I've been invisible, but not weak. I would hate for anyone to think that I was weak. The weak are not remembered. That's my irony.'

'Irony?'

She continued to stare at me with the most full, gleaming eyes. 'I became invisible to gain power.' She clicked her fingers and, in that moment, it seemed as if all the laws of nature had been suspended. I half-expected her form to dissolve into the night. But she remained.

'You don't need to hide,' I said. 'Who is this man who supports you? Where is he? I can take you to him, or to anyone else who will make you feel safe.'

Her face twitched as an icy gust blew across the path. 'Don't you worry about me,' she said, her teeth chattering. She pulled my coat tighter around her shoulders and raised her eyes to meet mine. 'You're not from here. How long will you stay?'

I told her I planned to leave first thing in the morning. I felt I should offer to stay until she felt secure, but I knew she would refuse. Indeed, she seemed relieved to hear that I would be leaving so soon. Once again, I was happy to please her.

'Then leave me here,' she said.

'But it's only a short way—'

'Leave,' she said simply, calmly. 'We're here. This is my home.'

'Are you sure? What about the ... blood?'

'I'm fine. It's not all mine. And it's not so terrible. In fact, it's the most natural thing I can imagine. To exist, yet disappear. To conclude, yet begin. To remain, yet move on. It's just life, isn't it?'

I'm not sure why, but I felt I needed to know who she was. There was something about her that seemed so displaced, in every sense of the word. There was her English accent, of course. And she moved like woodsmoke, as if the wind might blow her in any direction at any moment. 'What is your name?

'Laura,' she answered quickly. Then she repeated it: 'Laura, Laura, Laura, Laura...'

I felt that she said it for her benefit, not mine. I did not reply because she did not ask for my name in return. Instead, I merely watched her leave. Still wearing my coat, she eventually became a small, fluorescent-green dot in the distance. I saw her reach the village. I thought about calling to her, to ask for my coat, but I had an insurmountable urge to leave something of mine in that place. I couldn't understand it at the time, but now, as I think of my trusty jacket languishing at the back of a closet, I know that the woman was right. To remain, yet move on. That's life.

When I think of the mountains and the fog and the snow, I

realise that I too exist and disappear. I conclude journeys and begin new ones.

Sometimes I find myself wondering if I really met Laura. Maybe she was just a lonely traveller's sentimental apparition. However, if she was real, I can only wish that she, like us all, found comfort on her chosen path.

The pages seemed to tingle between Robert's fingers. He dropped the book and placed both palms on the table, his breathing shallow and dry. Trying to control the tremors, he flicked to the front of the book to find the publication date. As he thought: 2002. The year after Clara's murder. The mountaineer hadn't encountered a mysterious, ghostly entity. He'd bumped into Laura Stanley fleeing Clara's murder scene. And if he left for Spain a few hours later, as planned, he probably never heard about the crime. The description was clear: young, English, alluring, manipulative. Covered in blood. And she hadn't acted alone. There had been someone else behind the scenes, helping her, offering support.

Robert swore aloud and scanned the final chapter again, to confirm that he hadn't imagined it. There it was, in plain sight. 'It was Laura,' he announced to the room. He shook the book at his friends and repeated, 'It was Laura Stanley. She murdered Clara. It was Laura Stanley.'

'That name rings a bell,' said McCrae, already tapping his phone.

Eilidh looked at Robert, her eyes wide. 'Laura? The nanny? How? How do you know?'

'It's all in here.' He slammed the book on the table, barely able to control his excitement. 'She even tells him her name. Oh my God, I wish I'd read it faster. I think she's still here ... or back here. In Findrussie.' He threw the book to Eilidh, who began to leaf through the pages.

'I don't know any Lauras,' said Hammy. 'None who would be the right age, anyway. She'd be in her mid to late fifties by now, am I right?'

'About that,' confirmed Robert. 'She must have changed her name, kept a low profile. But even then, there can't be too many English women around here who match her description. We should be able to find her.'

'Woman, on the whole, is a timid thing, but, wronged in love, there is no heart more murderous,' Eilidh whispered, just loud enough for them all to hear. She looked up, surprised by herself. 'It's from the play,' she said, seriously. 'It's what Medea says when she decides to kill her own children out of revenge. She's murderous after Jason cheats on her. We know that Laura had a long-term affair with Anthony Rowley. Do you think she believed Anthony was unfaithful to her? Maybe she thought he was in love with her, that they'd end up together one day.'

'Their neighbour certainly said he heard the Rowleys arguing about her. Anthony and Laura were definitely a serious item,' recalled Robert. 'More serious than his other conquests.'

'Sounds like she had an accomplice, too,' said Eilidh, passing the book to Justine. 'That makes sense. I've been wondering how one person could have done all of this alone.'

'And Calan said something about an English woman before he died,' added McCrae, thoughtfully.

Eilidh looked at Robert, her cheeks pale but her eyes sharp. 'Mirabella said Clara had bumped into someone she knew that night. We all assumed it was Calan, and for more than twenty years he must have assumed he was the last person to see Clara alive. That would explain why he freaked out when I kept asking about her. But what if she met someone else ... after he'd proposed?'

'Laura, her childhood nanny,' said Robert, the nausea rising in his throat. 'Clara would have trusted her, possibly more than her own mother and father. It would have been easy for Laura to lure her to the bothy. She also knew all about Toby's violent outbursts and might even have witnessed his early experiments with drugs.'

'Christ,' whispered Justine. She reached over and took the book from Eilidh. 'It's been here all along; we just didn't know it.'

McCrae's thumbs were moving in slow, deliberate circles. He frowned slightly, looking at each of them in turn. 'You're definitely onto something,' he said. 'You've been working hard on this, haven't you, Robert?'

'We promised Mirabella,' said Robert simply. 'We said we'd finish what my dad started.'

McCrae pursed his lips together in thought. 'She's already got a hell of a body count under her belt if you're right. And it's self-evident that she's not a woman who gives up easily.' He sighed, folding his arms. 'But a chapter in a twenty-year-old book and an unsubstantiated theory won't interest the police. You're going to need to find some solid evidence to put her away.'

Justine wandered to the window, the book dangling from her fingers, and pressed her nose against the glass.

'It's okay, Justine,' said Robert, mustering as much reassurance as he could. 'Don't worry. We'll find her. Then the police can deal with it and we can all get back to normal.'

'But anything – any*one* – could be hiding out there,' said Justine, her voice cracking. 'It's suffocating, isn't it, the darkness?' She placed a hand on Robert's cheek. 'I don't like to admit it, Robbie, but I'm terrified.'

'We all are,' said Hammy, surveying the room. 'Nothing to be ashamed of.'

'Do you think we could...' Justine looked at the group.

For the first time in his life, Robert felt like *he* should be taking care of *her*. The woman's expression was so naive, so childlike. He wanted to hold her and tell her that everything would be fine, that he would make the darkness go away. 'Anything,' he said. 'Just name it. I'll do anything. I got all of you into this mess, after all.'

'Don't start that racket again,' moaned Hammy.

Justine continued, 'It's late anyway. There are blankets. It's warm. Do you think we could stay here tonight ... all five of us? Whenever I close my eyes, all I see are those poor, poor people. I can barely sleep.'

Robert was about to invite Justine to stay at his place instead, but then he realised that he actually preferred her suggestion. There was safety in numbers, not to mention eight huskies in the office. 'The doors are all locked. The bar's more secure than any of our houses, Dad made sure of that. I don't mind staying. What about the rest of you?'

McCrae seemed about to protest but then sat back down on his stool and hunched over his phone. 'At least there's plenty of booze,' he mumbled.

'I'll second that,' said Hammy.

'It'll be fun,' said Eilidh, already gathering some cushions and placing them on the floor. 'Laura can't attack all of us. That would be ridiculous. It's a great idea, Justine.'

Robert noticed that the older woman's eyes were glistening with grateful tears. She moved back to the armchair, sinking low into the fabric as if wishing she could disappear. Yet again, Robert felt a pang of guilt as he saw what he was putting all of them through. He rubbed his eyes and selected the bench beneath the bookshelves as his bed for the night. 'I suppose it's goodnight then,' he said, as cheerily as he could manage.

A chorus of murmurs sounded and he closed his eyes, hoping that the next day would bring some sort of resolution and an end to this fear.

Chapter Twenty-Eight

As Robert regained consciousness, confused did not begin to describe what he felt. He was dragged from oblivion, torn from a nest of black air and thoughtlessness. It took at least a minute for his brain to remember that he had once had a body, although the idea now seemed like a distant fancy. He travelled, weightless, through greyish-brown tunnels, half-acknowledging the echoes that drew him somewhere brighter, more solid. The sounds finally coalesced into something he recognised: the high-pitched, mournful whine of a pack of dogs. But there was another sound, too, one that was far less familiar. He stretched out his fingers. They detected warm, splintered wood. He was on the floorboards. He opened his eyes, panicking briefly about the unexpected heaviness of his eyelids, and scanned the room. It was the bar, but not as he remembered it. He winced as a curdled realisation fought its way to the surface. Deep, thick, suffocating smoke was filling every inch of the Pine Needle.

He tried to take a breath but immediately started to choke. He forced himself into what he thought was a seated position but there was no sense of up, no down, just billowing greys and blacks. The dogs were still whining urgently. Robert shook himself and tried to crawl towards them. 'Eilidh!' he shouted. 'Justine!' His cries turned into a painful cough but he continued to shuffle forwards, covering his mouth and nose with his sleeve. He was overcome by a horrible impulse to burst into tears but then thought he heard faint, muffled groans to his right. Stretching out a hand, he flailed about in obscurity, praying that he might touch flesh. A loud crash sounded somewhere nearby, as if something had fallen from a great height. It was so close that Robert felt the floorboards reverberate. He groaned and rolled onto his side as a sharp, hot object pierced his shin.

'Hammy!' he tried shouting again, this time into the crook of his elbow. 'Brian! Anyone!'

He continued to edge towards the dogs' whimpering, his nose pressed to the floor. After what seemed like an eternity, his hand finally met the skirting board. The bar was howling around him; wood snapped and groaned and swung in the thick darkness. He reached up, turned the handle, and swung open the office door, collapsing inside. The smoke was thinner here, allowing him the small concession of gurgled, wet gasps. The dogs jumped up, barking to be let free, but he slammed the door shut and frantically searched for something to stuff into the gap between it and the floor. Still coughing violently, he attempted to calm the dogs, then fell to the ground. His lungs tightened and throbbed, as if issuing a warning. He wheezed and buried his head into a dog's coat. His senses were beginning to wane; he felt himself being dragged beneath the surface.

'Dad,' he whispered, the word barely more than a rasp. 'Dad, I'm sorry. I'm so sorry. I didn't do it. I couldn't do it.'

He felt his eyelids flutter. The desire to surrender, to fall into the dark, hazy depths, was irresistible. The dogs' barking seemed more distant now. 'I know,' he said, still managing to stroke their heads. 'It's okay, boys.'

Suddenly he felt a sharp nip on his forearm. Then another.

And another. He opened his eyes and blinked at the dog's earnest face. It seemed to be giving him an opportunity to work it out for himself, but when he failed to react it sank its teeth deep into his shoulder and pulled him beneath the desk. The others barked loudly, excitedly, as if in encouragement, then two of them followed him under the desk and started howling, their nostrils flaring, their heads jerking from side to side. Robert's head fell forwards as the smoke from the bar started to creep under the door. The heat was already unbearable. Even the floor was hot to the touch. That's strange, he thought, the office is usually cooler than the rest of the building on account of the...

He eased the howling dogs to the side and immediately felt a cool breeze on his cheek. The dogs pressed their nostrils against the air vent, begging for more of the clean, fresh air.

Robert's vision began to blur at the edges. He rolled his eyes, forcing them to focus, then glanced back towards the door. A deathly orange halo surrounded the frame. Eilidh and the others were probably still inside, yet he had barricaded himself in here. He should have fought harder to save them. The office ceiling creaked ominously and the dogs barked even louder at the vent. Robert himself screamed – a wild, hopeless sound – then lowered himself back beneath the desk. He braced his shoulders against the underside, raised his knees to his chin, and kicked as hard as he could. The vent rattled but didn't buckle. He repeated the motion, then again, charcoal tears streaming down his cheeks. The vent began to loosen. The dogs began to bark excitedly. Robert continued to kick until he heard a crack in the plasterboard wall and felt a sudden gust of cold air beneath the desk. The dogs were already squeezing through the hole.

'Eilidh!' Robert shouted. 'Justine! Hammy!'

He crawled back to the door, but his flesh sizzled as soon as he grabbed the handle. He screamed and jolted backwards. 'Eilidh!' he shouted as he collapsed to the floor. All he could see now were dark, fiery shadows. Everything was shapeless, unformed. He heard a low buzzing somewhere deep within his brain. He found it quite pleasant. He closed his eyes and mouthed Eilidh's, Justine's and Hammy's names. As he heard the sirens, his last thought was that he had let his father down ... again.

❄

'She did it.' Robert was finding it impossible to distinguish between exhaustion and fury. 'I know she did.'

The detective inspector sighed and checked her phone again. 'I understand that you have very strong feelings about this, Mr Begg. But I assure you that every possible line of enquiry has been—'

'She did it,' repeated Robert. 'Laura Stanley. Why aren't you investigating her? She's killed so many—' He started to splutter again, which caused the machine on his left side to beep alarmingly. A nurse hurried into the room and placed a mask over his mouth. Robbed of the ability to speak, Robert continued to eyeball the detective furiously.

She folded her arms, a sympathetic frown forming on her face. 'Brian McCrae was a fantastic detective,' she said eventually. 'One of the best. But he badly misjudged this particular situation, not only by withholding information, but also by leading a group of untrained civilians on a wild goose chase. We are confident we have the killer, Mr Begg. You must relax.'

Robert blinked and tried not to cry.

The detective edged closer to him. 'I know it's difficult...'

He shook his head. She didn't know. How could she possibly know? He had learned that Eilidh was fighting for her life in an equally soulless room, down the soulless corridor. He had left her in the bar to die. The thought sickened him, made him wish that he was in that room instead. Hammy and Justine had somehow made it out with only minor injuries. The dogs' barking had woken Hammy and he had smashed his way through a window. Justine had crawled into the kitchen and passed out there. It was a miracle they both survived.

But then there was Brian McCrae. Robert felt his bottom lip tremble uncontrollably. He remembered the groans he had heard as he had crawled towards the office door, unable to see anything through the thick smoke. He remembered his hands flailing in the darkness, searching for one of his friends. Had it been McCrae's moans he had heard? How close had he been to finding him, saving him? He would never know. His eyelids quivered as he tried to push the fiery scene from his mind. McCrae was gone now. The thought left him feeling empty and hollow.

The detective cleared her throat. 'When you feel up to it, I'll need you to lead me through your meeting with him,' she said gently.

'Who?' mouthed Robert, confused.

'Dr Leonard Stougely,' said the detective patiently. 'You mentioned earlier that you visited his home ... in Wimbledon.'

Robert stared at the ceiling. A crack in the plaster stretched the length of the room. It reminded him of a hiking route on a map, except that this one began and ended nowhere. He remembered the old man's reaction when they had shown up at his door. Stougely had known Robert's name, and that Eilidh wasn't English, even though her accent was impeccable. Why had Robert not questioned *that* more thoroughly? Then there was his gait: drag, pull, shuffle. Robert had heard precisely the same sequence, albeit rather more hurried, in the whisky store. Even the way Stougely had spoken about Laura had been creepy. That should have given him a clue that this was a man who developed enduring obsessions, a man who didn't believe the rules applied to himself. Robert groaned as he realised that, had he been smarter, more competent, sharper, Eilidh would be fine right now. She would be preparing for her big audition in London, laughing, joking. Instead, she was hooked up to horrible, clinical tubes, her breathing regulated by pumps and electronics. He shook his head; he had no words.

The detective glanced at the door, presumably worried that she might be overstepping the mark by questioning such an ill patient. She tried a different tack. 'He clearly had a guilty conscience, Mr Begg. When he realised we'd spotted him, he didn't think twice about making a run for it. I'm just trying to clear up the details. Did he mention Mirabella Rowley at all?'

'Yes,' said Robert, removing the oxygen mask.

'What did he say about her?' She opened a notebook and took a seat next to Robert's hospital bed.

'He was their neighbour, so obviously he knew her.'

'Did he speak highly of her?' She leaned in.

Robert could tell that the detective considered this a significant question, though he couldn't work out why. 'Yes. Why?'

'What did he say?'

Robert closed his eyes and found himself transported back to the elegant road in Wimbledon. The crinkles in Stougely's face that had seemed so friendly, so kind, now resembled duplicitous crevices. 'He thought she was principled ... something like that.'

'So you got the impression that he knew her well?' Her voice was suddenly slightly breathless, eager. She clearly thought that she was onto something.

'Yes, he knew her well enough. And the children. But he was much more interested in discussing Laura. I think they might have been an item. Or at least she made him think—'

The detective interrupted abruptly. 'What's the likelihood he was in a relationship with Mirabella?'

Robert groaned and grimaced in frustration. 'Is that what you think? Why won't you listen to me? I've told you. The Spanish mountaineer met Laura. She was covered in blood. Why aren't you contacting him? She as good as admitted that she had an accomplice. Most likely, that person was Stougely. But now you've gone and run him off the road.'

'Mr Begg,' the detective said sternly, closing her notepad and dropping it in her bag. 'I've told you, we have our killer. Our *one* killer. When we saw him parked up in his car, he panicked, hit the accelerator, and drove straight into the nearest tree. If that's not an admission of guilt, I don't know what is. There was nobody else in the car with him. There was no sign of this Laura person. Please, try to focus on the facts rather than this fiction—'

'It's not fiction,' he shouted. 'And a good job you lot did, hounding him to his death. You can't ask him anything now, can you?' He tried to let out a sardonic laugh but found himself spluttering instead. Irritatingly, the detective passed him the spit tray and patted him on the back as the dark mucus worked its way up from his lungs. He wriggled to the other side of the bed.

After a few moments of silence, the detective sighed and looked him straight in the eye. 'It's over, Mr Begg. Laura Stanley was just the Rowleys' nanny. I believe that Stougely had an affair with Mirabella, but she eventually told him she had no intention of leaving her husband. In a premeditated act of revenge, he killed their daughter, Clara, and framed their son, Toby. He was a deeply troubled man, Mr Begg. He planned and executed a crime that would allow him to watch Mirabella and Anthony suffering, day in and out, possibly for years. Then, more than two decades later, that crime suddenly resurfaced. Maybe Mirabella told him that she was returning to Findrussie.

So he followed her here and murdered her, then turned his attention to anyone else who might come close to revealing that he was Clara's killer.' Her tone softened for a moment. 'I'll admit that I made an error of judgement about Calan Stuart. It's obvious now that Stougely was planning to frame him, just as he had framed Toby. I'll always regret not listening to Brian about that. But I'm not wrong about the rest of this.'

Robert gulped, unable to speak for fear of screaming in her face. He wanted to tell her that McCrae would still be alive were it not for her 'error of judgement'. Instead, in what he hoped was a measured tone, he simply said, 'He couldn't have done it alone. He was old. He had a limp.'

'Sordid motivations often override physical impediments. You learn that soon enough in this job.' She was doing her best to sound convincing, although she avoided Robert's glare as she spoke. 'Anyway, it's over. Stougely's dead. We have a motive and ample proof. There were enough petrol containers in the boot of his car to burn the whole village to the ground, along with traces of Calan's blood and a weapon that was consistent with his wounds. For a doctor, Stougely didn't clean up too well. I'm just glad we stopped him when we did. There was also a suitcase of lethal drugs in his car, along with more doses of the sedatives that knocked you out on the night of the fire. I presume he planned to poison all five of you if the blaze didn't kill you. It's beyond reasonable doubt, Mr Begg.'

'My name's Robert,' he said, suddenly exhausted. He hesitated before asking one last question. 'Do you think he killed my dad? For a while, I thought that Brian...' His voice trailed off into silence.

'Sorry,' she said, with a weak smile. She tapped her lapel with her pen. 'Detective Inspector Melrose. But you can call me Heather.' She seemed to be thinking carefully about whether to answer Robert's question. 'The same thought occurred to me. I looked over the notes relating to your father's death. To my mind, there are no signs of foul play. And there's no evidence of Stougely travelling to Findrussie last October. I suppose the only mystery that remains is why your dad rang Mirabella earlier that day. Any ideas?'

Robert shook his head. He found himself giving in to a great wave that cascaded through his whole body. He was desperate to believe that his dad had not been touched by any of this madness. Desperate to believe that he had died without too much fear. He closed his eyes and replied, 'No. Not a clue. I'm just glad that he died doing something he loved.'

Inspector Melrose let out a deep sigh and rose to her feet. 'Well, if you ever hear of anything, get in touch.'

Something suddenly occurred to him. 'Did you find the black coat?'

She stared at the clock above the door. 'Come again?'

'The CCTV footage from the brewery. Calan's assailant was dressed in black. They stabbed something in his arm and dragged him away.'

'I'm sure Stougely packed a few outfits,' she said casually.

'Wait!'

'It's over, Mr Begg,' she called as she walked through the door, without looking back. 'Try to focus on the future.'

The idea was certainly tempting. Robert studied the crack on the ceiling again and this time noticed that it stretched down the side of the wall and all the way to the window ledge.

Chapter Twenty-Nine

Over the next few weeks, Robert Begg's life took a turn towards what he supposed could be considered normality. Thankfully, both he and – more importantly – Eilidh made full recoveries. She then threw herself into music school applications with a sort of unquenchable enthusiasm. Initially concerned the fire may have damaged her vocal cords, she actually sounded better than ever, not least because she was following Justine's vocal exercises to the letter.

The arrival of spring brought with it lighter mornings and longer days. There was a brief flurry of heavy snow at the beginning of April, but then the chill in the air subsided. Sometimes, as Robert pounded up the slopes of his running route under clear blue skies, he wondered whether the start of the year had been no more than a dark, wintry dream.

Hammy and Justine seemed much the same as ever. They had helped Robert board up the bar so that he could decide what to do with it. The insurance would cover the fire damage, but that wouldn't make the business any more viable. For the time being, it remained a blackened, unused ruin, a burnt monument to what had passed.

Robert spent most of his time reading and running, without much in between. Of course, the question of how to earn a living played on his mind, but at present it was a relief to let life take its course without too much fuss or thought. He barely saw Eilidh at all. He wondered whether she remembered him sitting at her bedside as she recovered, unconscious, in the intensive-care unit. He read to her every day: initially just some random fiction that he had found in the hospital library, but then biographies of famous singers – Joni Mitchell, Aretha Franklin, Dusty Springfield. He was sure that her eyes fluttered with a little more interest whenever he read those aloud.

There was a slightly awkward meeting with Daniel Bell on one of these occasions. The bunch of roses in his hand and his cheeks were an almost identical shade of pink. His eyes widened in horror upon seeing Robert and he garbled a heartfelt apology before backing away to the door. Robert assured him that it was all water under the bridge, which it was: a bit of juvenile vandalism was child's play compared to everything else that had happened. However, he did enquire as to why Daniel was visiting, given that he and Eilidh were no longer an item. 'I just wanted to ... check in on her, you know?' Daniel offered, by way of explanation. Robert nodded briskly and accepted the roses on her behalf. Then, Daniel left without another word.

Those hours sitting by Eilidh's bedside seemed an age away now. It wasn't that Robert didn't want to see her; it just felt like a great, cold abyss had opened up between them. There was a danger of the same chill enveloping his friendships with Hammy and Justine, too, but Hammy clearly had no intention of letting a few murders and a deadly fire get in the way of a good chat. He visited Robert's house most nights, dogs always in tow, a bottle of whisky always in hand. Justine joined them whenever she had the time, though she was working quite a few evening jobs to make up for her lost shifts at the Pine Needle.

It was during one of these late-night visits that Hammy finally brought up the subject that had been festering in Robert's mind for months.

'One more?' Hammy held up his glass and Robert poured carefully, attempting to measure the smallest dram that would not trigger an objection. 'Come on, don't hold back, Robbie. Are you sure you won't join me?'

'I'm running tomorrow,' said Robert. 'And, as you know, I'm off whisky since—'

'Aye, the *fire*,' Hammy cut in, emphasising the word defiantly. He placed his glass on the coffee table and squinted. 'It was unlucky, wasn't it?'

'What's that?'

'That the bottle you chose was the one he'd spiked.'

'Detective Melrose said they took samples from all of the whiskies under the bar. They were *all* spiked. I could have chosen any one of them. It would have had the same effect.'

Hammy leaned back, frowning. 'That's just what I'm getting at, Robbie. How did this Stougely character know where we kept our whisky, the stuff separate from the customers'? How did he know *they* were the bottles to drug?'

'No idea,' said Robert, wishing that they could change the subject. 'But he'd been watching us, hadn't he?'

'Maybe,' said Hammy, unconvinced. 'Then there's the business of Calan.'

'What about Calan?' Robert folded his arms. He didn't want to dissect any of this. He wanted to move forwards, forget, live again. He saw no point in going over the same old details. Nothing good would come of it, he was certain of that. Maybe some questions were just meant to be left unanswered.

'You know what I'm talking about,' said Hammy, visibly frustrated. He stood to look out of the window.

'Yes, I do,' conceded Robert, sighing. He had been

pretending to himself that everything made sense, but Hammy was not so easy to fool. 'The English woman. Calan was terrified of a woman coming back, not a man.'

'Right,' said Hammy, holding out his hands as if he expected Robert to jump up immediately and do something.

'The police have closed the case,' said Robert, wearily. 'I admit there are still a few things I don't understand, but—'

'So, what are we doing about it?' Hammy spun on the spot and glared at him, his hands on his hips.

'Nothing,' said Robert, much more calmly than he had anticipated. 'Maybe it's just better to forget all about it. Better for everyone, I mean. Justine seems almost back to her old self. Remember what she was like at the height of it all? I just want her – and everyone else – to be happy.'

Hammy's face softened as he took a seat on the sofa next to Robert, extending an arm around his shoulders. 'Perhaps you're right,' he said. 'No good going over old ground.'

'Right,' said Robert, though he could still feel the niggles in his head. 'And anyway, nothing bad has happened for months, has it? So ... maybe the police had a point.' He slipped out from under Hammy's grasp and stood. 'You and the dogs are welcome to stay. I'm off to bed.'

'Thanks,' replied Hammy.

He pulled a blanket over his legs, as Robert knew he would. Staying over was becoming a habit. Robert had even invested in some food bowls for the dogs. He was just starting to make his way up the stairs when Hammy called, 'I wonder what Brian would have made of it? Do you think he'd have laid the case to rest?'

Robert shook his head without replying. Deep down, he knew the answer. But Brian McCrae wasn't here to do anything about it, because the Pine Needles had stuck their noses into business that was far too dangerous and complicated for them to handle. Perhaps there was virtue in letting old secrets lie.

❄

Robert couldn't shake Hammy's words on his morning run. There were so many mysteries to be unpicked. For example, why had his father phoned Mirabella rather than the police? And how on earth had he suddenly identified Stougely as the killer more than twenty years after the event? Then there was the invite. How could Stougely have written it on Peter Montgomery's headed notepaper? His feet pounded against the softening ground as he tried to outrun the doubts that continued to whirl around his brain.

For a moment, he thought must be seeing things, that his memory was playing tricks on him again. The blood in his legs seemed to thicken as he came to a halt at the viewing point. Down on the beach, he could see a figure dressed in black. They were staring over the water, holding something in their hands. Robert felt a thudding in his ears. The figure was kneeling very still on the sand. They didn't seem remotely concerned that someone might see them; on the contrary, it was almost as if they were staging a public performance.

Intrigue, rather than fear, carried Robert down the slope to the edge of the forest. He half expected the person to have disappeared by the time he arrived at the beach, but they were in precisely the same position when he emerged from the trees: a motionless figure in a black, hooded coat, kneeling on the sand. There was no reason to suspect them of any wrongdoing. There could be a thousand reasons why they were looking out over the loch. Perhaps they were simply enjoying the solitude and would be annoyed if Robert butted in. He'd almost decided to jog home without disturbing them when a voice made his heart clench in surprise.

'What are you doing standing all the way over there, Robbie? Come and give an old woman some company.'

Robert blinked at the figure who had turned to face him. Justine smiled and raised a glass to the water. Robert took a silent, hesitant step forwards, frowning.

Justine's smile turned instantly to concern. 'What's wrong, Robbie?'

He shook his head and felt the colour returning to his cheeks. Then he let out a howl of laughter and ran towards her. He knelt down beside her and gave her a long, tight hug, pressing his forehead into her shoulder. 'For God's sake, Justine, what are you *doing*? I thought...'

Almost bashfully, she tilted her head towards the loch. 'Your dad and I used to come here,' she said. 'Often before work, sometimes after. We talked through our problems, our triumphs, anything really. And you. We talked a lot about you.' She laughed and Robert noticed that her eyes were moist with tears. 'I've been coming here on my own since ... well, you know. Just for a blether with him, every now and again. We always share a dram, of course.' She nodded at the glass in her hand and another on the cairn. 'Sometimes he answers, sometimes he doesn't.'

Robert was caught between a deep longing to join her communion with his father and the humour of the situation. 'For crying out loud, Justine. I thought you were the hooded figure.'

'You what?' She frowned at him, concerned again.

'Look at your coat.' He laughed and tugged at the quilted hood. 'It must have been you I saw here before Burns Night. I thought ... well, I don't know what I thought. But I ended up in the loch. Hammy had to rescue me.'

'What?' Justine repeated. She was standing now, her voice shrill. 'In January? Robbie, no, you could have—'

'It's okay,' Robert reassured her, chuckling. 'I told Hammy not to tell you or Eilidh. Thought you'd think I'd gone mad.'

'You're not wrong there,' said Justine.

'But this black coat. When we saw that figure on the CCTV footage wearing something similar—'

'You thought it must be the person you'd seen by the loch?' Justine finished the sentence for him. She sighed and ruffled his hair. 'Coats like this aren't exactly uncommon up here in the winter, Robbie. You've got one yourself.'

Robert felt extremely stupid. No wonder Inspector Melrose had shown no interest in the coat.

Justine seemed to notice his discomfort. 'Focus on what you *did* find out. The police would never have found Stougely without your help. Come on, sit here.'

Justine perched on a rock and Robert joined her. The loch was less beautiful in the springtime. The diamond-like clarity of winter had disappeared. It was greener now, murkier. 'To Bennie!' said Justine, raising her glass again. 'Forever in our hearts. And Brian...' She looked over the water.

Robert took the other glass from the cairn and sniffed. 'Peaty,' he said. 'I should have realised it was you.'

'My favourite,' said Justine, nodding firmly. 'Your dad was a fan, too.' She turned to the water again. 'Your son's done you proud, Bennie, that's for sure. He's done us all proud.' She clinked her glass with Robert's.

After a few seconds of silence, he said, 'I think we should reopen the bar.'

'Oh?' Justine raised her eyebrows, though her smile suggested she had been waiting for this moment for a while.

'It's the right thing to do,' said Robert. 'It's what Dad would've wanted and ... well, with the insurance money covering all of the repairs, it's an opportunity to get the Pine Needle back on its feet. It'll take some work, but I think I'm ready.'

'Good to hear,' said Justine, kicking her feet with glee. 'When do you want to start?'

'No time like the present,' said Robert. A sensation he had almost forgotten began to glow within his chest. 'I'll make a start today. See what I can salvage from the fire.'

'Sounds good to me.' Justine whooped loudly and the sound echoed around the loch. 'I'll let Hammy know and...'

Robert noticed the sly look on her face. 'What?'

'Eilidh will probably—'

'No, Justine,' said Robert firmly. 'She's got her auditions to think about. She won't be interested in working at the bar any more.'

'You've asked her, have you?'

Robert didn't reply. Instead, he shook his head and began stretching.

'Well, I'll leave that to you to sort out,' said Justine. 'You're a grown man, after all. What do I know?'

Robert waved goodbye as he jogged back to the forest path, relieved she had taken the hint.

❄

There was no denying the bar had been damaged beyond belief. Thankfully, the building was still structurally sound, but all of the furniture had been lost in fire, the walls were stained with thick sludge, and Robert couldn't imagine how they'd ever get rid of the acrid smell of smoke. As he threw open the windows, he thought he heard McCrae's final moans pulsing from the charred walls. He clenched his jaw and looked around the bar determinedly, but the scene was dire. He carefully picked up a blackened glass from the floor, half expecting it to be hot, and placed it on what was left of the countertop. Although not broken, the glass was cracked. Robert flicked it with the tip of a finger and listened to the vibrations in the chalky air.

He placed his palms on the bar then immediately realised his mistake. Every surface was coated in the same oily, black substance. Sighing, he wiped his hands on his trousers and made for the kitchen to grab some cleaning products. He let out another sigh as he opened the door. The kitchen was in an even worse state than the main bar area: all of the cabinets and cupboards were charred and seared, their contents no more than ugly lumps of melted plastic and broken crockery. He berated himself under his breath and stood hopelessly for a few moments, considering the enormity of the task ahead. Nevertheless, he had a strong urge to clean *something* – no matter how small – right then, before heading to the shops to buy the necessary materials. Shaking his head, he made his way to the office, where he was sure he would find some cloths, if nothing else.

Amazingly, the office had been largely untouched by the fire, although there was no escaping the bitter taste of smoke. Robert had convinced his father they needed to keep electronic records, so it had been years since the old filing cabinet in the corner had been used for its original purpose. He started to open the bottom drawer and, to his relief, saw a few packets of J-cloths. But the drawer jammed. He tried to squeeze his wrist through the narrow gap, but it was no good: he couldn't even reach the materials he needed to begin the clear-up. He kicked the cabinet, his cheeks glowing with frustration. The metal clanged in response, as if mocking him, so he kicked it again, holding it with both hands as it shook. With a soft, unexpected clunk, the drawer slid open and fell to the floor. As he reached in, he saw what had caused the drawer to jam – a ring binder at the base of the cabinet. He sat back on his heels and retrieved it. It was plain and black, with no labels. Opening it, he flicked absently through the contents: printouts, photocopies, scribbled notes and photographs, all neatly arranged in frosted plastic sleeves. After a few seconds, he pulled one of the photos from its sleeve. He stared at it in stunned amazement: Laura Stanley, no doubt about it.

Robert worked his way quickly through the folder, pulling out each item in turn, then returning it carefully to its designated sleeve. All the notes were in his father's distinctive handwriting. The final page was a list of dates, a timeline:

1986/7?: Starts working for the Rowleys

1990: Visits Kinlogie on holiday with the family

1992 [highlighted]: Stops working for the Rowleys

December 2000: Rowleys visit Kinlogie for the final time

Robert flicked back to the first page and started to study the contents in greater detail. He struggled to understand all of the scribbled notes, addresses, question marks and marginalia, but he was sure of one thing: his dad clearly suspected Laura Stanley of Clara's murder.

The folder suddenly felt very heavy in Robert's hands. He placed it back where he'd found it, at the bottom of the filing cabinet, then slid the drawer into place. He reckoned his father must have had a very good reason to keep it secret and he was happy to follow suit, especially given all that had happened over the last few months.

'Robbie?' Hammy called from the bar. 'You in there?'

Robert grabbed the J-cloths and emerged from the office.

'There he is!' Justine was holding a mop and bucket, Marigolds already on her hands, raring to go. 'Ready to work up a bit of elbow grease, then?'

'I know I am.' Eilidh walked through the doorway. She was wearing overalls. 'Lucky *someone* remembered to invite me to the party...'

Justine cleared her throat noisily as Robert glowered at her. Then he turned to Eilidh and mumbled, 'I thought you were busy...'

'I'm perfectly capable of managing my own time, thank you very much.' She threw a soapy sponge at his face. 'And I choose to be here.'

Robert smiled as soap suds dripped down his cheeks, a gulp forming in his throat. 'That's ... well, thanks, Eilidh.'

'Right!' Hammy shouted, dipping his sponge into the bucket. 'Where do we begin? Looks like we've got our work cut out.'

'It's no bother,' said Justine. 'I'd take cleaning over crime fighting any day of the week.'

Chapter Thirty

Two weeks into the clean-up and the Pine Needle was already looking more like its old self, or even slightly better. Hammy had used some old barrels to build the base of the new bar, while Eilidh was painting a mural behind the stage area – pints, wine glasses and whisky tumblers rising from flickering orange flames. In one corner she'd added a gleaming police badge with McCrae's name written beneath it.

'Too much?' she asked Robert, standing back to admire her work.

'No,' he said. 'It's perfect.'

'We'll have a new specials board soon,' she said, nodding to the porch area where Hammy was working, surrounded by his dogs. 'He's framing it with some of the damaged floorboards; I think it'll look pretty cool. I like the idea of embracing the fire. Shows we're not afraid of anything.'

Justine was working her way through the Hogmanay photographs. Fortunately, most of the pictures seemed to have emerged unscathed, with only the frames damaged by the fire. Robert nudged her as he walked past, a crate of bottles in his hands. 'It'll feel just like old times when they're all reframed and back on the wall.'

'Aye,' said Justine, clipping another picture into its new frame. 'Wouldn't be the same without them.'

Hammy burst through the door, dragging the new specials board behind him. 'Where do you want this, Robbie?'

Robert rushed to help him hang the board on the wall next to the office.

'Looks good,' squealed Eilidh, clapping her hands. 'I reckon we're almost there.'

'Me too,' said Justine, spinning in a circle. 'Robbie, when do you think we can open?'

He shrugged and looked around the bar. 'We'll need to put a food order in, but most of the drinks are already stocked. We're just waiting on the casks I've ordered from Liam and Sammy. I suppose we could put the word out that we'll be opening next week.'

They all cheered and Hammy gave Justine a little spin. 'Well done us,' he said, pulling out a piece of chalk and handing it to her. 'Do the honours then, Justine. This board needs a title.'

Laughing, Justine took the chalk and Robert held her hand as she stood on a chair to christen the new specials board. She looked down at him, smiling, and announced, 'It's a fresh start, Robbie.' He watched her head tilt this way and that as she wrote the message. Then she gripped his arm and jumped down from the chair. 'Right, I think this calls for a celebratory drink.'

'Took the words right out of my mouth,' cried Hammy.

'Wouldn't say no,' agreed Eilidh.

But Robert found himself rooted to the spot. He couldn't tear his eyes from Justine's message. There was something strangely familiar about it, especially the words 'Family Favourites'. He took a step back and held his breath as he felt a sharp twang deep within his chest.

'What are you drinking, Robbie?' Justine asked. 'I think there's a bottle of Prosecco somewhere.'

Robert jumped when he heard the pop, then struggled to maintain a façade of calm as Justine handed him a glass. 'To the Pine Needles,' she declared.

Hammy and Eilidh echoed her words, let out a loud cheer and clinked glasses.

The sharp sound crawled over Robert's skin like insects. He avoided Justine's gaze, though he was sure she was studying him. Trying his best to appear normal, he took a tiny sip of his drink.

'Everything okay?' asked Hammy with a nudge.

'Yes, yes,' replied Robert, a little too quickly. 'Just excited.' He tried to compose himself and forced out a laugh. 'But you know what? In keeping with tradition, I think I'll disappear to the office for a few minutes. Might as well get on with the admin. It's got to be done some time.'

'Not now though, surely?' said Eilidh, frowning. 'Can't it wait?'

'No, I really must...' He was already making his way to the door, his chest tightening with every step. 'There are just a couple of things.'

'Need any help?'

He jumped at the sound of Justine's voice but then turned and forced his mouth into a wide grin. 'Just enjoy yourselves.' He didn't wait for a reply. Instead, he slipped through the office door, closed it and leaned back against the wood as he tried to regulate his breathing. The words were still fresh in his mind: 'Family Favourites'. He had seen 'family' written in precisely the same way before. He wrenched open the top drawer of the desk and fumbled around for the invitation that Eilidh had pocketed during their meeting with Felicity Montgomery. There it was:

I trust you and the family are well. The Montgomerys cordially invite you to spend Christmas and Hogmanay with them at Kinlogie.

The 'f' was rendered as an elaborate volute, which meant it resembled an 's' – just like the first letters of the two words on the specials board.

'Robbie!'

Footsteps were approaching the office. Robert shoved the invite back in the drawer and ran over to the door, throwing his weight against it, berating himself for neglecting to lock it earlier. The handle rattled.

'What are you up to in there?' asked Justine. 'Come out and join the celebrations.'

Robert blinked as hot and itchy tears formed in the corners of his eyes. 'I'll be out in a minute, Justine,' he said, sliding the bolt discreetly to the right. 'Just got a few things to—'

She knocked sharply. 'We want to do another toast, Robbie.'

He backed away from the door, tiptoed to the filing cabinet and pulled out the bottom drawer to retrieve the folder. He flicked through the plastic sleeves until he came across the first photograph of Laura. It was the family portrait in which the Rowleys were posing in front of Kinlogie House in 1990. He raised it close to his face and squinted at Laura's profile. He couldn't be sure, but there was definitely a resemblance.

'Just let me in, Robbie.' Justine's voice was shrill, pleading.

'One second, Justine.' He looked through the rest of the folder until he found another photograph. This one was a theatrical headshot of Laura Stanley, dated 1984. He studied the black-and-white image closely, half-hoping he would see nothing familiar in the youthful face. But there was the long, slender nose, slightly upturned at the end. The high forehead, too. The young woman in the picture was blonde, but it was easy enough to dye hair and maintain the new colour for years, even decades ... as long as you never missed an appointment at the hairdresser's. He read his father's scrawled note underneath the photograph:

> *1984 production of Medea, Conway Hall, Holborn.*
> *Laura Stanley played the lead: Medea.*

Robert swayed as a wave of nausea hit him. He knew he must think quickly and clearly. His hands sweating, he placed the folder back in the cabinet. 'Just coming,' he said. He needed to calm himself before letting her in.

He started to recite his animals – it was a 'C' day – but his lips froze over the word 'caterpillar'. Another child, another young boy, had been taught how to self-soothe. He recalled Mr Stougely telling him that Laura had calmed Toby's tantrums by teaching him a counting method she had learned in drama school. Robert began to shake. They had shared the same teacher, albeit more than a decade apart. Yet, it didn't make any sense. How could Justine be Laura? Justine was kind. Justine was his friend, his protector. He had to be mistaken.

'Robert, open this door this instant. You're starting to worry me.' Justine's voice was firm and blunt.

He looked around the office in a desperate search for an alternative explanation. This surely couldn't be. It was ... it was too much to take in.

Justine banged on the door so vehemently that the hinges rattled. 'Robert Begg. Open ... this ... door.'

Robert gathered himself, unsure of what else he could do, and forced himself to stand straight. He opened the door wide, his face arranged in as serene an expression as he could manage. 'Sorry, Justine, I'm feeling a bit under the weather.'

Her eyes narrowed as she looked past him, towards the desk. '*Under the weather?*' she repeated. 'How so?'

'Oh, you know. It's been a long day...' His voice trailed off as her eyes continued to stare at the desk. 'But you're right. Let's have another toast.' He made to squeeze past her, but she blocked him with her arm. He laughed nervously and suddenly realised the bar was strangely quiet.

'Doing some paperwork?' Justine asked, nodding towards the drawer.

Robert met her eyes without blinking. 'Yes, I told you I had a couple of things to sort out. Where are—'

'Sent them to the brewery to fetch the beer,' Justine interrupted. 'They'll be a while.'

Robert felt his heartbeat quicken erratically. He motioned to walk past her again, but she kicked the door shut neatly. This close to her, Robert could smell the strange, citrusy aroma he had first noticed on Burns Night. He took a step back to create some space between them and wondered what Justine might have been cooking.

She flashed her best smile, although it was sicklier than Robert remembered, and grabbed him by the elbow to guide him towards the drawer. 'Show me what's been taking you so long, then,' she said, still gripping his arm firmly.

Robert gazed at the drawer. He had placed the invite on top of a pile of documents. If Justine opened it, she would surely realise he had recognised her handwriting. He pulled himself away from her and chuckled, probably a little too loudly. 'Come on, the Prosecco's waiting...'

Her expression changed in a split second. It was in that moment Robert understood why the Spanish mountaineer had mistaken her for a supernatural being. He had never seen anything like the look in her eyes. It was sharp, ludicrously intent, as if, by some dark force, she could read his mind, sense his fears, stifle his dreams. 'Such a shame,' she said, licking her lips daintily. 'You look just like your father did when he finally realised, you know. They call it an anagnorisis in the theatre.'

Robert flinched at the sudden transformation of her voice. The familiar gravelly intonation had disappeared. Instead, she was speaking with a cut-glass southern English accent. 'What was it?' She pulled open the drawer and let out a small laugh. 'Of course, the invite. Silly, silly me.' She placed her hands on her hips and tutted, slowly, luxuriously.

Her face no longer resembled anything Robert recognised. She was holding herself differently, her shoulders more open, her chin more defiant. She seemed younger, too, more vibrant. 'Justine...'

She shook her head as a smirk formed on her lips, her eyes glittering.

'Laura,' he said, as if to confirm what he already knew. Saying it aloud caused him to tremble. 'You're Laura Stanley. You...'

'Yes.' She said the word with unmistakable pride. 'You're right, Robert.' She was eerily calm, displaying the infinite patience of someone who knew she was in complete control.

Robert realised he would have only one chance to escape. In that instant, he barged past her and threw himself towards the door. He fumbled desperately at the bolt and scrambled into the bar, knocking over furniture as he went. He reached the front door and was halfway to turning the handle when Justine's voice – *his* Justine's voice – called out, 'Robbie, please, wait. I can explain.'

Instinct, habit, caused him to hesitate at the threshold. Then he felt the blunt force on the back of his skull. He crashed to the floor, coming to rest between Justine's feet, and surrendered to the spinning world.

Chapter Thirty-One

Findrussie, 31 December 2000

Clara Rowley blew cigarette smoke into the icy snow as it continued to sting her face. She folded her arms across her midriff and marched towards the house. She was struggling to identify the emotion she was feeling. Anger? Disbelief? Incredulity? The thought that someone like Calan Stuart might think *she* would marry *him*. She couldn't wait to tell her friends in Wimbledon about it. She let out a shrill giggle as a powerful gust of wind almost blew her off her feet. Slapping a hand over her mouth, she continued to laugh as she caught her breath.

It was flattering, of course. And Calan had clearly gone to some trouble. That ring must have cost him – what? – at least a few months of whatever he earned selling his gear. But what did he think she would do? Break down in tears, slip it on her finger and promise to move to Findrussie to be with him? She stopped outside the bar. They'd all be traipsing over here later, pretending they were happy, or at least festive. With a bit of luck, Toby might share some of his 'synthetic happiness' with her.

Her friends in Wimbledon would be in the pub right now, tricking strangers to buy them booze, already getting tipsy on jugs of cocktails. Why her parents wanted to come up here to stay with that weird couple was beyond her. The summers had been pleasant enough, when she was a kid at least, but she'd always hated the winters. The ski slopes weren't exactly the Alps. The weather wasn't just wintry; it was brutal. She looked around and muttered that even the locals couldn't stand it: she was the only person on the street. The sooner they could leave, the better. The last thing she wanted was Calan turning up at the house and making a scene. Her mother would kill her, even though she was pretty sure she would have gone for exactly the same type back in the day ... just for a bit of fun.

A shout from the bar's porch suddenly distracted Clara from her reverie. She looked up to see a chunky, red-haired woman waddling towards her. 'Clara? Clara Rowley? Is that you? It's me ... Laura.'

Clara's mouth fell open as she recognised the voice, if nothing else. 'Oh my God!' She threw her arms around her old au pair. The smell of her neck brought back a rush of childhood memories. 'What have you done to your hair?' It seemed a better option than asking about the weight gain.

'Like it?' Laura patted her new hairdo.

In truth, Clara much preferred Laura as a blonde, but she nodded and grinned. 'It's gorgeous. Very ... bold ... and festive!'

Laura laughed and held Clara's cheeks between her hands. 'You've turned into such a beautiful young woman. I can't believe it. How long has it been? Eight years?'

'I think so.' The question made Clara feel a little awkward. She remembered nobody in the house had been allowed to mention Laura's name after she left. She had always assumed she must have done something very wrong. As she'd grown older, she'd reached the conclusion the thing in question had probably been her father. Of course, she'd never sought confirmation. 'Daddy's just Daddy,' as her mother always said.

'Listen,' Laura continued, excitedly. 'I can't stop now, but I'd love to catch up, hear how you've been doing. I'm sure you have plenty of stories to tell.'

'Oh, I don't know about that...'

'Come on, Clara, don't give me that. A girl like you. I'd love to hear how you've been getting on. I always loved looking after you.'

Again, Clara shifted uncomfortably on the spot. She remembered loving Laura so much as a child, but right now she seemed rather odd, standing there all alone in this cold, isolated village. Indeed, Clara couldn't help wondering what she was doing there. 'Are you here on holiday?'

'Yes!' Laura's answer was shrill. 'I always enjoyed those summers at Kinlogie so I decided to make the trip, but I never dreamed I would see you up here in the middle of winter.'

Clara suspected that Laura knew very well that the whole family was there. All of a sudden, her once-glamorous childhood role model seemed a pathetic shadow of her former self. Didn't she have a life of her own? Her own places to visit? The one thing her family didn't need was one of her father's old lovers showing up on New Year's Eve. 'Well!' she said brightly. 'It was lovely to bump into—'

'When would you like to meet up?' Laura's voice reeked of desperation.

Clara held her smile as steady as she could and met Laura's eye, looking down her nose for good measure. 'I'm afraid I'm busy with the family, what with it being New Year. You know how it is.'

'Ah.' Laura looked at her feet. 'I see. I understand. Of course.' She seemed close to tears. 'How silly of me to put you in such an awkward position. I was just staff, after—'

'No,' Clara interrupted.

'It's fine, Clara. Really.' Laura squeezed her hand and flashed a pained smile. 'It was just so nice to see you, little one, that's all.'

Clara's head jerked up. She had always loved being Laura's 'little one'. Every night, when Laura tucked her in, she would say, 'Nighty night, little one, little friend, ray of sun.' Clara would howl with laughter and practise her own rhymes. She'd forgotten how much she had shared with this woman, and now all Laura wanted was a little of her time. 'Well, we're all coming here, to this pub, before dinner,' she said, nodding at the building behind Laura. '*All* of us,' she emphasised, just so there could be no doubt.

'Understood,' said Laura. 'How about a secret rendezvous after dinner, then? The last thing I'd want to do is cause you any trouble with your parents, Clara. You're staying at Kinlogie?'

'Yes, as always. Err, sure. Do you have somewhere in mind?'

'You know, I have the perfect place.' Laura clapped her hands, already excited at the prospect of their meeting.

Clara was pleased to see that she'd brought her a bit of festive cheer.

'It's not far from the house, actually. Do you know the Ryvune bothy at the edge of the estate? Why don't you bring Toby along, too? I'd love to see him. Give us a chance to address some old grievances.'

Clara Rowley momentarily thought this was an odd thing to say, but she didn't ponder it too much. As she made her way down the Kinlogie Road, she realised she had something of a bounce in her step. A proposal and a blast from the past in the space of a couple of hours. This trip was turning out to be more exciting than she had expected.

Chapter Thirty-Two

Robert groaned as his throbbing head rolled forwards onto his chest. He tried to wipe his mouth with his hands but found them impossible to move. He blinked at his lap and realised he was bound to a chair. He was still in the bar. 'Help,' he tried in a weak, husky voice.

'I wouldn't bother.' Laura's voice came from behind him.

Unable to turn his head, Robert heard her dragging another chair so she could sit facing him.

'I sent Hammy and Eilidh home for the night,' she said matter-of-factly. 'I told them you were busy with the accounts and didn't want to be disturbed. There's nobody around to hear you.'

Heavy rain pounded on the roof of the bar. Robert's heart sank as he realised no one would hear him scream over it, even if they happened to be passing, which was unlikely. Nevertheless, he blinked at Laura and screamed, 'Let me go!'

'I'm afraid I can't do that, Robert,' said Laura. She crossed her legs and watched him with great curiosity. She moved fluidly, with occasional tiny flourishes: the flick of finger, the turn of a wrist. The hooded figure who had abducted Calan had injected him with a similarly graceful movement. Laura sighed and leaned backwards. 'You know, I wish you had just left it alone. I didn't want it to come to this.'

Robert swore loudly as he squirmed in the chair, writhing against the ropes. Finally giving in, he stopped struggling and looked at her. 'You don't care about anyone,' he said. 'Stop pretending.'

'Now, Robert.' Her eyes widened. It was unclear whether she was mocking him or genuinely hurt. 'That's not true. I care about you. I cared about Bennie.'

'Don't!' Robert looked miserably at his shoes and allowed his tears to drip onto the floorboards. He didn't want her to see him cry. He shook his head, then raised it to meet her eye, hoping that the fury in his heart was visible in his face. 'It was you. You killed him. You killed my dad.'

Laura stood abruptly and turned her back to him. If he hadn't known better, he would have thought she was weeping, too. Her shoulders shuddered and she sniffed. Talking to the wall, she said, 'He was too generous, that was his problem.'

Robert didn't reply. Instead, he watched her walk slowly towards the Hogmanay pictures she had reframed and rehung only a few hours earlier. She traced a finger around one of the frames.

'Nineteen ninety-two,' she said. 'Nothing particularly special about that year. Unless, of course, you know it was the year when Laura Stanley stopped working for the Rowleys and disappeared forever. And, of course, unless you are already questioning the identity of your trusted cleaner. Do you have any idea how difficult it was to gain all this weight, Robbie?' She grabbed her stomach and made a sound that wavered somewhere between disgust and amusement. 'I had to make sure no one would recognise me. I evolved, you might say. I needed to fester here until I could be sure no one would suspect the old nanny. My God, the patience required...' She spun suddenly, making Robert yelp in surprise. 'He shouldn't have tried to help me, Robbie.' She was speaking in Justine's voice again. 'I was fine. I didn't need shares in this place, I told him that. He shouldn't have stuck his nose into my business. He started to ask all sorts of questions, you know? How could I afford my flat on my wages? Where had I worked before arriving in Findrussie? Had I ever considered another career? Why was I working as a cleaner when I was obviously as sharp as a tack? His suspicions increased. I smelled them. But he didn't put two and two together until he accidentally knocked *this* Hogmanay photo off the wall. I watched him pick it up. It was like he'd seen a ghost. The ghost of Laura Stanley in a photo taken just months after she had disappeared. He'd already been researching her, you see. I'd caught him Googling her name a few weeks earlier. I suppose he remembered her from all of those Rowley family holidays with the Montgomerys in the eighties and early nineties. She was quite memorable, after all,' she said with a smile. 'But then, from 1992 onwards, it had just been the Rowleys. No more Laura. It must have seemed strange to him.'

She paused and looked intently at Robert.

'I really didn't want to kill him, I promise you that. Still, I steeled myself, just in case. After he saw the photo, he tried to pretend everything was normal, excused himself and rushed to the office. I followed him, saw him make a call. I assumed he was phoning the police, so I had to stop him, I had no choice, you understand? He forced my hand, Robbie. I never wanted to hurt him. He was such a great man ... and a dear, dear friend. It was only when I saw the open visitors' book that I realised he'd been trying to phone Mirabella. I suppose he thought she'd listen to whatever he had to say, whereas the police would probably dismiss him as a deluded crackpot. Clever, really. But she never picked up.'

'So, you killed him?' Robert repeated. The longer he could keep her talking, the better. He had already been wriggling his wrists, stretching the ropes behind his back, for the past five minutes.

'I had to.' Justine had transformed herself back into Laura. Her voice was clear and sharp. 'Although I never meant to. I'm no serial killer. The children had to die; that was unavoidable. It was the only way to harm Anthony irreparably. I had to inflict the same amount of pain he had inflicted on me.'

'Inspired by that play?' Robert loosened the ropes a little more and managed to squeeze a finger between the resulting gap in the knot.

'Ha!' Laura clapped her hands in delight. 'Yes, Robert. Well spotted. One exacts revenge by destroying the things the other loves the most. Brutal, isn't it? Wonderfully brutal. You know, I thought it might be a bit self-indulgent to press ahead with the production, especially with Mirabella sniffing around, but, as ever, she was so self-absorbed that she didn't notice a thing. Barely deigned to glance at the fat, old cleaner. That's the trouble with people like her – they're *entitled*, Robert. They exist only in their own little world.' She flashed Robert a smile and became Justine again, but only for a split second. 'I enjoyed toying with her, standing right next to her, while she was so, so ... unaware. Is that awful? But I never meant to kill again. This has all been so ... *unfortunate*.' She threw her hands in the air and sat opposite him once more. 'I tried to warn you off. God knows I tried.' She looked to the ceiling, then traced her gaze slowly down Robert's face. 'When Leonard killed Calan, I allowed myself to believe he'd finally managed to draw a line under it all. I thought he'd gifted me my freedom again.'

'He was your accomplice,' Robert said. He kept his eyes

locked on Laura's even as his wrists continued to strain against the ropes behind his back. 'Leonard Stougely. He supported you financially when you left London. Helped you change your identity. Carried on helping you for decades. You warned him we were heading to the whisky store, didn't you? Told him he had to kill Calan.'

'He was an old idiot,' Laura said with disdain. 'But that was precisely what I needed. Every Medea needs an Aegeus, like in the play – a sponsor, a fool she can manipulate, a safety-net. It's all there in the play. It's how she gets away with murder. Leonard was the perfect Aegeus. I noticed him ogling me when I was still working for the Rowleys and sensed an opportunity. I needed someone to set a few false trails down in London until I became established as Justine up here. I'd already tested his morals as his patient. It didn't take him long to make the first move, believe me. I could have threatened to inform the General Medical Council he had touched me inappropriately. That might have worked for a while, but I knew I needed him for the long haul. So I decided to use desire rather than fear; convinced him we'd end up together if he did everything I said. Although, I must admit, I never thought he would still be doing my bidding thirty years later.'

'Like stringing up Mirabella in a tree? Mowing down an old lady? Killing my dad?' Robert tried to remain calm but he could feel the anger and pain rising again. His voice was shaking and shrill. 'You got him to set fire to this bar with all of us in it.'

'Yes, all of that.' Laura waved a dismissive hand in the air. 'The bar was the most difficult one,' she continued, as if suddenly struck by guilt. 'But you were getting so close. I granted you the kindness of sleeping through it, though, didn't I? I never dreamed you'd wake up, Robert. You must have been terrified.'

'You drugged us.' Robert felt his legs begin to shake. 'You wanted us all to die. You planned it.'

She nodded, smiling, seemingly pleased that he had fully understood. 'I didn't know you'd wake up so soon,' she said, 'but Leonard miscalculated the doses. I told you, he was an old fool. Thankfully, he couldn't even make a proper escape – crashing his car! – so he became the perfect scapegoat. As I said, he had his uses. Oh...' she shrieked gleefully as if a thought had suddenly occurred to her. 'It was so exciting to hear my walker friend from all those years ago remembered me. To think that I had such a big impact on him and never knew it. But you see, Robert, that was when I knew you had to burn. I had no choice. You were just so ... *persistent*. I suppose we have that in common.'

She sighed deeply and rolled her eyes, then removed a small syringe from her pocket. She gave it three quick taps and held it in front of Robert's face. 'This won't hurt, Robert, I promise. It's the same stuff as I gave your dad. Luckily for him, he had the benefit of not knowing what was coming. A quick prick to the neck and ... well, you'll see...'

He exhaled through his mouth and desperately tried to think of more questions to ask. 'Hang on! What about the ring? The one Brian gave to Mirabella. Why did you remove it from her body? What was the point in that?'

Laura chuckled. 'Oh yes, the ring. I enjoyed seeing that wild goose chase unfold, I must admit. It was an accident, Robert. The stupid thing came off in my hand when we were fighting and I just tossed it into the woods. Careless, of course, in hindsight. But who knew Hammy's dogs were so eagle-eyed? Anyway, it all played to my advantage in the end. You suspected Brian McCrae for quite some time, didn't you?'

Robert gave up trying to escape surreptitiously and shook the chair with all his might, pressing his limbs as hard as he could against the ropes. Laura ignored him and readied the syringe. 'What is that?' he murmured quietly as she placed a steadying hand against his neck.

'Succinylcholine,' she said gently. 'Keep still, please, Robert. This is Leonard's last gift to me. It's untraceable, you see. They never found a drop of it in your dad's blood. It relaxes the muscles, paralyses the whole body. I'll carry you to the loch after dark. It will be poetic. Like father, like son, in death. I'll place some rocks in your pockets. The story will be that you wanted to die like Bennie. The mounting pressure of reopening the bar became too much. Eilidh and Hammy will confirm that you seemed distant, moody, when you locked yourself in the office. It's all okay, Robert. It's all okay.'

She stroked his hair reassuringly, as she had when he was a child, but he let out a scream and flung himself to the side, so that he and the chair crashed to the floor. He tasted blood in his mouth and spat out a tooth, groaning.

Laura placed a hand on his ribs and rocked him gently. 'Shhh,' she said. 'Robert, shhh. It's over.'

Robert felt the prick of the needle as it entered his neck. The fluid was ice-cold in his veins.

'Let it settle,' Laura whispered into his ear.

The liquid spread throughout his body, numbing his limbs, rendering him completely vulnerable. She gave him a lingering kiss on the cheek, and once again he smelled that odd, citrusy aroma. He stared blankly at the bottom shelf of the bar, unable even to turn his head.

For a moment, he thought the sound of the door banging open must be a figment of his imagination. However, if that were true, there would have been no reason for Laura to spring to her feet. The voices were muffled, and he listened with no more than vague interest. He was more concerned with the fact he was dribbling profusely onto the floorboards. He idly wondered whether the drug would kill him before she put him in the loch. His heart seemed to be beating at a very slow and lazy rate.

There was a sudden, loud crash from somewhere in the room. Someone called his name. Dogs barked. He imagined responding, telling whoever it was that Justine was Laura and that most of his childhood and all of his adult life had been a lie, but he was just ... so ... tired. Nothing really mattered any more. He seemed to float in mid-air. It felt like the most natural thing in the world. He watched his static body below. He looked so small and helpless from such a great height. But who else was in the room? Blue lights filled the space. That was strange. Robert had always imagined that he would move towards a *white* light. He heard a loud rattling, then realised it must be his own breathing. Blue, it turned out, was a fine colour on which to end.

Epilogue

Hammy's eyes were red and puffy as he brought the tray over to Eilidh. Robert was lying on the couch, a deep purple bruise covering the right side of his face. His wrists still felt raw. He took a mug gratefully.

'Can't believe it, even now,' Hammy said. 'You're sure you're all right? A couple of nights seems a bit soon.'

'It's a couple of nights too many in that hospital,' said Robert. 'And I'm still struggling to believe it, too.'

'She's just ... gone,' said Eilidh.

'She never existed,' replied Robert. 'Laura, however, will be locked up for the rest of her life.'

Eilidh looked like she was about to say something else but she settled on letting the steam from her tea warm her face.

'How did you know?' Robert asked them both. 'Why did you come back?'

Hammy raised his eyebrows and looked at Eilidh, who nodded. 'It started to rain just after Justine told us to go and fetch the beer. Eilidh wanted to wait for you, but Justine insisted it was urgent and gave us her umbrella. The thing is, the dogs couldn't get enough of it. As soon as I walked out of the bar, they were sniffing it, barking, the whole works. It reminded me of how they'd behaved around Felicity Montgomery ... and when they found Mirabella's ring.'

'I noticed it too,' said Eilidh. 'They'd definitely picked up a scent.'

'Aye. Now, obviously, I didn't think it meant anything sinister, but it got my juices flowing, so to speak. I thought it was worth finding out where that umbrella had been. I still thought there were a few bits and bobs we'd not cleared up, as you know. I meant to ask her about it when we arrived back with the beer kegs, but she was in such a rush to get rid of us I never got the chance. I guess you were already unconscious by then, Robbie.'

'Probably,' said Robert, rubbing his wrists.

'Anyway, I got home, started to make my dinner, but something just didn't seem quite right. I kept thinking back to Felicity's house and how the dogs wouldn't leave the poor woman alone. Then I remembered who was standing next to Felicity the whole time. Justine! I told myself to get a grip because ... well, I thought Justine was a good friend, you know? But the dogs were still sniffing the umbrella and I couldn't let it go. I needed to know whether it was Justine's or not. So, I tried her flat. Nobody home, which was unusual. Then, on my way back here, I see the lights are on in the bar. The rest, as they say, is history.'

'The scent!' Robert sat up too quickly, almost spilling his tea.

'What do you mean?' asked Eilidh.

'Your dogs have good hearing and an excellent sense of smell, don't they?'

'Definitely,' Hammy nodded. 'My dogs are the most intelligent around.'

Robert nodded, finally understanding. 'We thought they were barking at Felicity in her cabin, but it was Justine, you're right Hammy! Dogs can sense danger ... you said you were asleep when Mirabella would have been killed, but the spot's so close to your cabin that the dogs would have known about it. They probably heard it, *saw* it from the window...'

Hammy started nodding very quickly. 'You're right ...they jump at the smallest of sounds. The doggy door's always open, so they might even have been outside. A struggle – a murder – they'd know about.'

'And then they would have associated Justine's scent with it, wouldn't they? They were there with us in the aftermath, in the woods. They would have picked up her smell there. That's why they sniffed out the ring ... Justine was the last person to touch it!'

Eilidh blew through her lips. 'It makes sense.'

Robert gave a bitter laugh, shaking his head. 'It wasn't her cooking. I kept smelling a weird lemony smell on her after we visited Felicity. Lemons put dogs off, don't they? She was applying it to keep them away, to divert suspicion.'

'Clever,' Hammy said. 'It's true, though. They hate lemon. Brian even told us he used citrus spray because of his dog allergy.'

'She was lying to us the whole time,' said Eilidh miserably.

'Nearly my whole life,' said Robert.

A long and full silence filled Hammy's living room.

Robert hung his head and stroked the lacerations on his wrists. 'She was evil. She killed the whole Rowley family and for what? Revenge? Passion? Pride?'

'It takes a monster,' said Eilidh. 'Apparently she dosed poor Toby with so many substances that he was out of his senses when she killed his sister. That's why he thought he'd done it. How could anyone be so calculating?'

'No use moping about,' said Hammy suddenly, slapping his

knees, although Robert noticed he wiped his eyes quickly. 'Eilidh, are you going to tell him?'

'Oh!' Eilidh blushed but smiled. 'All right. The thing is, Hammy and I have had an idea.'

'It's a good one,' said Hammy.

'I think so too,' agreed Eilidh. 'You see, Robbie, we know the bar isn't the easiest way to make money. So...'

Hammy rose to his feet and rifled through his kitchen cupboards before bringing out what looked like a large sign.

'What's that?' Robert asked.

'Our solution!' Eilidh announced, barely able to contain herself. She winked at Hammy, who turned the sign around. It read 'THE PINE NEEDLE BAR AND PRIVATE INVESTIGATION SERVICES'.

'I don't understand,' said Robert.

'I got the idea from Mirabella,' said Eilidh. 'She was willing to pay us for our services and, well, after speaking to Inspector Melrose the other night, it sounds like we did a cracking job.'

'You can say that again,' said Hammy. 'And that was while the murderer was right in our midst, sending us down dead ends at every opportunity.'

'We thought we could keep the bar but combine it with ... well, something we've shown ourselves to be pretty talented at,' Eilidh explained.

'The press is already hounding us,' said Hammy.

Eilidh smiled. 'We've had a few calls. Someone even wants us to turn the whole story into a book.' She held up her hands. 'I'm not saying we should definitely do it. But I am saying it's good publicity. Maybe we should seize the day.'

Robert stared at them both like they were lunatics. 'You want to do all of this *again*? I ... you ... we almost died.'

'I told you he'd need some time.' Eilidh looked at Hammy.

'What about London?' Robert asked, squashing the mild irritation that they'd formulated this plan without him.

She shrugged. 'Singing's great, but I love it here. And I think I prefer solving mysteries. If it's not your cup of tea, though, I suppose I could always rearrange those auditions...'

'No!' Robert cleared his throat and felt his cheeks glowing red. 'I suppose it's not the worst idea in the world. And we could pick and choose our cases, couldn't we? No more dangerous psychopaths.'

'Aye, of course,' said Hammy, a little evasively.

'That's right, not a hint of danger for the Pine Needles, Robbie.' Eilidh giggled.

Robert looked at the sign again and smiled. 'The Pine Needle Investigation Services' certainly had a nice ring to it. And it was just the sort of venture that would have made his dad proud.

THE END

Also by V. J. Randle

The Hellenic Mysteries series

The Athenian Murders

The Saturn House Killings

Author's Note

Thank you so much for reading *Cold Secrets*. You may already have tried Googling Findrussie and, if so, you'll know it's a fictional village. I'm lucky enough to call the town of Elgin, Moray my home; Findrussie is an amalgamation of Elgin's community spirit and the topography of Aviemore in the Highlands. In particular, the Pine Needle bar is inspired both by the Pine Marten on Loch Morlich and The Drouthy Cobbler in Elgin (I'd suggest visiting both!).

Your reviews make all the difference to a little murder mystery book like this. If you enjoyed *Cold Secrets*, I would be so appreciative of you leaving a review on Amazon. If you'd like to receive news of my upcoming releases, consider subscribing to my newsletter at *randlebooks.substack.com*.

Acknowledgements

To my late Dad, who was always the first to read the initial drafts of my novels, thank you. This is the last book I'll release which will benefit from your unparalleled intellect and eagle-eyed attention to detail. I promise I'll keep writing.

To Abbie Rutherford of Abbie Editorial, thank you for the beautiful typesetting and expertise. To Betsy and her team at Bloodhound Books, thanks for providing this fantastic cover and for your ongoing support. To Curtis Rosenthal for the beautiful illustrated map of Findrussie, I am forever grateful. To the wonderful editor Philip Parr, so many thanks – I recommend him to any authors out there! To my husband, Will, thank you for believing in this book.

To my readers (especially those who began reading this as a serialised novel!), you have no idea how grateful I am to you for reading my story – thank you from the bottom of my heart.